THIMBLETON

DOWN THE WELL

VERONICA KING

INIMITABLE
BOOKS
UNFORGETTABLE STORIES

Published by Inimitable Books, LLC
www.inimitablebooksllc.com

Library of Congress Cataloguing-in-Publication Data is available.

First edition, 2023
Cover design by Keylin Rivers

ISBN 978-1-958607-22-0 (hardcover)
10 9 8 7 6 7 6 5 4 3 2 1

To anyone who was told,
"It's just your imagination."

TRIGGER WARNING

Verbal and physical domestic abuse, predatory/creepy behavior by older (male) characters toward the younger (female) main character, descriptions of drowning, graphic description of a murder victim

ONE

They say there are two ways to bring a family together: a wedding or a death. Well, whoever said that forgot about illness. Which was why Lore was stuck in a truck with her parents and everything they owned.

She pressed her forehead against the window and watched the thick line of pine trees pass by in a blur. The radio played some country singer she wasn't a fan of. The whole genre sounded like the same songs recycled over and over again to her.

"Cheer up, Lorette. Hazel Borough will be good for us." Her mom assured from the front seat with an optimistic drumroll on her thighs. As if that would make her words true.

"Mom, please. It's Lore." *I don't understand what's so hard to grasp. Someone named Charlotte could prefer to go by Charlie, and no one would think twice. I wanna go by Lore and it's such a big fucking deal.*

Her mother said nothing, but Lore knew she was rolling her eyes.

Lore and her parents were moving to the quaint little town because her grandma took a nasty fall on some slick February ice back around Lore's eighteenth birthday, and since then her recovery had been rocky. The doctors said she'd recover faster if she had an aide to help her. Instead, the Deodarán family was uprooting their whole life to be near her.

Lore's father had applied for the first job opening he was qualified for. And less than a week later, he'd landed a new position.

She furrowed her brow as a sigh escaped her. She wouldn't be walking with her graduating class next month. The faces of her friends floated in her mind. No matching graduation cap designs, no silly photos to look back on past years down the road. She wouldn't get to hug her English teacher, excited that she had done it. She'd struggled through most of her classes, but it was thanks to the multiple after-school tutor sessions Mrs. Bellomy did on her own time that really helped Lore get her act together.

No. She would graduate from a school where she knew no one and wouldn't have the time to make connections.

Her dad reminded her constantly it wasn't a big deal. She just had to get through two weeks, then she'd walk across a stage and—in her parents' words—*finally learn what being an adult is like.*

Lore's forehead thudded against the window as her dad hit a pothole hard.

Her mom shrieked while her hands braced her against the dash and passenger door. "Christ's sake, Andrew! It's like you purposely hit those!"

Her dad bellowed a laugh. "Well, if you could pull a trailer, then maybe you could drive. But here we are." The end of his words held a sugarcoated venom. He loved reminding his wife of the things she couldn't do.

He had what most would call adulterous affairs, maybe even sinful acts, but Lore preferred to call them what they really were. A new flavor of the month to feed his narcissistic ego. She knew her mother knew, and yet there her mother sat. In the front seat of his pickup. Lore grew up hearing their arguments. She now thought that their hatred for each other outweighed any love they could hold for someone else.

The worn wooden sign was soon in sight.

WELCOME TO HAZEL BOROUGH!
SLOW DOWN AND SMELL THE DAFFODILS.

Well, most of the sign's yellow text was legible. Some vowels were almost gone, faded from the years of sun and storms.

Lore could already smell the apple crisp her grandma would pull from the oven and hear sweet tea pouring over ice. *Wouldn't be much longer now.*

DOWN THE WELL

The truck took the next left turn sharply, and Lore turned to peek out the window, expecting to see the trailer carrying everything from their old life unhitched and flipped in the road. Luckily, that wasn't the case.

"Do you have to drive like such a maniac?" her mom hissed.

Unsurprisingly, her dad said nothing and just turned the radio up. They'd been in the truck for about two hours now and were cruising on eggshells. As the truck slowed down, they drove through a picturesque downtown that you'd see in some cheesy holiday movie. For a weekend, the area seemed pretty dead.

She fidgeted with the end of her braid that hung just over her stomach. They took a few more turns, and then her dad threw the truck into park. He didn't wait for any small talk before jumping out. She felt the truck rock as he put the trailer gate down.

"Come on, I'm not moving all this shit myself!" he called.

Her mom finished sending a quick text and flipped the phone shut. Then, with a huff, she opened the door.

Lore lingered a moment longer, taking in the sight of what would be her new home. *Hopefully, not for long.* Her eyes scanned over the cracked windows and the mismatched siding. It was very faint, but Lore noticed the cream vinyl paneling butted up against the eggshell white paneling and it made her want to bite her nails with how god-awful it looked.

"Lorette!" her dad yelled. "Are you even paying attention? Come get your shit!"

Lore sighed deeply and slid from the backseat. She brushed past her dad's infamous stink eye and looked among the piles and piles of boxes for the ones with her name written on them. She didn't have much. Maybe a grand total of three boxes.

Nowhere near her mom, who seemed to have every article of clothing from her *glory days*, as she called them. Rebecca Deodarán was always going on about how one day she'd fit back into them, and it would miraculously fix her marriage.

I almost feel bad for her. Lore picked up the first box and headed to the porch. She looked at the paint peeling off the boards as she waited for her

3

mom to unlock the door.

"Will probably need a fresh coat of paint, eh?" Lore asked as she balanced the box on her leg. The weight was getting to be a bit much. *What did I put in here, anyway?*

Her mom started cursing as she jerked on the house keys.

"Are they stuck?" Lore prodded.

"No, I don't think these are the right ones." Her mom jiggled the key and the door handle again. Her cheeks were flushed, and she was muttering to herself.

Lore sat the box down. "Here, mom, let me help."

"No, I can do it."

She crossed her arms and looked back to the truck and she saw her dad eyeing them as he carried boxes to the bottom porch step.

"Mom, just let me see."

"No!" her mom shrieked as she jerked on the door more.

Lore finally pushed past her and rubbed her temples. It was clear her mom had put in the wrong key. She pulled, and she jiggled it some more. To no avail.

"See!" her mom shouted and pointed at the door. "I told you!"

Her dad's heavy footsteps up onto the porch sent a chill down Lore's spine. His tight grip on her shoulders forced an audible yelp from her lips.

He shoved her out of the way. "What'd you fuck up now, Becky?"

Lore looked at her mom, who was chewing her nails—where she'd undoubtedly gotten the trait from.

"I think she put the wrong key in," her mother answered.

She felt her face turn white hot and her eyes grow. "*Who* put the wrong key in?"

"You were just getting impatient and put the wrong key in, 'cause you couldn't wait for me to do it." Her mom sounded very relieved as she crafted the lie.

Before Lore could point out her mom's bullshit, her dad turned, anger glinting in his eyes. "Give me your flannel," he demanded.

Lore crossed her arms, "But I didn't—"

Her father grabbed her arm and pulled off one sleeve. It didn't matter to him if she did or didn't do it.

Lore felt the uncomfortable eyes of onlookers on her. A woman working in her flowerbeds peering from behind the safety of a rosebush. A man lingering at his mailbox. A couple pushing a stroller on the other side of the road slowed down.

"Stop it!" she yelled.

If her father could literally fume, he would have been at this point. He grabbed the collar and gave it a tug that forced her onto the ground. The flannel finally slipped off. He wrapped it around his fist, punched through the glass of the door, and unlocked it from the other side. The door creaked open.

Lore shot her mom a disgusted glare as she quickly picked up her box and rushed past her dad so that her parents couldn't see the tears welling up in her eyes.

As she darted up the staircase, she could hear her dad yell out to the neighbors.

"Nothing to see here!"

Once Lore got to the loft, she picked the nearest door and busted through it. She dropped the box on the floor. Then stormed over to the twin bed on the rusted powdered blue frame and collapsed on it. She screamed into the mattress until she couldn't anymore. When that moment came, she brought her knees close to her chest and just lay there in the empty orange room. Her eyes felt heavy from all the tears. That's when she heard a knock at the door. She shot up, swinging her legs over the bedside. Letting her feet dangle just above the scratched-up floorboards. Lore wiped her face using her black tank top.

"What?" she called.

Her mother opened the door and pushed the rest of Lore's boxes inside with her foot. "I brought these for you." When Lore said nothing, she continued. "And this, too." Her mom held out the green plaid flannel—a peace offering.

Anger burned beneath Lore's skin, and the fire was itching to spread.

She pursed her lips, moved close enough to snatch the shirt back, and slid the flannel back on. She noticed a tear near a button. Her gaze fluttered back up to her mom, who was just about to see herself out. "What was that about?" she spat, her eyes still stinging from the bitter tears.

Her mom stopped in the doorway but didn't turn around. "What do you mean?"

"Telling dad I put the wrong key in when you did it. I was just trying to help." She chewed her lip, waiting for any sort of response.

Her mom waved a hand. "You're just overreacting."

The taste of copper seeped into Lore's mouth. She had broken skin. "*Mom.*"

Rebecca Deodarán turned, only showing her profile, covered by her long bleached hair. "Well, you saw what he did to you. What do you think he would have done to me?"

Lore's breathing grew ragged and uneven. Her heart felt like it was trying to escape the prison that was her ribcage. "So..." She shoved trembling hands into her pockets. "I'm just supposed to be your sacrificial lamb?" Her cracking voice undercut her anger, and all she could hear was the sad desperation of a child longing for her mother's affection.

Her mother stood there for a moment longer, her back still to Lore. "You should decorate your room. It'll make you feel better."

Before Lore could muster any sort of retort or protest, her mother had closed the door behind her. Lore walked back to the bed and let her body thud against the flimsy mattress. She traced circles on the back of her hand and steadied her breathing.

Worst day ever.

TWO

Lore fiddled with the hole in her plaid flannel. The frayed green thread tickled the tip of her index finger. She lay on the feeble mattress and pulled the thin sheet over herself. There was a bottomless pit in her stomach that made her just want to crawl into the void.

She sighed and tried to focus on taking the rest of the slasher films and novels from the box. Lore held them in her hands, scanning the empty room for anywhere to put them. There was a nightstand that stood under the only window in the room. And on the opposite wall was a prefab dresser that the previous owners left behind. *Good 'nuff.* She shrugged and placed the stack of movies and novels atop it — an assortment of true crime, mystery, and thriller.

Wonder what Maccon is up to. She wished he was here helping her unpack, at least if he were here it'd feel a bit more like home. Lore closed her eyes and remembered him carefully putting her belongings in the cardboard boxes.

"You really don't have to be so dainty with my stuff." She reassured as she tossed her wrinkled laundry into the box on the floor beside her.

He ran his hand through his unkempt raven hair. "These are your things. You should take better care of them." His voice lacked the usual pep.

Lore rolled her eyes. "Exactly. They're my things and I'll take care of them how I please." She paused, holding onto a tie-dye tee shirt they did together in fifth grade. She quickly folded it and placed it in the box at her feet, feeling his eyes on her.

"You still have that?" he teased.

She quickly threw a pair of jeans atop it. "Don't know what you are talking about."

His warm laughter filled the room as he walked behind her.

She turned to give him a playful jab in his shoulder, but held her tongue when she saw his gentle gaze.

Her friend said nothing as he slid off his flannel and tied it 'round her waist.

Lore's brow raised. "Uh, the fuck you doin'?"

Maccon laughed. "Giving you something that you'll take care of, Fire Flower."

Back in the present, her eyelids fluttered, fighting back tears. Lore's finger traced around the hole in her green flannel while begrudgingly looking at the boxes she still had to unpack. *The only thing she had of her childhood best friend, and now it was ruined.*

She could practically hear him telling her it wasn't anything she couldn't fix with a thimble, needle, and thread.

If this were some cheesy movie he liked to watch, there'd also be sunlight peering in through the window. Representing hope or something cliché. Lore looked out the window to her left. No sunlight, just the beige siding of her new neighbor's house.

She felt her stomach surge with nausea as a loud grumble filled the somber orange room. Today was Saturday, which meant her mom would find some excuse to go spend money, and her dad was probably drinking the family into more debt. Shoving her feelings into a bottle, she put on the best face she could muster and opened the bedroom door. No one was around. A chilly hush filled the house.

Lore silently tiptoed down the steps. When her foot stepped on the old wood floor, a loud *creeeaaak* gave way. To her right, she heard a glass bottle hit the ground, and her heart raced. She stood there for maybe a moment, but the anxiety buzzing in her stomach would have her believe twenty minutes had passed. Her eyes locked on the door. She was only a few steps away. She could make it. Lore could hear the blood flow in her ears as she hastily shuffled to freedom. Just as her hand touched the doorknob, she leaned to the right a bit and saw her dad passed out on a plastic moving tote. Glass bottles littered the floor around him. Her eyes followed along the wall where it seemed he had hung up old pictures. Her parents' wedding photo.

A family portrait, too. She shuddered, recalling the day that photo was taken. That had to be one of the worst days of her life. Just the sight of the pink frilled dress her mother forced her in made her skin itch. Rebecca Deodarán had a smile that would strike the fear of any bedtime monster in the hearts of children everywhere, but Lore and her father shared the same grimace. She hated she had anything in common with him.

Her eyes continued to trace the pictures. She saw one of her grandma smiling at her. Even though it was just a picture, it made her tingling stomach ease.

Suddenly, the door shoved open.

"Oh, afternoon, sweetheart. How did you sleep?" Her mom asked as she pushed past, her arms full of shopping bags.

"Good, I guess."

She watched her set the bags down at the foot of the stairwell. "What d'ya get?" Lore waved a hand at what she was certain was money wasted.

Her mom peeked around the arched entry to the living room and looked back at Lore with a grin. "Well," she began as she went back to her precious bags, "just a few things to make this place feel more homey." Her eyes faintly sparkled.

"What about the things we brought with us?"

"Those things were from our old life." Her mom waved a hand at her. "Too bland for our family."

Lore rocked on her heels, her feet itching to step out the door and leave this conversation where it lay.

Rebecca pulled out some bright yellow curtains and folded them over in her arm. "You know, Lorette, I saw just the cutest little bakery down the road. They are having walk-in interviews."

"Ok... and?"

"You should apply! That way, when you aren't helping your grandma, you can stay busy."

Lore sucked on the inside of her cheek.

"You know what they say," her mom began.

Lore grumbled and turned away.

"Idle hands are the devil's playground."

She leaned on the doorframe. "Okay, yeah, I'll look into it. I'm gonna go now."

Her mom rubbed the fabric of the curtains. "Just remember we are going to your grandma's this evening to let her know we're ready to help her."

"Sure." Lore rolled her eyes and had a foot out the door. *You mean that you both are ready for me to help her.* Her dad was a hit or miss, but Lore knew for a fact her mother never cared for visiting Mamó. Let alone care for her.

She didn't hear another word from her mom, just the sound of distant humming.

She closed the door behind her with a gentle hand. *Should have slammed it shut and woken dad up so he could see the shopping bags that sat at the bottom of the staircase like presents under a Christmas tree.* Lore wrestled with the what-ifs as she headed down the narrow sidewalk that would take her to Hazel Borough's downtown.

The afternoon sun kissed Lore's cheeks, and the locals were flooding the streets.

"Good gods, is there a festival happening or something?" she muttered.

"It's the last weekend of May," a voice tickled the back of Lore's neck, making her arm hairs stand up.

She whirled around to see an older man. His hair reminded Lore of white walls in a smoker's house.

"Ok, thanks for that." She squinted and walked away from the friendly stranger dressed in an elaborate purple suit, who gave a warm wave with a jewelry-clad hand as she put distance between them. The sound of clanging bracelets carried in the air as Lore pushed past fond faces.

DOWN THE WELL

All that weirdo was missing was a staff and some horns, and he'd be some sort of discount store villain who curses animated princesses.

Her eyes followed along the brick buildings. A large window with a painting of a blonde in a poodle skirt holding up a tray of donuts caught her attention. Yeah, mom would find that dated skirt cute. PRICILLA'S PLACE arched over the woman in big, bold block lettering. Her hand hovered above the doorknob for a moment as she read the recruitment sign.

HELP WANTED

MUST BE WILLING TO WORK WEEKENDS, HAVE A CAN-DO ATTITUDE,

AND BE A TEAM PLAYER!

WALK-IN INTERVIEWS — TODAY ONLY.

Lore shoved any snide thoughts deep, deep down. At least if she got a job, with the money her parents didn't siphon away, she could save up to leave. The bell that the door hit was barely audible over the full lobby of sweet-loving shoppers. Their food must have been really great—or the only bakery in town.

She drifted to the corner with a pop machine and waited. She watched as the three women behind the counter glided around each other to get the pastries, coffee, or bread they were after—the way they smiled at every customer, no matter how ridiculous the request was.

Lore chewed the inside of her cheek and crossed her arms. She wasn't all that graceful. Or, at least, that's what she was always told. She also wasn't sure how well her customer service smile would hide her true feelings, either. *Maybe this was a bad idea.* Her nails dug into her arms, and she gently rocked on her heels. *But the money.* Her cheeks flushed.

She heard a clear voice cut through the air and her anxious thoughts. "Can I help you, honey?"

Lore looked up and saw that she was now the only one lingering in the lobby "Oh, uh—me?"

The tattooed woman smiled, her eyes like warm, welcoming pots of honey. "What can I get ya?"

11

Lore walked up to the glass case lined with sweets. "I was here for the walk-in interview."

"Oh, well, just take a seat right over there."

She followed her gesture and saw a bistro table that was hidden from the crowd earlier.

"I'll be with ya in just a second."

The woman turned, revealing a long purple ponytail protruding from the back of her baseball cap.

Lore turned on her heels and felt her cheeks warm as she thought the other two women were staring at her. *Why must I be so god-forsakenly awkward?* She pulled out the bright blue metal chair, and it scraped against the tile, making the sound echo in the small shop. *It's like I'm cursed or something.* She quickly sat down and wished she would have just opted to go to her grandma's early. At least then, she would have been able to actually relax. She rested her head on her hand and looked at the intricate design on the tabletop. Lore traced a finger along the swirling blue sprayed metal. Her leg began to shake.

A clipboard slid onto the table. Lore looked up, and the tattooed woman sat across from her.

"Nice to meet you. I am Mavi, the manager. Thanks for taking an interest in our part-time position." Her eyes dipped to her clipboard, then back to Lore. "So, tell me a bit about yourself."

"Well, there's not really much to tell. My name is Lore. I just moved to the area."

"You got a last name, Lore?" Her voice was soft but clear.

"Deoradán."

"That's a mouthful." The purple-haired woman laughed. "Do you have any experience in customer service?"

Lore could feel her face getting warmer. "Not really."

"Any work experience?"

I babysat my cousins there briefly—but is it even babysitting since we're so close in age? That probably didn't count.

She scratched the base of her neck. "No."

The manager pursed her lips and scribbled down on her paper. "Do you consider yourself a team player?"

"Yeah." She tried her best to be convincing. No. I hate being around people. "I work better in a group." *Why did I say that? Ugh, now I'm even more of a liar.*

"Well, you said you just moved here so we can skip this next question," the woman mused.

"Okay, great." Lore's eyes drifted to her tattooed covered arms. Vivid flowers, fruits, and little sayings decorated her skin. A specific one caught Lore's eye. He who tr snaked around the manager's tricep, but the shoulder-length sleeve of Mavi's perky pink tee hid the rest of the phrase.

"What's that from?" Lore gestured to the cursive writing on Mavi's arm.

The woman pushed up the fabric, revealing the rest of the letters. "He who travels has stories to tell." She smiled at Lore's star-filled eyes. "It's an Irish proverb."

"I like it." She directed her gaze back to the woman's warm brown eyes.

"Alright. Last question. It's not something official the owner has on the application to ask, but I think it says a lot about a person."

Lore nodded.

Mavi laid the clipboard down on the table flat and leveled an intense and magnetic gaze that danced in the light like a freshly tumbled tiger's eye gemstone. Her lips curled into a playful smile as she pointed her pen at Lore. "What do you wanna be when you grow up?"

Lore gulped. She'd never really given much thought to it before.

She remembered teachers would ask generic questions like that in all her classes on the first day of school. Some of her classmates knew exactly what they wanted to be, and their answers never changed throughout the years. Others bounced back and forth between careers. She didn't have an answer then, and she didn't have one now. Would she ever?

Lore let an anxious laugh slip. "I—uh—I don't know." She looked down at the hole in Maccon's flannel and began fidgeting with it.

"Everyone wants to be something. Or has a dream to aspire to." Mavi's voice was gentle and reassuring.

VERONICA KING

The echos of screaming matches began in the basement of her mind and traveled up bringing with them the flood of a disappointing childhood. It swirled around her like rushing water, eager to pull her under. Lore decided what she wanted. She could hear her mother's voice tell her that her answer was stupid before it left her mouth, but didn't let that stop her.

"Happy," she said, the words almost a whisper.

Mavi leaned back in her seat and nodded. "I think a lot more people should aspire for that." She scribbled in the corner a few times, trying to produce ink from the pen. "So, what's a good cell number to reach you on?"

"I don't have a flip phone."

"Oh sorry, that's right. You kids have all the latest tech. What's the newest one called? The one that kicks to the side?"

Lore drummed her fingers on the metal table. "No, like, I don't have a cell phone."

"Oh."

"My parents thought it would be a waste of money."

"Well, I can put down your parents' cell number if you know it?" Mavi suggested.

Lore laughed and leaned the chair back on its hind legs. "I'd rather not. Can I just come back here tomorrow or something to check?"

The manager sat there for a minute, tapping her pen against the paper. "I don't think I can do that." Then she shot up and walked behind the counter. Lore's gut twisted together, making a knot so big it dwarfed the rat's nest made of the many mistakes in her parents' marriage. She felt like she swallowed a cactus as she gingerly got up. Unsure if her not having a cell phone was a deal breaker or not.

Lore opened the door, signaling her exit.

"Hold on." Mavi quickly walked back around the counter and tossed a shirt and hat at her.

She barely caught them.

"You can come in tomorrow morning for your first shift."

THREE

Lore stood on the front porch of the new-to-her house. She looked down at the bright pink tee shirt with the same poodle skirt-wearing blonde on roller skates holding up a platter of donuts that was plastered in vinyl on PRICILLA'S PLACE's front window. The baseball cap had identical bold and blocky lettering as the display window. *I should be excited to tell them about my first job. Her stomach started doing flips. But they're just gonna ask about how much it pays—when I'll get paid, and how many days I'm working. Stuff that I still don't know yet.*

"What are you doing?" Her dad's voice came from behind her.

She turned, thinking her father had already seen her new work uniform in hand. "What are you doing?" she asked, returning his question to avoid answering.

He raised a brow and a grocery bag. "Your mom was so busy buying every material item possible, she forgot something for dinner." His voice was flat.

Lore said nothing, just nodded along, and let him shoulder past her into the house.

He kicked off his boots in the doorway. "Are you comin', or you just gonna stand out there with a stupid look on your face?"

Lore let out a sigh. *Maybe he didn't notice.* She followed behind him and slid out of her off-brand flats.

Her father's back was facing her as he began taking food out of the bag. He was busy setting them on the dining table.

He probably won't notice. She took the first quiet step to go up the stairs. Truth was she didn't feel hungry. But the first step let out a groan. Lore froze like a deer in headlights. Damn house is creakier than an old church.

"Where ya goin', Lorette?"

"My room."

"No, ya ain't. We're gonna have dinner together before we go see your grandma." He crossed his hairy forearms.

Her eyes looked at the carton of eggs, loaf of bread, and pack of hot dogs on the dining room table.

"Yeah, it's just fuckin' eggs and toast, but we're gonna start eating together." He grumbled as if he could read her mind.

Lore bit her lip, placed the tee shirt and ball cap on the first step of the staircase, and went to the dining room to pick her seat. She sat with her back to a window with an open view of the front door and kitchen and waited for dinner.

Her mom came out and took the carton of eggs off the table that had seen so many of their family fights.

Lore traced her finger over a marker drawing of an alligator she'd done as a seven-year-old. She thought about the question the store manager had asked, "What do you wanna be when you grow up?" At one point, she thought she'd be an artist. But they hadn't encouraged it. She remembered her mom screaming at her until her face was as red as a tomato. Her father kept promising he was going to sand it off and stain the whole thing new, but he'd been saying that for years now.

He plopped in the seat across from her. He said nothing, just sat there tapping his fingers on the wood. Eventually, he asked, "So, what do ya think?"

She could smell the alcohol on his breath. "The house is nice," she said, not meeting his gaze. Instead, she opted to run her hand over a few indentations on the table.

He nodded. "Well, Monday, your mom calls the school to finalize everything there."

Lore bobbed her head along, acting interested. She liked to think she'd become an excellent actress over the years.

Down The Well

"That therapy place we are sending you to is open on the weekends, though, so tomorrow will be your first appointment."

Lore's fingers stopped along a deep gash on the table, her eyes wide. *Therapy places were never open on the weekends.* "What time?"

"Do you have something going on tomorrow?" her mother asked with a laugh as she came in with their meals. First, she put a paper plate in front of her dad and slid him a beer bottle. Then she placed Lore's eggs and toast down in front of her.

Lore sat there with both her parents' eyes boring into her. "Well, I—uh." She looked down at the alligator doodle she had done as a child. "I got a job and start first thing tomorrow morning."

Her dad popped the cap off his beer. "I'll drink to that! Good job, Lorette. Now you'll know what being an adult is all about."

Her eyes shot open wide, her jaw went slack, and she sat up a little straighter. *I don't even care that he got my name wrong.* She could never recall a time he said he was proud of her.

Her mom sat beside her, her back facing the small black and white kitchen that looked straight out of the fifties. "Your appointment is at two."

Her dad waved his fork in the air as he got ready to dig in. "Nah, our daughter is a working lady now. The therapy place can wait."

Her mom sipped some lemon water. When she sat the glass back down, she folded her hands together on the table and smiled as sweetly as she could. "Andrew, honey, remember she has to be in therapy as long as she is still under our roof."

"She's eighteen now."

Lore's eyes darted back to her mom.

"She still lives with us."

He took a swig of beer. "Eh, she's close enough to bein' out on her own."

Her mother's tongue clicked. "Andrew." Her eyes were stern yet pleading he hold her stare. "It's court-ordered, so unless you want one of us to end up with fines or in jail, she needs to go."

Her dad stayed silent, drinking deeply before swallowing. "Fine," he said through gritted teeth, slamming the bottle down on the table.

17

Lore didn't flinch.

Her mother was quiet and started dipping her toast into her egg yolk. "So, how much are they paying you?"

There it was.

"I'm not sure yet."

"Do you know when they'll be paying you?" her mom pressed.

"No." Lore's eyes fell to her paper plate.

Her mom kicked her father under the table.

His head shot up. "Didn't we teach you better? You should have known to ask these things during the interview," he said in between bites, as if they really had taught her anything during her eighteen years aside from how to avoid conflict.

Lore pushed her egg around with her fork. She hated sunny side up. Yet that's what her mom has always given her. Because she liked it, so obviously her daughter must, too.

"You didn't really teach me how to do anything, Dad," she muttered, the words slipping out before she could catch them.

"Nonsense," he bellowed.

She didn't say anything else. Even with the argument about her schedule, this was the least problematic dinner they'd had together in a long time. *I don't want to ruin it.*

Time passed rather quickly, and it never took anyone long to eat eggs and toast. Soon they were pushing in their seats and piling up in the powdered blue truck that has seen its fair share of rust.

Lore would be lying if she said she wasn't excited. It seemed like the only time her parents behaved was when her grandma was around. A few quick turns, over a rushing gray river, and through a meadow of daffodils that sat on the edge of a pine forest. The brick-built town of Hazel Borough faded behind them as they went to her grandmother's.

The cabin sat at the other end of the flowers. She remembered as a child saying her grandma lived in the sunshine fields. A smile spread across her face.

Once the truck parked, Lore didn't wait for her parents as she practically leaped out. She ran up onto the porch, the wind chimes singing to her in the gentle evening breeze. She burst through the door. "Mamó?" she called.

Her mom's voice was soft as she walked around Lore. "She's most likely laying in her room. Now, be quiet. She's sick."

Lore's bottom lip pouted.

A raspy voice chuckled from the hall. "Sick! Who's sick?"

Lore's head wiped to her left, and she saw her grandma bent over a walker fitted with tennis balls coming from the bathroom.

Lore hurriedly shuffled around her to shut off the bathroom light. "Mamó! How are you feeling?"

"Oh, leave it on, Moon Drop," her grandmother said gently as she continued to the living room.

"We are all moved in," Lore's mom chimed in.

Mamó sat on her floral couch and sighed. "That's nice, dear." Her drooping gray eyes drifted to the window to watch her son—Lore's father—on the porch, sitting on the swing.

"I can go get him." Rebecca's voice held a sense of urgency. She was already heading out the door when she stopped.

Lore's grandma waved. "It's fine, dear." Then Mamó's eyebrows then shot up. "You know what would be really helpful? There's a nightgown I've been wanting to wear for the past few nights."

Her mom nodded and set her purse down on the kitchen counter.

"You know," Mamó hummed, "I was about your age when I started getting the photoflashes. Even in the crisp spring nights, I get so warm in here."

Lore watched her mother wince at the comment regarding her age, and then Mamó continued. "Anyway, it's in the very back of my closet on one of the upper shelves and I just can't reach it. Would you mind going and finding it for me? It's a light green with yellow and pink flowers sprinkled across it."

"Not a problem!" Lore's mom disappeared to Mamó's room on the other side of the open kitchen.

Lore smiled, and her grandma patted the spot beside her.

"How have you been?" Lore asked, sitting down and looking at her grandma's hip.

"Oh, been better, but as good as I can." Her gaze drifted back to Lore's dad, sitting just on the other side of the window.

"You know, if you want that sleeping shirt, I can actually go find it. Mom is terrible at finding things."

Her grandma laughed, then whispered, "She'll be back there awhile. Antsy hands need something to do. I don't think I even have a nightgown that's green with yellow and pink flowers."

Lore grinned ear to ear. Leave it to her grandma to get her mom out of their way. "Do you need a drink or anything?"

Mamó pursed her lips and shook her head. Her pale, moonlike hair fell bit by bit from the bun she had sitting atop her head. "Tell me," her gray eyes fixed on Lore and held a sparkle, "what's been new with you?"

"I got my first job." She leaned closer to her grandma. "At that little bakery downtown."

Her grandma's eyes lit up. "Oh, so you can bring some of those teeny tiny chocolate chip cookies when you come to see me." She playfully patted Lore's leg.

"Whatever you want, Mamó."

Her mom came out into the kitchen dumbfounded. "I can't find the nightshirt you were talking about, but I found this purple one with cats on it." Her voice cracked as if she were afraid of a reprimand for failing. She certainly would have gotten one from Lore's dad.

But Mamó wasn't like her son and just nodded. "That one is fine. Just lay it out on the bed." Then she waved her off. Once her daughter-in-law was gone, she leaned closer. "I'm gonna have to come up with a long list of nonsense to keep her busy."

Lore snorted with laughter. "It's gonna have to be as long as those receipts you get from the pharmacy."

Then the screen door creaked open.

"Ah, Andrew. Finally decide to join us?" her grandma mused.

Her dad silently sat in the matching floral rocker next to the couch. His eyes were stone cold and focused on the coffee table. "The doctors called me today, Mom."

"Oh?" Mamó's stark white eyebrows pulled tight. "And what did those loons have to say for themselves?" She stomped the walker on the carpet. Her thin, bony arms quivered as she did so.

Her father didn't reply. Just interlocked his hands and fidgeted with his wedding band.

Lore's mom was hovering silently back in the kitchen. "Anyone want water?" she asked.

Mamó got up with a huff and shuffled to the kitchen. "Get the kettle. I'm going to make some tea."

Her dad shot up. "Mom, you really should sit down." His voice was different from normal. Lore couldn't quite place it.

Her grandma stopped and turned, shaking a wrinkled finger at him. "I didn't spend years wiping your ass and cleaning your messes for you to tell me what to do."

The air thickened with tension like a warm stew perfect to go over mashed potatoes. Her grandma hobbled around her dad's tall figure and called out, "Moon Drop?"

Lore's ears pricked up. Her Mamó has been calling her that as long as she could remember.

"Can you go out to my herb garden and grab some lemon balm and peppermint?"

She jumped to put on her shoes. "Sure thing."

Her grandma's white bun moved with her nodding head. "Good, good. I'm afraid your mom would bring back the wrong herbs." She tried to laugh between coughs.

Lore didn't think too much about it. *Mom probably would have brought back lavender, or maybe even a dandelion.* Lore walked around the cabin where a round garden bed spiraled upward. A distant memory floated to the forefront of her mind.

It was summer, Lore was eight, and it was prime early nineties. She

VERONICA KING

cringed, remembering the vivid red overalls she wore. Her grandma's forehead glistened in the July sun as they moved dirt to the bed. Lore was in charge of puzzle-piecing together the river rocks as a wall to keep the dirt in one place.

"Remember, Moon Drop, as I pile in the dirt, we will have to build a little mound in the center. And the stones will spiral up it."

"Okay Mamó," she'd called with a toothy smile.

Remembering the sound of her innocent child's voice was like hearing a ghost. Lore ignored the shivers it gave her and knelt down to the herbs that looked like they were just planted yesterday. She picked a few of the largest, best-looking leaves.

Beyond the garden bed was the blue brick well they used to water the garden. Lore walked over with a handful of peppermint and lemon balm. She ran her free hand along the painted concrete slabs. The deep blue color was chipping off. *Maybe I should paint it for her this summer.*

A breeze whipped her braid. She picked up a flat stone and tossed it in. When she heard the water splash, she closed her eyes tightly.

"I wish for something new, something good to happen." As she said the words, her mind drifted to the inked words on Mavi's tricep: He who travels has stories to tell. *What did I want my story to be? What stories do I want to share when I'm old and gray?*

The sound of a breaking branch made her open her eyes. Along the tree line, maybe a few hundred feet from her, she saw a large animal moving through the thicket. It appeared to be carrying a small forest of its own atop its head as a crown. *Probably a moose or something.* Lore slowly walked backward, her eyes following the colossal figure as it pushed past more low-hanging branches. When the rose bushes planted just at the start of her grandma's porch kissed her hand, she turned to dart up the steps.

The screen door snapped shut behind her, drawing her attention back to the house. Her eyes landed on her grandma, who was sitting back on the couch. A handful of pill bottles sat on the coffee table.

Puzzlement crossed Lore's face, but she didn't comment on them. "Here's the peppermint and lemon balm." She gestured with the hand

22

holding the herbs.

"I'll take them," her mom called from the kitchen, the kettle screaming in the background.

Lore hesitated but walked through the living room to the kitchen, and laid the leaves on the counter.

"Lore, you do it," her grandma spoke up. "Your mom always botches it."

Lore said nothing and blindly reached into the cabinet for Mamó's snowflake mug. Her hands brushed against unfamiliar plastic. Her eyes looked up and narrowed at more pill bottles. She pushed them aside to get the mug.

Next, she poured in the hot water. She then stripped the leaves from the stems and put them in the metal mesh ball. She placed it in the steaming water and carefully stirred in some honey.

Her mom quickly took the cup and sat it on the coffee table.

The sinking sun cast an amber glow in the living room.

"Mom, you have to take your meds." Her dad's voice was low. "You aren't going to get better if you refuse the medicine."

Mamó crossed her arms. "I'm telling ya, those ain't gonna do a damn thing."

Her dad knelt on the floor beside the couch. "Mom, please."

Lore held her breath, watching the unfamiliar softness in her father play out.

Her grandma looked up, and they locked eyes.

Was that confusion or fear on her face? Maybe her grandma didn't feel like fighting with her son, but she ended up taking medicine from the handful of pill bottles.

She stood at the counter, gripping the countertop, and watched as her parents helped Mamó back to her bedroom. Then they left the cabin in a blur. Lore's dad never liked to linger. The night air nipped at the apples of Lore's cheeks as they loaded up in the truck. The drive back felt brief as Lore kept replaying when she pushed aside the pill bottles in the cabinet.

Her mind was racing about how quickly she could get over to her grandma's house in case of an emergency. As Lore slid her shoes off at the door, her parents dispersed. Her dad got a beer from the kitchen and her mom raced up the stairwell, surely going to take a shower and use up all the available hot water.

Her work uniform stared back at her from the first step. *Well, fuck. That puts a wrench in my plans.* She picked up the clothes and bounced up the stairs. When she opened the door to her room, she wanted to rip her hair out. *And there was therapy after work!*

She found herself drawn to the window. She opened it and climbed out onto the angled roof. It had random patches missing in its shingling. She brought her knees to her chest and looked up at the clear night sky. Admiring the stars was one of the many things she and Maccon had done together. *The year his mom got him a telescope was the best summer ever.* She recalled all the comets they saw and the constellations they renamed. Their makeshift star log in a long-forgotten sketchbook sat on the back of Maccon's mom's bookshelf.

Then a quiet purr accompanied by a fluffy furred body pressed against her arm took Lore's attention from the distant stars above her.

"Oh, hello." She said, petting the calico cat. The stray mewed as if she understood her, and it brought a smile to her face. "Do you wanna star gaze with me?"

The cat slowly blinked as it stared at her with grass-green eyes.

Lore shrugged. "Kinda in the market for friends right now."

The cat then curled up next to her, warming her side. "Do you 'ave a name?" she whispered. The cat gave no response and Lore grinned. "I think I'll call you Dinadrometa."

The cat gave a judgmental, disapproving stare.

"Fine. Dina it is." Lore mused, running her fingers through the cat's colorful coat.

FOUR

Pounding on her door jolted her awake. The morning breeze made the room feel like an icebox, and her reluctant to leave the bed.

"Get up or you'll be late!" her mom yelled through the wood.

Lore searched her room for Dina, but the animal was nowhere to be found. *Maybe she'll come back tonight.* Lore closed her window but left a cat-sized gap. *In case she wants a warm place while I'm gone.*

"I'm coming!" she called. She quickly slid the peppy pink shirt on and tucked her braid through the hole of the baseball cap. Once dressed, she burst through her door past her mom, ran down the stairs, and raced out the door without a second thought—right into some heavy rain. *You gotta be kidding me!* As she sped walked along the narrow sidewalk, she untied the green flannel from around her waist and quickly put it on. Spring rains were always a bit chilly.

The streets were emptier than yesterday, so she managed to slip into Priscilla's Place in a heart-pounding, fifteen-minute speed walk. The air-conditioned draft of the café chilled Lore to her bones. Getting caught in the downpour only made her colder.

"Well, don't you just look like a little mouse who's been caught in the rain?" Mavi called out.

Lore didn't see her until she popped out from behind a donut rack. "Sorry. I didn't know what time I needed to show up or anything because after the interview, I kinda just left in a tizzy." Lore's face reddened as she shuffled behind the counter.

Mavi glanced at the clock. "Eh, it's eight. Most of the early birds have already come and gone." A brief pause filled the shop as the manager eyed the empty sidewalks. "Come on. I'll show you where to punch your card."

Lore followed her through the swinging door to the back. There were so many more people working and packaging food than she thought could fit into the building.

Mavi laughed. "Don't worry, you'll get used to all this chaos." She handed Lore a sheet and a pen. "Just write your name down and today's date all the way through next Saturday." She tilted her head to a calendar on the wall beside them.

Lore scribbled down the dates.

"And you just punch it in this." Mavi pointed to the time clock the same way a game show girl points to a prize.

It made Lore laugh, and the machine made a clicking sound as it stamped her card. She put her card in the manilla folder that sat in a holder above the time clock.

The front bell rang, barely audible in the back.

"Ope, c'mon, we have a customer!" Mavi raced back up to the front and Lore followed her, giving shy smiles to the other workers she almost ran into.

When Lore pushed past the wooden door, she froze in place.

It was the old man with rings on every finger from before. A ridiculous number of bangle bracelets adorned both wrists. He smiled at her. "Well, nice to see you again," he purred.

She moved closer to Mavi. "Hi," she squeaked.

"Lore, this is Mr. Dempsey." Mavi swiped a paper bag and put a donut in it, leaving it on the glass counter, and then she left Lore's side to go to the coffee machine.

Lore stayed where she was, looking at Mavi awkwardly.

"So, I have something to tell you," Mr. Dempsey said, leaning on the counter, his swirled mustache twitching as he spoke.

Before she could ask what, he continued.

"Meet the shadow at the wishing well, for he has secrets to tell." He leaned even closer, stopping just an inch away from her face. "Secrets of time undone and spells that were spun," he continued.

She could now smell the caramel candy he was tossing around his mouth.

His voice dropped even lower, his gaze boring into her. "Meet that shadow, not the shell, after the last farewell."

Lore stood there, trying to process the cryptic message. Before she could ask him to elaborate, Mavi was back at her side.

"That'll be the usual, Mr. Dempsey."

The man nodded and slid Mavi a twenty-dollar bill. "Keep the change, darling!" He then turned to leave, humming a tune. His choice caught Lore off guard.

It was the same song her Mamó would sing to her as a child.

Mavi's voice interrupted Lore's thoughts. "And that's that. You'll have your usuals who come in. They're pretty easy and lax with newbies. Nothing to stress over."

Lore looked at the rows of pastries and inhaled the smell of fresh coffee filling the air. "What about a full lobby?" she asked, taking in the picturesque little café.

Mavi laughed and started wiping down the counters. She handed Lore a rag. "Don't worry about the crowd. Focus on one customer at a time. It makes the whole thing less intimidating."

Lore nodded in agreement as she swiped her wet rag in circular motions over the countertop. "There is something that I didn't find out until last night. I have to go to therapy, and my first appointment is today." Lore hugged herself as her nerves ratcheted up. She looked up, expecting to see anger and annoyance across Mavi's face.

Instead, her manager regarded her with a warmth that made her uncomfortable. She didn't know what to do with gentleness and almost would have preferred a scolding.

Then Mavi nodded and sprayed the counter. "What time is it?"

"Two."

Her manager smiled. "Oh, sweetheart, your shift today is only til about one-thirty."

Is my luck finally beginning to turn 'round?

"Really?" Lore gasped. "Do you know where Raven's Ridge Behavioral Therapy is?"

Mavi smiled. "Sure do."

The door opened, ringing the bell, and Mavi gestured to her. "You got this!"

Lore still had nerves floating in her stomach, but more so from doing something new. She never thought she'd be able to say she was excited about interacting with strangers.

"Hi! What can I get you today?" Lore beamed, hardly believing the chipper voice that came from her lips was hers as she spoke to a mother and her young child.

"Hi, honey." The woman gave a gentle tap on her toddler's shoulder. "Go on. You can tell the nice ladies what you want."

The child stepped forward, standing on their tippy toes. "Uh, can I have a pumpkin muffin?"

Lore looked at the rows of muffins in front of her.

"Pumpkin isn't there, baby," the mom cooed.

Mavi winked at Lore. "You know what, little one? We may not have pumpkin in season right now, but if orange is what you're after," she bent down and reached into the case, "then might I suggest this orange zest surprise!"

"Oh, it's so perfect!" the child shouted. Their toothy grin gave Lore a joyful buzz. She put the plump treat in a paper bag for them and Mavi rang it up.

"Alright. That'll be a buck, twenty-five!"

The woman went to pay, but her child tugged on her raincoat. The mother leaned down and listened to some whispered instruction before hoisting the little one up and handed the child the money. With a smile as wide as the first quarter moon, the child handed over the cash and reached for the bag Lore was holding.

She gave it over, and the two thanked them.

"Haves a nice day!" the child called as they left out the door.

"See?" Mavi mused. "Easy."

And the rest of the morning *was* easy.

Lore's mind would still drift back to the words Mr. Dempsey said — and the eerie way he hummed her grandma's song. *Maybe they knew each other?* Regardless, she made it a point to make a note on her hand to ask her Mamó about him when she went to see her tonight.

The lobby of about five people cleared and Mavi looked at Lore as she got a water bottle from the cooler that was also lined with pops, lemonades, and teas. "Looks like it's time for you to go, Miss Lore." She pointed to the clock above the door leading to the back of the café.

"Already?" Lore turned to see for herself. "Wow, it went by so quickly."

Mavi laughed. "Time flies when you're havin' fun."

Lore went to clock out, but the manager waved her off.

"Don't worry about it. I can get it!"

She stopped and looked at Mavi, who was scribbling on the back of a piece of scrap paper.

"Here, this is a little map to get to Raven's Ridge from here. You'll have to leave now though if you wanna make it by two."

Lore took the paper from her. "Thank you."

"Not a problem."

Lore felt a sense of relief wash over her. "No, really, thank you." She then looked at the makeshift map and headed out the door. Trying to let her smile cover the dread that was eating away at her when she laid eyes on Mavi's faint pencil-drawn mess.

"See ya same time tomorrow!" Mavi called behind her.

"See ya tomorrow!" Lore waved as she walked out the door and down the dreary gray street.

Large droplets made the black ink spread like thin little roots across the page, making the map even more illegible. Lore sighed and looked around the square. All the buildings looked the same to her, and she didn't see any sign of Raven's Ridge. She slowly turned in a circle. The courthouse clock showed she only had ten minutes before her appointment. Lore's hands started trembling. *No, no, I can't be late.* The heavy gray clouds didn't show any signs of letting up, so she took shelter under a tree that had a cute bench sitting below it. *If it weren't for the gusts of wind, it wouldn't be too terrible right now.*

Footsteps approached her, but she couldn't see who it was through the downpour.

Mr. Dempsey stopped by the bench shielded from the rain with his enormous umbrella. "Why, hello again." He smiled.

Her fingers crumbled the edges of the scrap paper map. *For fuck's sake, am I gonna have to get a restraining order?*

There was something not right about Mr. Dempsey. "Hello." Her voice was flat.

"What are you doing out in this rain?"

Lore cocked an eyebrow. "Could ask you the same."

His laugh was audible over the thunder. "Well, at least I am equipped to deal with the inclement weather." He gave his umbrella a playful spin.

"I'm just fine."

He leaned down and looked her over from the top of her head to her toes, gave her a look of pity, and clicked his tongue. Then, from the corner of his mouth, he said, "You look like a drowned rat, my dear."

Lore bit her lip, chewing back every unkind thought she had. "What do you want?"

"A pleasant conversation, but it seems I won't be getting that here."

"Sorry?" Lore's eyebrows knitted together. *I wish he'd just leave, so I can find this therapy place already.*

Mr. Dempsey lingered for a moment and turned his nose up at Lore. Which wasn't new. People had been doing that to her for years. "Oh, I know," he said in a honeyed voice. Looking at her with gleaming eyes. "You're lost, aren't you?"

"Nope."

"You are." He chuckled. "It's okay. Where do you want to go?" His tone now sounded less like some smug old asshole and more like a concerned grandpa. It should have given Lore whiplash, but it didn't. Her parents did this nonsense all the time.

Lore let out a sigh as the clock on the courthouse struck two, the bells ringing out. She slumped on the wooden bench. "It doesn't matter now."

He shrugged his shoulders underneath his umbrella. "Then I suppose it doesn't matter which direction you go."

She thought about the words for a moment. "Yeah, I suppose you're right."

"I usually am!" he called as he began walking away from her, disappearing in the distance thanks to the falling rain.

Sitting here moping in the weather wouldn't get her anywhere, except maybe a downward spiral to depression central. She shot up and blindly walked in a direction. The map crumpled in her fist. She had walked north, east, and even retraced her steps from the south. And yet, every time, she still ended up back at the town square. This is ridiculous. Her eyes locked on the clock that looked more like the moon in the heavy rain. Lore paced back and forth for a moment on the red brick path.

The clock struck two thirty. *Oh gods, she could hear her mom now. "OFF WITH IT! Whatever nonsense is swirling around in that head of yours, turn the switch off!"* Her mother's face always got so red when she yells. It was a miracle her parents didn't lose their voice more often.

"Look!" she heard a small voice call.

Lore turned around to spot the mother and child she had helped earlier at the café.

"Oh, hello," Lore stopped in her tracks. Desperate not to look like a lost puppy.

"Finding everything okay?" the mother asked.

"Yeah, everything's fine!"

The wind blew, and the mom held onto her child with one arm and her coat hood with her free hand. "You sure, honey?"

Lore felt her stomach sink. The weather wasn't letting up and her dad was going to be at the therapy place to pick her up at four when her session was supposed to be over. "No."

"What can we help you with?"

"I need to find Raven's Ridge."

"Well, lucky you, we're heading that way. Come on!" She gestured for Lore to follow.

They began walking in the direction Mr. Dempsey had walked after he was giving Lore a rough time.

Figures.

"We live in the duplex right across from Raven's Ridge actually," the mom said casually. "It's a real cute building, ya know?"

"I bet everything here looks so perfect. I feel like I don't really fit." Lore laughed it off.

"Oh darlin', your age is showin'." The woman laughed a bit and held onto her child a little tighter, who was now asleep in her arms. "Not everything is as it seems. This place has cracks and dents, but everyone is putting their best face on." She spoke with experience that Lore couldn't argue with.

"I'm sure you're right."

The mom came to a halt, and so did Lore. She dug around in her pocket and pulled out a set of keys. "Well, it's just across that crosswalk, sweetheart. You shouldn't be able to miss it."

"Thank you!" Lore waved as the mom went into her dry home. *Next time, I'll have to give them an extra muffin on me.* She quickly crossed the street and flapping in the wind was a wooden sign in the shape of a raven with the words RAVEN'S RIDGE BEHAVIORAL HEALTH CENTER printed as clearly as a midsummer's day.

Eager to get out of the rain, Lore pushed through the doors. But the stale air made her body freeze like an opossum playing dead. She forgot how much she hated these kinds of places. Her hand reached for the handle again when a friendly "Hello!" came from behind the counter.

Lore sighed. If only she'd been quicker out the door and back into the storm.

FIVE

"How can I help you today?" The receptionist chimed, brushing their curly hair away from their rounded glasses.

Lore gulped and walked over to the counter. She felt everyone's eyes on her. "I'm late."

"That's okay. What's your name?"

Her mouth went dry. "Lorette Deoradán," she forced out.

"How do you—?"

"D-E-O-R-A-D-A with an upward symbol from left to right-N." By now, it was like reciting the same dusty song and breaking out the musty shoes to dance to it. Everyone seemed to have trouble spelling her name. But it took the cake when someone recognized it.

The receptionist smiled. "Any connection to Rowan Deoradán?"

Lore rocked back on her heels. That was her grandfather she'd always heard so much about. "Hm? Not sure," she lied, nervous laughter erupting from her.

Fingers typed away behind the desk. The clicking reverberated off the pale green walls of the lobby. *A nice color. Maybe if I had seen it in a different place, I'd've liked it enough to paint my new room the same shade.* The green walls felt like they were closing in.

She started picking at the hole in Maccon's flannel again. Eventually, she mustered up the courage to peek over her shoulder. Only the faces of strangers awaited her, and none of them were even looking at her. Lore counted her breaths as she tried to focus on who she was sharing this space with. There was a child asking their mother a million and one questions, and a burly man sitting in the corner with his back to a wall. A couple sitting close enough together to signify they were together but far enough apart that they appeared to enjoy the company of their flip phones over each other's spoken words. A woman sat close to the stairwell. The bags she carried weren't designer, but were under sunken eyes that looked like they had not felt a good night's sleep in some time.

The receptionist perked up on the other side of the counter. "Alright, hun! Gotcha all signed in."

Lore's eyes drifted back, "Okay, thank you."

"Not a problem!" they mused with a smile. "Your case manager will be right out."

Lore gulped. Like she had swallowed a pill that went down sideways. "I'm sorry? I thought they transferred all my files, and I'd just start speaking to a therapist?"

The receptionist adjusted their circular glasses. "Your assigned therapist is actually out today as a part of their vacation. She left on Friday."

"Oh." Lore's voice was flat. *I suppose it really didn't matter that I showed up late.*

"If you'd like to speak to someone today, though, I can see if anyone else can take on clients." The words were spoken with such kindness, Lore wasn't sure how to respond.

"Um…" She rocked on her heels, feeling like the burden her parents swore her to be. "That's okay. I can wait for my therapist to come back."

The receptionist gave a soft smile. Like a gentle summer's rain. "Alright, well, your case manager will be out shortly." They gestured to the seats.

Lore turned, biting her lip. *I don't even want to be here.* She felt the muscles in her hand twitch until she folded her slender fingers into a fist. *If dad could control himself, I wouldn't even be here.* The tears welling up in the corner of her eyes retreated so they could be shed on another poorly timed occasion. Then she felt an abrupt ache in her shoulder.

She turned and caught a pair of ocean-blue eyes holding hers. *She looks eerily familiar.*

"Oh, I'm sorry." Lore heard herself say words but didn't recall speaking them.

Her long blonde hair fell perfectly around her softened face. Rebecca Deoradán would've been floored if Lore looked anything like the perfect young woman standing before her.

"Are you okay?" Lore asked in a hushed tone, not wanting to make a big scene.

The girl's face became flushed with what Lore could only assume to be embarrassment. The woman rushed out the door and into the rain clouds without another word.

Lore turned back to the lobby of people who still held as little interest in her as before and took the seat closest to her.

A man wearing a rather unnecessary top hat sat beside her, their face buried in a magazine. "Don't worry. That's Miss Pricilla Cline."

Lore's eyes grew to the size of a fifty-cent piece. "Pricilla? As in Pricilla's Place? The little café downtown?" Her hands gripped the metal armrests. *Did I fuck up and just lose my job?*

The stranger turned the page. "I wouldn't be too pressed about it." He ran a freckled hand through his ginger beard and gave a deep laugh, his eyes still fixed on the photos of himself in the magazine.

Looks like a red carpet event from like three years ago. His green silk shirt had a crocodile scale pattern, which had to be even more dated.

"She thinks no one knows the princess of the borough comes to therapy." His voice was gruff. Like sandpaper had been rubbing it down.

Lore tilted her head. "Why are you telling me this?"

Amber eyes paired with a mischievous grin sent a chill down her spine as if the first wind of winter was at the doors of Raven's Ridge. "If you've got me, you want to share me. If you share me, you haven't kept me. What am I?"

Lore scrunched her face. *What does that even mean? Why are all the interactions with the people of this shitty little town so damn frustrating?*

She crossed her arms and averted her gaze toward the receptionist, taking calls and scribbling down notes. You know those jobs. Underpaid with the expectation to happily pile on more work.

A breath prickled on the back of her neck. "What am I?"

The red-haired man was now leaning in close to her space. *Too close for comfort.*

Lore continued looking away from the man. "You know crocodile scales are tacky."

He let out a playful gasp. "The woman at the store assured me it was an alligator."

Lore whipped her head around.

His eyes glowed under the rim of the black top hat, like a fire that knew it had spread itself too far. He laughed under his breath. "You remind me of a little rodent."

Lore's brow pulled together, and she tried to ignore the dryness in her throat. *I've about had enough of these weirdos.*

As her lips parted to muster something unsavory, a candied voice called into the lobby. "Lorette!"

She slipped away from the redhead's offbeat presence.

"Hello!" she peeped as she scurried to the woman calling for her.

"My name is Penny. Nice to meet you!"

Penny was all smiles and sunshine, but the silver cross that hung around her neck made Lore feel like a noose was being tied around hers. Penny turned, giving her denim skirt a whirl. "Right this way!"

Lore looked over her shoulder to see that the man with curly red hair was gone, and the doors were slowly closing shut. *He's pretty silent for a clumsy giant.* A muscle in her hand twitched again, and she crossed her arms as she followed Penny.

The woman held a clipboard close to her chest as she led Lore through a door and down a hall. The hall was bone white, which made Lore's hands feel clammy, and the imaginary noose felt like it was tightening. *Too much like hospitals.* The only decoration they had were the posters you'd find in the classrooms of elementary teachers across the states. Corny sayings like "Hang in there" with a cat playfully hanging for a tree branch, the word "unique" with a group of normal forks, then one in the center whose base was curled in on itself and prongs bent in different directions. All

Lore could think, though, was how broken the single fork looked next to the rest. *And they call it unique.*

Penny opened the door to her office. Blush pink walls embraced Lore, and she moved an oversized plush pillow. Its case was fluffy braided yarn, and the corners had little tassels.

Lore plopped in the chair and looked at her case manager, who was still as peppy as ever. *No one is that happy.*

Lore rested her cheek on her hand as she slouched. Her eyes scanned the walls. Bible verses and pictures of angels covered the wall. Lore's eyes searched until her gaze fixed on the photo of Jesus. A crown of thorns with blood droplets dripping on his white skin. It made Lore roll her eyes every time.

Mamó always said that the town is full of religious nuts.

"So, from what I see here, you just moved in!" Penny mused, her eyes still on her computer screen. Scrolling through Lore's long, long, long file.

"Unfortunately."

"What brought you here?"

Lore narrowed her eyes. "My parents."

"Right, right." The woman kept typing away. "I see here that finances aren't an issue since you have state insurance."

Lore nodded, her gaze scrutinizing the spines of the books lining the small shelf on the opposite wall. They all were missing dust jackets and were organized from tallest to shortest. *I would have done it by color. It would look better.*

"So, your therapist isn't here today," Penny said, her tone carefully tempered.

"Yeah, that's what the front desk person said." Lore shrugged it off and pursed her lips at the bookshelf. It was far enough away that she couldn't make out the tiny golden and silver embossed letters, but close enough for her to wonder what books they were.

"You're a reader?" Penny asked, pulling back her long, dark hair.

"Sometimes," Lore started, sitting up straighter. "The best stories I've heard don't come from pages of books. They come from my grandma."

Penny nodded along. "Some people are gifted storytellers. I'm guessing she is one of those people."

The ticking clock behind Penny struck four, and the sound of chimes danced through the pink room. Lore was quick to her feet.

"In a hurry, I see."

"My father isn't the fondest of waiting,"

Penny nodded and stood to open the door for Lore. "You can just go out the way we came." She pointed down the hallway.

"Thanks," Lore called as she took the first left down the hall. The white walls felt like they were closing in on her with every step. *Just got to get to the lobby. It shouldn't be much farther.* Her breathing was uneven, but a bit of relief washed over her when she saw the exit. With every step she took, the door seemed to move away from her.

Then a hand fell on her shoulder. "Hey, you took a wrong turn." Penny's voice was a cool breeze on a hot summer's day.

Lore couldn't collect anything to say, but she let out a relieved sigh. *Who knows how long I would have walked around in this labyrinth? It would have been absolute torture.*

The woman's calming presence made the anxiety melt away as she brought Lore to the correct door. "Here you are. If you need anything, remember that I can squeeze you in on shorter notice than your therapist."

Lore turned, her eyes softening. "Thank you," she mouthed.

Penny smiled and called the next name on her clipboard.

Lore fixed to the door of Raven's Ridge and walked out of there as quickly as she could.

"Oh, excuse me!" the receptionist called.

Lore paused, her hand hovering above the doorknob.

"Same time next week, okay?" They had a slip of paper waving it towards Lore.

"Yeah, sure." Lore slid out the door without a second thought.

She scanned the rainy streets, not seeing the rusted blue pickup.

This never happens. He's normally ten minutes early and pissy because I wasn't.

Then she heard screeching brakes, followed by the sound of a broken muffler that some may mistake for a gunshot. She wiped her head, causing freed strands of hair to stick to her cheek. A single headlight shone coming around the turn. If one thing was certain, it was her father's truck. But when it came to a halt, she saw her mom sitting in the driver's seat.

Lore opened the door and over the crashing rain asked. "I thought dad was picking me up after his shift?"

Her mother threw the truck into drive. It was a shame her mom didn't bring any books. She needed at least three to sit on to actually see the road properly.

"I'm getting him after I drop you off at your grandma's," she explained, rather flustered. "He called abruptly, waking me up during my afternoon nap."

Lore rolled her eyes and turned the heat up. *My bones feel like popsicles.*

"So of course, I answer. If I'm being honest, I didn't want to, but—"

Lore acted interested. "But?"

"But the factory is keeping him over for an extra hour or two and he wanted to let me know to pick you up and take you to your grandma's. Then come and get him."

Lore took her work hat off and let it slide into her lap. "Isn't that good? Won't he get overtime or something?"

Her mother huffed. "Yes, but really quite an *inconvenience*, if you ask me."

"Sorry picking me up was such an inconvenience," Lore muttered.

"Oh, Lorette, stop that. You know what I meant." Her mother pointed a hand to the windshield. "I mean, just look at this weather. Utterly terrible."

As if on cue, thunder rumbled above them as if it were shaking the trees and not the high winds.

"You know," Lore started picking at her fingertips, "if I had a cell phone, dad could have just called me."

Her mother laughed. "Oh, darling, you know how that is."

Lore said nothing, just looked out the window, currently being pelted with large water droplets. She didn't expect a different answer this time, nor the next time she would ask. It was always easier bringing up these kinds of topics with her mother. If she even attempted to talk to her father about it, she'd get a long, drawn-out explanation about money and responsibility. She sighed.

They were out of Hazel Borough now, just rolling fields and trees of the countryside. The brittle tree branches were blowing around, resembling flexible bamboo bending. Then, as if the radio had read her thoughts, an abrupt alert ran across the radio followed by a robotic voice.

"This is your national weather center. The following areas have a severe thunderstorm warning, and we urge residents to seek shelter imm—"

Her mother cut the radio off, and the truck slowed down as her mom put on the blinker.

"Mom, maybe you should stay with Mamó and me." Lore's voice was shakier than she would have liked.

Her mom threw the truck into park as the rain continued to assault the top of the old truck. "Nonsense, it's just a bit of rain. Besides, I don't think your dad would be very happy if I left him stranded at the factory."

Lore pursed her lips but opened the door. "Okay, I guess I'll see you tomorrow after work." She then pushed the door open and ran to take cover on the porch.

Her mom rolled down the window. "Love you!" she yelled over the grumbling sky.

Lore waved a hand as she jogged up the slick wood steps. "Love you," she silently echoed as she watched her mom go down the gravel drive from the safety of the covered porch.

SIX

Lore opened the screen door with a creek. The smell of apple cinnamon filled her nose. "Mamó!" she called, sliding her shoes off. She made her way to the kitchen and started wringing out her green flannel in the sink.

"In the bathroom, Moon Drop." Her honeyed voice carried down the hall. A few moments later, her grandma appeared, scooting along with the walker. "That bad out, eh?" She plopped on the couch. "Where's your dad?"

"There was a weather alert on our way over." Lore sighed, leaving Maccon's gift where it was to get out two plates and two forks. "And from what mom said," she began as she opened the oven, letting the ridicule heat warm her damp skin, "dad ended up having to work overtime. She is on her way to go get him now." She scooped out the warm apple crumble, the satisfying sound of the cooked crumble crunching as she did so.

Mamó rolled her eyes and flipped on the TV. "Only your mother would be in denial so deep that even when bad weather pelts the windshield, she chooses to not see it."

Lore came in and gave her a plate of the sweet and cinnamon-sticky dessert. Lore laughed. "I mean, you aren't wrong." Her jaw tightened as the weather reporter on the TV talked about how long this storm is going to last. *I do hope they make it home okay.*

Her grandmother took a bite, and she did the same. The first bite sent a subtle woody flavor of nutmeg dancing along her tongue. It sent a warmth through her soul. "It's really good, Mamó. Thank you."

"Well, I know it's a favorite of yours." Her grandma mused as she fidgeted with the remote. "This dang thing," she muttered.

"Here." Lore reached for the remote. "What'd ya wanna watch?"

"Let's watch that trivia show. On channel seven, I think." Mamó handed the remote over to Lore with shaking hands. "You know, I think the pills just make it worse."

"Why do you think that?"

Every wrinkle in her grandmother's face scrunched. "I didn't take them until after I made the apple crumble. And now look." She held her hand up.

They both watched it as it trembled.

"Well, it's s'posed to be better than that hip of yours worsening," Lore offered, then promptly took another bite.

Her grandma sat there, holding her breath and, by doing so, holding onto a secret. She let out a sigh. "You're a smart kid," she finally managed.

Lore smiled. "I'm glad someone thinks so."

The rest of the evening went rather normally. Almost as if it were a summer night that had long since passed. Lore was a child again as they watched hours of game shows. Mamó seemed to know all the answers.

They laughed, and Lore cleaned up the kitchen a bit.

Then the old grandfather clock struck eight, and her grandmother had a cup of tea before bed.

"Lemon balm and mint?" Lore asked as the wrinkled crone stirred in a spoonful of honey.

"Wouldn't have anything else." Mamó winked a tired gray eye as her thin lips took a sip from the milky white glass that had pink flowers 'round the rim.

Lore helped her grandmother back to her room. It was clean as usual, and a vanilla candle burned on her nightstand beside her black jewelry box.

"You know," Mamó croaked out as she fluffed her pillow, "there's so much I'd like to tell you before I go."

Lore furrowed her brow. "Mamó you've just busted a hip." Lore closed the pink linen curtains, her fingers gripping the fabric tightly. "You'll get better, you'll see." Her voice sounded more of a plea than one of certainty.

DOWN THE WELL

There was a thud, and she turned, her eyes wide. She didn't see her grandmother on the floor, which was a relief. Instead, Mamó rummaged through silver chains and charms. The top of the jewelry box rested against the pale yellow wall.

"I may not have enough time tonight. I'd like to give you something."

Lore sat at the foot of the bed, watching her grandma's back as the woman continued pulling out necklaces, bracelets, and earrings.

With jittery hands, Mamó set them to the side. "It's been a while since I last wore it," she admitted. "A bit of a family heirloom, really."

Her voice carried a certain sort of tenderness to it.

Family heirloom.

"I didn't know families like ours had heirlooms," Lore joked.

Her grandma hobbled to the bedside table and reached for Lore's hand, rubbing her thumb over the knuckles.

It had been a long time since she'd held her Mamó's hand. They were colder than she remembered, and a few more wrinkles and spots had appeared on them.

"Families like ours have deep roots that are often forgotten about. But I want you to have this." She released Lore's hand and reached into her nightgown pocket. From it, she pulled out a chunky silver chain. A single charm that caught the candlelight just right. "My grandmother gave this to me, and she got it from her grandmother before that." She looped the chain around Lore's wrist. "Now, I give this to you, Lore Deoradán."

It was lighter than it looked.

"Thank you, Mamó. I won't let anything happen to it."

Her grandmother's tired gray eyes softened, and she nodded as she climbed into bed. "That was my hope."

Lore shut the thin door quietly behind her as she admired the bracelet. She lay on the couch like a caterpillar in the cocoon of blue patchwork squares, her feet just hanging over the side, and pulled down the quilt that always sat on the back of the couch. She pulled her wrist out and fiddled with the circular charm. Her fingertips met warm, embossed metal. The design was a single antler and two daffodils wrapped around it.

43

Thunder shook the tiny cabin. Lightning flashed through the white curtains of the living room. The colors from the mosaic lampshade flittered against the faded living room wall panels.

Lore smiled, and her mind drifted back to a warmer summer day when she was around twelve.

She had been dipping her paintbrush in the bucket when her grandma gingerly picked it back up to pour some of the liquid sunshine into a pan for her paint roller. Lore remembered the sound of her voice. Like a songbird singing as she worked. Coating the brown faux wood with bright paint.

"Sing me a song of a time undone, Sing me a song of a place forgotten, sing me a song cause the world's got me downtrodden, sing me a song that calls me home…"

Lore reached behind her, flipped off the lamp, and burrowed herself more in the cozy quilt.

The rain hammering away on the cabin roof was enough to lull Lore into a welcome sleep.

A thud woke her up. Lore's eyes shoot open. Another sound quickly followed the first. Then Mamó let out a shrill scream, jolting the last remnants of sleepy from her mind and propelled her into action.

She couldn't get to her feet fast enough, sliding in her socks across the kitchen linoleum to reach the bedroom. She flung the door open to see her grandma and dresser drawers on the floor. The jewelry Mamó had so carefully placed on her nightstand was strewn across the carpet.

On the other side of her bed was a smaller shadow. It had large, pointed ears that made up half its size and gleaming golden eyes that cut right through her.

The sight of the figure held Lore frozen. *What was that? And what was it doing here?*

"Lore," Mamó's voice was strained as she clawed at her chest. "Moon Drop…" Her pleas were almost a whisper now.

What did it do?

Lore's knees hit the carpet as she tried to help her up onto the bed. Under her hand, her grandmother's skin was cold yet covered in sweat.

Mamó's breathing was short and uneven.

Thunder shook the house once more.

The figure slunk out the open window and disappeared into the forest.

She watched, the feeling of icy water settling in her veins. Her heart was racing.

Mamó groaned in pain, drawing her attention back to the problem at hand.

Lore's hands trembled as she bolted to the kitchen to get the landline phone. She hated to leave Mamó behind but she needed to do the only thing she could—dial 911.

She just hoped help would get there fast enough.

SEVEN

Lore bounced her leg as she sat in the world's coldest chair. The cushion was as soft as a river stone. The hospital walls were as hollow as her heart, sitting there in the waiting room with a heaviness that weighed on her chest. Alone. She couldn't say how long she had been there, either. She stopped looking at the clock hours ago.

The ride over was so nerve-wracking, her arms still felt like they were being pricked by thousands of needles. She had called her parents upon arriving at the hospital, her fingertips pressing the sticky buttons replayed in her mind. They had rushed over, and—for once—pressed no questions. When she watched them leave to go see Mamó's condition, it was like seeing them fight gravity as they pushed past the door. Their limbs swung slowly, their tense faces still and unmoving.

Her eyes stung as she looked out the large windows. The thunderstorm had finally dwindled down to a light mist paired with low-rolling fog. The clear sky had millions of glittering stars that looked intentionally placed around the luminous glow of the moon's crisp edges. Lore wipes her nose with her sleeve as she gave a sniffle. It had been a while since she last saw the moon's waning crescent smile.

What do I tell them? It all happened so quickly.

She blinked back to tears welling in the corners of her eyes. *Was it even real, or was it just my imagination?* Was the shadow just something to blame for what happened to Mamó? *No, no—that can't be it.* Mamó wouldn't have pulled out her drawers and scattered her jewelry. Lore played again with the cool metal charm of the bracelet Mamó had given her.

It had to be real.

Just before bed.

I need *it to be real.*

Before *it* happened.

She felt a hand gently rest on her shoulder, and she jerked her head to see it was her mother. The streams of tears from her bloodshot eyes told Lore whatever it was, it wasn't good.

"What?" Lore mouthed, barely able to muster her voice.

"Baby," her mom started and knelt beside her, taking Lore's hands in hers. "Your grandma has died."

No. She can't be dead. I told her she was gonna be on the mend. We were going to have another summer together. Lore's lip trembled as her eyes became clouded with tears. *I didn't even get to say goodbye.*

She sat there stunned by sadness and her blood surging with rage all at the same time.

I didn't get to say goodbye.

She took a ragged breath and looked past her mother to the tranquil night on the other side of the glass. *I'll never share a plate of apple crumble and watch game shows with her again.*

"It's alright, Lorette." Her mom attempted a hug, but her daughter wasn't there.

Lore was too busy thinking about the way Mamó smiled, the way her voice sounded—frantically recounting every precious detail she was so afraid of forgetting.

EIGHT

Lore's reflection in the mirror looked like swarms of dust bunnies had attacked it. It had been a little over a week. And still, somehow, none of it felt real.

She examined the black dress she wore. *Terrible thing, really.* Could hear her grandma's voice teasing, "Dark colors don't suit you, Moon Drop."

Lore fought the pooling tears at the corner of her eyes as she fussed over the itchy lace. *I look so stupid in this.* She splashed some cool water over her face, then tied Maccon's green flannel around her waist. Already better.

Her mom's voice carried through the screen door of Mamó's tiny cabin as she yelled for Lore's father. "Darling, your sister is about here. Then we can spread the ashes."

Lore's stomach dropped. She had forgotten about her aunt. She could picture her dad's annoyed expression. His brows pulled tight, his sharp gray eyes boring into anyone who dared look at him, and the single line that wrinkled across his forehead.

She looked back in the dusted mirror where her soft, unpolished gray eyes stared back at her. Her mother had often called them her father's eyes, making her hate them. *But maybe I have Mamó's eyes.* She adjusted the chained charm bracelet, stood up as tall as she could, and held her head as high as a sunflower, searching for the sun. She needed that right now. A bright side. Her heart ached for her friends that she left just a little over a week ago.

The worn screen door creaked open.

DOWN THE WELL

"I'm comin'!" Lore insisted as she pulled the bathroom door closed behind her. As she turned to face who she thought to be her mother, her jaw slackened and her eyes grew. *No, it can't be.*

"I told you we should have asked my mom if you could've moved into our basement instead." Maccon's voice was like a sun's ray after a rainy day.

She smiled, tears welling up again. She practically jumped to hug him. "It has felt a bit chaotic, and I'm sure chaos doesn't live in your basement," she muttered into his chest.

He rubbed her shoulders and laughed. "Chaos rides on your coattails, Fire Flower."

Lore let out a breath. She had found the ray of sunshine she was missing. "How — I mean — why are you here?"

"Your mom called mine late the other night. My dad let me borrow the pickup, and now I'm here," he said nonchalantly, then ran a hand through his inky unkempt hair. "My best friend needed me."

She stepped back away from his warm hug and kind words, rubbed her arms, and looked out the window. Her father was sitting on one of Mamó's wooden lawn chairs in front of the field of daffodils with a case of beer. Her mom was beside him and made a fuss over his shirt. The morning dew still clung to the grass.

"Maccon." Her voice broke the silence, and his pale eyes stayed fixed on her.

"Hm?"

Lore chewed her lip for a moment. *I know he'll believe me.* She met his gaze. "I saw something," Lore said, almost whispering the words.

His thick, bushy brow raised. "What'd ya mean?"

Lore stepped closer like they both were in grade school again and she was about to share some big secret. And she was. "There was a shadowy figure when Mamó had her heart attack."

Her friend stayed silent for a moment, then his eyes melted into a gentle stare. "Why are you whispering? We're the only ones in the house."

Lore's heart thudded in her chest as she stormed past him to sit on the couch. *I'm sharing a very vulnerable detail with him and he decides he wants to be funny?*

"Did you not hear what I just said?!" Her tone was an angry shade of red, and she wished she had a better ability at concealing her true feelings.

Maccon sat beside her. His frame made the couch appear two sizes smaller than it actually was. "Lore," he started, his voice gentle with caution. "I think you've been through a lot. Moving away from your childhood home, your friends, and now this."

She watched him rub his calloused hands on his jeans in a circular motion. "Not to mention or touch the steaming pile of shit your family dynamics have always been." His voice was low, but all Lore saw was the same circular motion he used to soothe himself when confused or upset about something.

Lore felt a cool numbness rush to her fingertips, and she placed her hands in her lap. "You don't believe me." Defeat echoed in the tiny living room.

Her best friend chewed on the inside of his cheek. "I didn't say I don't believe you." His jaw tightened a bit. "I said you've been through a lot and maybe we should focus on that and what you are feeling before we worry about hunting some shadow."

Some shadow. His flippancy stung her skin. He was talking as if they were in middle school going to go to the woods on the outskirts of town and hunt down beasts from fairytales.

This was different.

This was real.

Before Lore could spout off anything else, the sound of gravel kicking up the driveway got her attention. Out the front window, she could see her aunt's absurdly-sized black SUV.

"Great," Lore muttered, playing with the charm bracelet.

"That the aunt that used to waitress at the country club before she met her city-slicker husband at said country club?" Maccon asked.

"Yup." Lore rolled her eyes. "Only aunt I have."

Lore got up from the couch and walked to the screen door. "Let's go get this over with." Her voice sounded as bitter as her tears had tasted.

Maccon followed her out.

DOWN THE WELL

Her aunt's bleached hair sat in a neat low bun, and a large-brimmed black beach hat sat atop her head like the cap of a mushroom whose stem was a bit too slender to hold it up. She closed the passenger door and adjusted her black lace gloves as she looked up to see Lore.

"Oh, there she is!" she called, her thin lips curled into a smile that made Lore's fists clench.

Lore liked to call her aunt's tone 'sham chic,' all hollow words and empty promises.

"Hi, aunt Caraline." Lore's voice was flat, and her eyes uninterested.

The driver stayed in the car as her aunt clicked over to Lore and Maccon in her six-inch pumps.

The sound of two more doors slamming shut felt like a casket top closing over Lore. *Her cousins.*

They used to all play well together, but as they got older and her cousins became more aware of their familial wealth, the more they teased and shunned her.

"How you been, baby?" her aunt asked as she reached over to brush Lore's braid off her shoulder.

Lore huffed as she threw her braid back over her shoulder. She liked the way it felt when it fell in front of her chest. Her eyes narrowed. "Been better."

Her aunt's beady eyes darted over Maccon as she laughed. "I see you landed yourself a fine young man."

Lore rolled her eyes, and Maccon laughed nervously.

"Actually, we're just friends." Lore's voice didn't hide her annoyance.

"Best friends, actually," Maccon added.

Her twin cousins peered out from behind their mother. Looking Maccon up and down like he was some show pony that their daddy could buy for them.

Lore's brow furrowed.

"Well, isn't that lucky for us?" her cousin purred through bubble-gum-painted lips.

"I'd say so." The other sister dropped her large square sunglasses down her nose to get a better look. "Unless they're friends-with-benefits or something." She gestured as if Lore and Maccon couldn't hear the way they were being talked about.

Lore grit her teeth. "Really? On the day we spread grandma's ashes?"

Her aunt's thin lips pulled tight as she tried her best to give a sweet smile. "Girls, girls," she mused, "your cousin is right, you know. We are here to mourn our loss today." She pulled a white tissue from her small clutch and dabbed her face.

"Wiping away sweat rather than tears, I see." Lore almost couldn't believe the words that fell from her mouth, but the growing heat in her face assured her she'd spoken.

Her aunt squinted her eyes a bit as she clutched the tissue. "You think you're a clever girl, don't you?" Her words were like a sharp edge of a knife dancing along Lore's forearm, inviting her to continue.

If it wasn't for Maccon, she may have just waltzed into the blade.

"My mom always says during the darkest moments," her friend said, "the worst can sway us to do things that may be out of character." His eyes looked over Lore, before returning his gaze to her relatives. "But it's important to remember that these dark moments aren't permanent and each of us can share a light from within to see the group through." He nodded, pleased he could piece his mother's words together to a tee. "We each have a candle. Everyone's candle is a different color and has a unique scent, but alone we just have a candle. Together, we have a glorious fire."

Her aunt nodded and adjusted her gloves once more. "Well, on a lighter note…" She sniffled a bit. "I have good news that could act as a candle of light during this dark time of mourning."

Lore's face was still flat as she said, "Uh huh."

By now, Lore's mother was on her other side. "Oh, what's the news?" she pushed a bit too eagerly for Lore's taste.

"Well, girls, should I tell them, or do you want to?" The twins went to open their mouths, but then their mother's voice continued. "Oh, you both are right, I'll tell them."

Lore watch as her cousins' faces fell, and she'd be lying if she said their disappointment didn't put her in a better mood.

"The twins were accepted into Oakwick University!" Her aunt beamed with pride.

Not a surprise. They can go on daddy's dollar.

"That's wonderful! Isn't that an Orchid League school?" Lore's mother mused.

Her aunt's lips curled up into another unsettling smile. "It is, indeed." Her eyes slithered across until her gaze landed on Lore. "Do tell—which school have you made it into?"

"Oh," her mom's voice faltered a bit. "Lorette hasn't really had the time to look into such things." Her mother then did her best to compare a walnut that's kicked around the forest floor to a juicy peach. "But she does have her first job."

"Oh, and what job is fit for such a clever girl like you?" her aunt inquired.

Lore said nothing, but her face felt hotter than before and a fire burned within her gut. Before right as she was going to spit out a retort, Maccon's firm but gentle grip clasped her shoulder as he directed her to go stand by her father.

"Hey," he whispered.

She whipped her head up to him. "Really?! Your mom's candle spiel?"

His face scrunched. "I was try'n'a diffuse the situation?"

"That was good for when we fought over something stupid as kids. Not for family squabbles."

Maccon's expression softened. "I don't really think you're mad at me for trying to diffuse the situation. I think you're mad at your family."

She ignored him and crossed her arms, glaring out into the open field. Her cousins' giggles and clicking of their texting on their sidekick phones ate away at her eardrums as they approached. Lore's family had not been together since her tenth birthday.

Her friend's hand rubbed her upper back as he leaned down to her ear. "Don't worry about them. Okay, Fire Flower? Let's make this as special as we can for your Mamó."

Lore wiped a pesky tear from her cheek. "I'm happy you're here."

"Me, too."

He was right, though. I'm not mad at him. I'll have to apologize later.

The sky was a light pastel blue, and there wasn't a cloud in sight. The breeze tenderly rustled the treetops of the forest line and, if not for current circumstances, it would have been the start of a perfect day.

Her father and aunt sat in the lawn chairs Mamó put out every summer. Her mother shuffled around in front of her aunt and father, holding the white ceramic urn. It was rather plain and thoroughly unsuited for someone as vibrant as Mamó. Lore, Maccon, and her awful twin cousins stood behind the adults.

"Thanks for making the long trip up, Caraline," Rebecca said meekly.

Her aunt waved modestly.

Lore's dad frowned. "I'd hope she'd be able to spare a few hours' drive to spread her mother's ashes." His words seethed with aliving hatred. "She can't hurt her image of being the ideal everything, so of course, she's here."

Lore didn't agree with her father on much, but this was a sentiment she could get behind.

No one said anything. Only the spring breeze rustled the daffodils infant of them.

"Let's get on with it, then." Her dad cracked open another beer.

The whispers of her cousins made Lore gritted her teeth against each other as their hushed words echoed in her ears.

"Drunk."

"Reeks of booze. You think he showers?"

One flipped her strawberry hair as her pair adjusted her beach hat. Then they continued to whisper ill of her dad.

She felt her palms beg her nails to stop digging into them. *He is a drunk—and yeah, he may only shower a few times a week—and he is an all-around terrible dad.* She could feel her face become flush with anger. *But he is my father and if anyone is gonna talk about what a piece of shit he is, it's me. No one else.*

As her cousins stood there whispering, clicking their tongues, and blowing bubbles with bright pink gum. They were completely oblivious to Lore's feelings. That, or they just didn't pay Lore any mind. A toss-up, really.

Suddenly, a shadow caught her attention from the corner of her eye. The figure's tall ears stood alert. In front of everyone. Her heart felt like an icicle had stabbed it. Her eyes darted to look at Maccon, then to her aunt and father. *Did they not see him? He was right there!*

Its golden eyes appeared to glow in the sunlight, disappearing briefly when the figure winked at her, driving the icicle of grief deeper. It had split her heart without care or precision. Then the shadowy creature darted between her dad and aunt.

Toward her.

The shadow felt like nothing more than a sudden gust of wind, and her wrist suddenly felt lighter. She looked down and saw it was now bare. Her jaw clenched, and she whirled to see the shadow dashing behind her grandmother's cabin.

She wished she had been the type of person to just save face. Just turned her cheek and tried to enjoy what she could. But she wasn't that person. Her feet were already carrying her away from her family and the field of yellow flowers.

She heard the heavy footsteps of Maccon behind her before he spoke. "Where are you going?"

Half of her desperately wanted to chase after this shadow creature. The other half yearned to stay with her friend, her personal ray of sunshine.

"The bathroom," she lied. "I'll be back. Just need a few." She didn't turn to see his sad puppy dog face she was certain he was making.

"Okay," he sighed. The sound of his steps halted.

Maccon drove up to see her. Ready to be a blanket of comfort. And yet, her feet continued to take her farther and farther away from those tethering her to this miserable place. Her eyes felt like bees had stung them, and her throat felt like a swollen lump.

Mamó gave me that bracelet. It's *mine*. And this thing can't just take it.

It had already taken her.

The creature sat atop the blue brick well behind the cabin. Dancing along the rim, taunting Lore.

"Give it back," she spat.

The shadow held out empty hands and rocked back and forth on its heels. As if to say its pockets were empty.

"I know you took it," she said through gritted teeth. "You took it and you took her!" she yelled.

The creature held up a single finger to Lore, signaling her to wait, then pulled out the charm bracelet and dangled it over the well.

"You vile little thing!" She launched herself at the creature, who, quicker than a fly to shit, gracefully leaped to the other side of the stone rim.

Lore stayed there, wisps of her hair falling around her face from her braid, arms hanging over the edge of the well.

The creature waved a finger at her again and held the bracelet over the water once more.

"Don't!" Lore snapped. But her bark was empty, no bite to back it up. And the shadow seemed to know that.

Time slowed as the figure loosened its grip on the thick chain.

When she reached up to grab the creature, Lore felt like she was moving through water. Her hand wrapped tightly around the shadow as she stood. *It's not that big. I can take it in a fight.*

The shadow wrapped its other hand around hers and smirked, flashing a single white fang, making her curse her last thought.

The chill of a cold winter's night shot down her spine.

"No," she mouthed, terrified.

The shadow said nothing. Just winked a golden eye and, with the strength of ten men, pulled Lore down the well.

NINE

The crisp water nipped at Lore's cheeks, reminding her of how church grannies pinched the cheeks of young kids. She snapped her eyes open, but her sight was useless in the dark waters of the well. She felt the weight of the shadowy figure still gripping tightly onto her wrist, now an unwanted anchor. Her limbs flailed as she tried to swim back up to the surface. But the pressure of the water made her limbs move slower and soon they, too, felt heavy.

Her vision tunneled as her lungs begged for air. Right as she danced along unconsciousness, her body erupted from the icy water of the well, and her body thudded against a hard surface. Lore raised her head, but her neck felt like a slice of jello, so she quickly lowered it again and rested her cheek against the gray, smooth cobblestone. As her eyes fought to stay open, she could only think of one thing. *That damned shadow.*

She sighed through gritted teeth and tried to summon any remaining strength. Lore steadied herself on all fours, her arms trembling under her own weight. Her eyes drifted down again to see the bracelet Mamó gave her was gone. Her heart was in her throat and she wanted to wail and scream, but only silent tears fell from her face. Lore pushed herself up to rest on her legs, her face turned toward a familiar night sky. It was exactly the same as she had always seen it since a child. Until she saw the stars were no longer stark white on a canvas of black and blue. Some looked to have made swirling patterns, and others clusters of green, white, purple, and orange dots. *Beautiful.*

From the corner of her eye, she saw the shadow creature scurry off to a cliff face adorned with a garland of mangled trees.

What really caught her attention, though, was the pair of moons hanging in the sky. One was so large and close it was like she could reach out. Maybe if she jumped, she could touch it. The other moon was more familiar to her, far away and like one she'd see on a clear summer's night.

The breeze carried a conversation on it. It swirled around her, and the echo of voices seemed to raise her spirits.

Lore rose to her feet, careful to steady herself on the well as her fingers gripped the painted brick. She rested her weight against the wooden post that held up its little roof. "Where am I?" she muttered between ragged breaths.

Wait a damn minute.

Lore slowly looked around her. Old vintage street lamps flickered in the night. They were tall, slender poles. The glass compartments encasing the flames were like little heads atop bodies, and the piece covering the glass looked like a tiny metal crown of sorts.

The cobblestone reached under what appeared to be some business stalls lining the outer rim surrounding the well. Little flags and banners flapped along with dried leaves in the frigid night air.

Beyond the stalls were little stone buildings whose roofs were so vibrant Lore could see the colors pop in the dim lighting. The roofs varied from rich purples to bright greens. Their slopes and pitches were a little unnatural. *That can't be structurally sound.*

Lore stepped forward a bit and furrowed her brow. *What kind of messed up dream is this?*

Sounds of merriment and cheer continued riding the chilled breeze. The wind sent goosebumps down her arms.

Right, people. I need to find the people.

She untied Maccon's green flannel from around her waist and scrunched her nose. Sopping wet. As she slid her arms into the flannel, giving her some sort of coverage, it hit her. *I told him I'd be right back.* She whirled around to face the wishing well. *I've got to go back.*

DOWN THE WELL

But if recalling what she told Maccon was a hit to her gut, what she saw next was being hit by a train. *No. that's not right.* The only similarity between the well in Mamó's backyard and this one was the little wooden roof. The paint here wasn't peeling. In fact, it looked like it was done within the last few days. She carefully ran a hand along the beaming orange bricks, her fingertips dipping over what appeared to be a diamond-shaped crack in the center of a brick. *How peculiar.*

Another gust blew. This time, the wind carried in an awful howl. She turned, not sure where to begin her search for people. Then her eyes darted around the shopping square. The lamp had changed, but just slightly. The curved decorative pieces of metal no longer mirrored each other as if its hands were resting on its hips. Now, the left iron bar pointed to an alley. Lore looked at it and said, "thanks," not thinking twice about it. As she slipped through the small space between the wooden market stalls and walked down the pocket of space between the building. The flickering lantern used the other, more rusted, metal arm to tip its "crown" to her back.

She took a quick turn down the dark alley, following the sounds of laughter. *Even if they don't help me, maybe I can piece together some sort of sense to all this.*

She halted in her steps as the smell of beer and fried food filled her nose. Then she saw it from the little alleyway she was emerging from, a neon sign waving in the night. It read DINA'S PUB & ENTERTAINMENT in an unforgettable shade of neon pink. *The twins would love that color.*

Lore crept to peek into a window of the building. Her breath hitched as she rubbed her arms with cold, pink hands. The only sound her body made was the loud and slow beat of her heart ramming against her chest. The sight made her stumble backward. *What the—no, no—it has to be exhaustion. I'm hallucinating or something.* She peered back into the window. Thick smoke swirled like grey clouds inside the building. The little puffs that found their way out the window made Lore's eyes itch and her throat dryer than a dessert.

Inside, a handful of busybodies rushed around. Other figures sat admiring the sultry voice paired with the slow dancing of the vixen on the stage. Tall hats towered over the smoke clouds, and long trench coats swept the floor from the backs of chairs. Everything about this scene would have been normal, aside from the smoke caking the back of her throat.

But what made all this even harder to swallow was that there were no people at all. *They were animals. The whole lot.*

Her hands trembled as she hugged herself. Lore moved away from the building, her stomach jumping in panic. She looked at the red and brown bricks of the building as if the answer to all her problems was written in some sort of invisible ink. *Invisible ink. Nonsense.*

But then, what was sensible anymore? She put her hands behind her back as she slowly backed up, wanting to find something to lean on. When her hand rested on the cool metal lid, she adjusted her weight a bit and took a deep breath in. Getting back home certainly won't be easy. She stretched out her neck, racking her brain for any sort of ideas. *I guess the first step would be to go back through that cursed well.*

Then she felt a warm, slender touch fall across her hand.

Lore adjusted her vision to the window she had just been peeking in. The reflection came to focus, revealing a toddler-sized mouse in a bright red jacket, looking at her a bit too intently atop trash cans.

Being the fan of horror movies that she was, Lore was a bit too familiar with the scenario of a young girl in the alleyway. But she wasn't expecting a mouse to be the killer. Still, Lore let out a shriek. The last thing she heard was the swooshing of the makeshift club the mouse used to hit her over the head.

TEN

Lore was awake but still paralyzed. She heard a door fly open over the familiar jazz music of Felicity's Pub & Entertainment.

"Mathilde," a deep voice groaned, rattling Lore to the bone. "How did I know you were the root of this mischief?" A moment of silence passed before the bellowing voice spoke again, this time a bit more hastily. "Go on, explain yourself."

Lore couldn't paint a picture of the owner of the voice, but it seemed familiar.

"I was exploring," replied a female voice that sounded like an innocent child. Lore could only assume to be the mouse who assaulted her and pictured the tiny mouse crossing her arms.

"Exploring?" the other voice questioned. "More like snooping in on CHS affairs, little lady. I thought I told you to stay home."

"Yes, maybe I was, *but* if I weren't snooping around, the human I found stalking about would have caused a panic." Lore felt the mouse's tiny furry hands tugging at her sleeve, but she couldn't muster the strength to shake the mouse off, let alone get up.

The cobblestone felt like it was shaking from the footsteps of the stranger. Lore couldn't move. She winced as a large stranger knelt beside her and, with what felt like a long dull knife, turned her face toward him.

Lore began doing another back-and-forth dance with unconsciousness. Her vision was still blurred and all she could see were shapes and shadows. She guessed she was staring straight down a snout of an alligator.

"Mathilde, do you know what this means?"

She listened to the conversation unfolding as the large animal lifted her into the air.

"Yeah, Gannon. it means humans aren't extinct like we originally thought." The mouse—Mathilde—sounded very excited. "Are we going to tell the Society?"

"Do you know *who* this is?" the alligator—Gannon—asked in a soft rush, ignoring the mouse's question.

"Uh…" Lore could picture Mathilde scratching her chin. "A lady kind of human?" The mouse didn't sound very certain. "But I don't wanna assume," she added.

The gator grumbled something Lore couldn't quite make out.

"Well, I haven't gotten that far yet," Mathilde admitted, voice lifting in defensiveness. "I was going to take it back to the house, bandage it up, and then show you when you got back."

The alligator let out a deep groan. "Bandages won't heal this up. We'll need to be careful." Silence settled for a moment more before the large alligator added, "We'll have to send a carrier crow. It shouldn't take that long."

Crows? Normal crows? Un-humanlike crows?

The sudden shifting of the alligator's weight made her head jerk hard to the left. Creaking wood filled Lore's ears as she lay slumped over the alligator's back.

"But Mathilde—"

"Yes?" the mouse's voice sounded like a wounded animal. Most likely, though, the only thing hurt was the mouse's pride.

Down The Well

"No matter what, you can't let anything else happen to this human once she's well again. No matter what *anyone* tells you." He spoke quickly in a near whisper.

A door opened and closed behind them.

Lore bounced against the cotton cushions of what she guessed was a couch.

"Go fetch CC and bring me some paper and my quill," the deep voice ordered. "Quickly, now."

The pitter-patter of small footsteps echoed on the floor.

"So when will we tell the Society?" Mathilde asked again.

"*We* won't be telling them anything." The alligator's voice was stern. "But I will let the other elders know. This is vital to the work I set out to do."

"Yes, and I think it's important I be there, too." The mouse's voice had a certain sharpness to it, but more like the sharpness of a needle than a sword. A small annoyance rather than a threat.

"Mathilde, my dear, bring CC here, please. This can't wait."

Lore could hear the frantic scribbles on paper.

"Alright," the deep voice started again, "now this shouldn't be a long wait, but I am tasking you to look after this human. They certainly aren't from here and will need guidance."

"But—"

The alligator cut off the mouse. "No buts."

The sound of a window being slid open scratched against Lore's ears.

"You expect me to babysit?" the mouse protested. "I'm not a babysitter—I'm an explorer." She huffed, trying desperately to find a better term. "I'm an adventurer."

Lore could hear Gannon's words, spoken with the warmth of a smile. "Sometimes, my girl, the biggest adventure you can take is getting to know someone else."

She could image the mouse's large round ears drooping.

That's okay. I don't know how I feel about the mouse being my lifeline to this place, anyway. So, I s'pose we're both out of luck.

The door opened again, and a musky smell tickled Lore's nose.

"Oh, Gannon! A human? But how?" a raspy voice asked, reminding her of any man who had picked up a pack of cigarettes at the young age of ten.

"Can you help or not?" The alligator's deep voice was suddenly void of patience.

"Of course I can." A cackle filled the air. "After you take the human to a bed, I'll need you to fetch a few things from Sable's for me," the mysterious voice purred.

Lore started fading in and out again, and soon the words became jumbled. The two words regularly floating around her ears were "important," and "secret." She didn't know how to feel about that, but that didn't matter because the next thing she knew, she was floating in a sea of darkness.

While she swam through this dark pit of nothing, soon she saw giant pieces of beautiful silver necklace chains, gaudy rings, and gold bracelets with intricate carvings on them. Then they smacked together. The clanging metal made her wince and grab her ears.

Then she began coughing as green smoke swirled around her, swallowing her up like she was on the menu for some monster's dinner. Lore suddenly wished for the loud and tacky jewelry instead of the smog that made her wheeze.

As if on cue, she saw something familiar in the distance. The blue brick wishing well.

She flapped her arms against the nothingness surrounding her and, through sheer desperation, gripped the side of the well. Lore looked behind her and saw the green mist still had a grip on her ankle, like a snake's tail coiled around its prey. She kicked and pulled against it, but nothing worked. She twisted enough with it still holding her to peek down the well.

What followed was a blinding, bright light.

Then she saw nothing. Felt nothing. *Is this where I die?*

ELEVEN

Lore shot up from a sweat-drenched pillow, hair clinging to the back of her neck. She blindly felt around, still wiping the sleep from her eyes. *Where is it?* She pulled the blanket up and rolled herself tightly in it. Then she took in a deep breath ready to be lulled back to sleep.

The comforter cocoon smelled like spiced orange peels steeped in honey. Not the usual second-hand smoke and burnt breakfast scent she was familiar with first thing in the morning. She threw the cover off of her like it was a boa wrapping itself around her moments ago.

Wait a minute.

Her eyes fluttered open again.

But wasn't it all just a dream?

The tea-stained colored walls had vined flowers sprawling across them that twisted and wove over each other, directing Lore's heavy eyes to the window on the wall to her left, where sunlight glowed behind the thick curtain. The rich coffee fabric spilt against the wall and pooled at the bottom along the dull wooden floor. An intricate light green braided design gathered the curtain up in the center, that allowed just enough sunlight in to make the wallpaper come to life.

The blush blossoms on the walls started to twitch and blossom open. Lore's jaw relaxed. Lore's mind race, and the only cohesive thought she had was, *A lovely shade of green.* She slid from the bed and silently went to the curtains. She ran a hand along the warm metal. The shade of green slightly changed hue depending on where the light struck it.

She heard some mumbling through the boards. Naturally, she bent down with an ear to the floor, her fingertips tracing along the ground. The scratches and notches in the floor varied from deep and old to light and probably sanded away by hand.

Then a familiar voice traveled up towards her like heat rising. "He was fine when I saw him last."

Her heart thumped hard against her ribs. Begging to be free from its skeletal prison. *No mistaking it.* Lore's thoughts drifted back to the haunting reflection in the glass pane before she felt the blunt end of the heavy club. *That voice belonged to the mouse in the bright red jacket.*

She rose to her feet and looked back at the bed. It sat on rather plain wooden bones. But the bluish green photo frame on the nightstand was very ornate with soft curves and pointed edges.

Lore shuffled along the floor and saw it was a family portrait that included an alligator the size of an oak tree, wearing a rather well tailored suit. Her mind replayed the fuzzy figures of the night prior. She could finally pair the deep bone rattling voice to a face. The alligator's painted smile beamed with pride, and five mice all piled in front of him, each one wearing a big cheesy smile, all aside from one. Mathilde grinned with a spark alive in her large almond-shaped eyes. It was rather unsettling. *Who knows what that stick-swinging lunatic was scheming?*

Lore's brow furrowed as she crossed her arms. This is not the dream I wanna be stuck in.

Without warning, the bedroom door flew open as if a strong gale of wind had blown through the house, up the stairs, just to frighten Lore. As quickly as it had opened, she saw the mouse from the night before slip in and shut the door so hard it made Lore jump. Then, it sounded like a stampede was heading up the creaking steps.

The mouse stood with her back to the door, digging her heels in as it violently rattled. Even the gray painted trim trembled. The animal jerked her head and locked eyes with Lore. "Oh!" she gasped, her petite body jolted with each shake of the wood door. "You're awake!" The creature sounded a bit bewildered by the discovery.

Lore tilted her head, not sure what to make of this. What to make of her attacker—and host.

"What is it you are hiding in there, Mathilde?" A splintery voice demanded from the other side of the door.

"So, how did you sleep?" the mouse asked Lore as if they were meeting for a casual catch-up chat over brunch.

Lore flatted her lips and knit her brow. *Good, I guess. But do I really give that away or tell her everything about this place is terrible, and I wanna leave right away?*

The loud thuds against the door kept pulling Lore away from her thoughts. She gestured to the door. "Who are they?" she mouthed.

The little gray mouse's eyes were wide as she quickly locked the door behind her. Then she skipped to Lore's side, her jaw practically dragging along the floor in amazement. "You *do* understand!" She lifted Lore's arm and further inspected.

Lore swatted her away immediately. "Stop it, I'm not some animal at a fair," she grumbled.

"And you do speak rather well!" Mathilde mused, leaping on the bed, so she was almost eye level with Lore.

"And no, you wouldn't be an animal at a fair," she agreed, then again locked eyes with Lore as she rubbed her fuzzy chin. "C'mon, have you seen a raccoon ravage the fried chicken stand at any fair or festival?" Her eyes fluttered over Lore from top to bottom. "You look a little underfed to be the part," she admitted casually as she plopped down, the mattress subtly bouncing her.

Lore crossed her arms, the feeling of embarrassment gnawing in her gut. "You're such a rude little thing, aren't you?" she snapped.

The pounding on the door continued,

"Open this door, Mathilde!"

"I hope she's hiding Father in there," a voice whined.

"I hope it's Father with a castle of waffles!" another proclaimed.

Lore looked at the brittle wood door. "Who are they?"

Mathilde twiddled her boney little fingers. "No one."

"Well, 'no one' seems to enjoy talking," Lore chided.

Mathilde pinched the scruffy fur between her eyes and paced over to the door. With her hands firmly on her hips, she called over the ruckus. "That's the problem with you lot!" Her voice was sharp. "You wouldn't know a grand discovery if it hit you upside the face!"

Harsh words.

"I've found it!" another unfamiliar voice cheered.

The tops of Mathilde's large round ears curled as if she had found herself in a trap, her eyes filled with sudden worry. "Brace yourself," she said, scampering over to stand between Lore and the owners of the voices. "They're savages, I tell you!"

The lock clicked and the door burst open. Lore didn't know how much more the poor old wooden planks of the door could take.

Three mice piled inside, shoving each other, all trying to lead the charge.

Then, from the doorway, a fourth mouse walked in. This one was taller than the rest and the flowing yellow fabric of her dress popped against long, fluffy coal fur. Her smaller, rounded ears were flat like an annoyed cat's. All that mouse had to do was clear her throat, and the three others moved to the side and out of her way rather quickly.

They looked down at their feet and twiddled their fingers, avoiding any sort of eye contact.

Silver eyes that were sharp like daggers drilled into Lore.

A fuzzy memory centered itself in her thoughts. She was fighting with a figure over a well... but the memory was just out of reach that her fingertips could barely graze against it.

"And just exactly how did you smuggle a human into Charmsend?" The question was directed down towards Mathilde, who was now standing to make herself as big as possible.

Her large ears pricked upright, but Lore could see the way her tail quivered. "I discovered this human," the red-clad mouse snapped.

The coal-colored one leaned down so the tips of their noses barely touched. "You can't discover something that's been extinct."

Down The Well

Extinct? Lore felt like shrinking into a corner.

A silvery blue mouse scampered to Lore's side and poked her with a boney finger right in the ribs. "It doesn't feel extinct."

"Hey! Stop that!" Mathilde insisted, swatting the furry hand away.

"This human have anything to do with our missing father?" The coal-colored mouse's voice was frigid.

"No, Minifred." Mathilde was quick to answer, her voice unwavering, and the tension growing to the size of an elephant.

Another silver mouse came to stand beside its pair. Lore's eyes lingered on two mice. She hugged herself, hoping it'd deter any more poking and prodding.

The second mouse rubbed its chin and knelt down, looking at Lore's knobby knees and eyes, watching carefully, then pulled away.

Lore cornered herself between the bed, the nightstand, and Mathilde. She was, unfortunately, trapped. The feeling stirred in her stomach like a swirling wind, making the dry fall leaves rise and fall during autumn.

The mouse, clearly ignoring the social cues, walked over and stuck its finger against Lore's rump.

"Hey!" Lore chided. The adrenaline rushed through her, tickling her fingertips. "The fuck is wrong with you? You can't just do that!"

The mouse turned to its pair. "Nope! It definitely feels extinct," it said matter-of-factly.

Mathilde whirled around and shooed the two silver mice away. "It's not extinct because that means it'd have to be dead, and it's very much alive. Now leave the human be."

The two silver mice whispered back and forth to each other.

Wait a minute. Where did the cinnamon-colored one go?

Lore scanned the room and her eyes landed on the cinnamon-furred mouse huddled by the window. With the curtain resting against her back.

"Something's happening in the square," she said with a squeak. "The whole town is down there, I think."

Minifred's nose twitched. She huffed. "Oh, what could it be now?"

69

She shot over to peer out the window herself. Then she muttered something Lore couldn't quite make out.

The twin silver mice scurried over, practically trying to climb overtop of the largest mouse to get a look.

"Mildred is right," Minifred announced. She went to stand by the door, her arms crossing. "It looks like a large gathering. More so than the standard market hour, so we should go see what it's about. Maybe we can get a lead on where Father wandered off to." Her voice tapered off towards the end. Lore could hear the exhaustion in the mouse's voice.

Maybe she actually isn't a hard ass.

Mathilde stayed silent, and Lore wondered if she was holding her breath, waiting to see what the older mouse said next.

"Sisters!" Minifred called. "Let's go,"

The other three mice filed out of the room more civilly than they entered. Before pulling the door shut behind her, Minifred spoke to Mathilde, but stayed fixated on Lore.

"Be downstairs in two minutes." Her voice was softer, like the steel edge in her tone had melted by the fires of fatigue. "The human clearly stays in the house." With that, she quietly shut the door, leaving Mathilde and Lore alone.

Mathilde didn't miss a beat, she jumped back atop the mattress so she and Lore were at eye-level. "Okay, so as much as I hate to admit it," she sounded defeated, "Minifred is right. You've got to stay put, at least until we figure out what happened to our father. Okay?"

Lore looked past Mathilde, and even with the curtain only partially gathered, she could see rows of animal bodies crowding the streets outside. "Then what?" she asked, not looking away from the window.

"We'll see what the commotion is about first, then worry about that later," Mathilde insisted.

The statement alone made Lore feel like a caged songbird, but she wouldn't know the first place to start when walking out into the world beyond the walls of the house. She rocked back on her heels. "Fine."

"Wonderful." Mathilde picked at the fraying cuffs of her bright red jacket. "I cannot emphasize enough how important it is that you agreed. For the safety of the townsfolk. But, more importantly, for yourself." Her eyes flickered away as if she were debating sharing something she shouldn't.

"*Mathilde!*" Minifred's voice boomed.

"Well, I must be off then." The mouse in question slid off the bed and scampered to the door. She looked back over her shoulder at Lore. "We'll talk more when I get back, Human. Don't worry, you're safe within the walls of this house."

Lore silently walked around the wooden frame of the bed to pick up the comforter. She pulled it neatly across the mattress. Mathilde shut the door and Lore quickly tiptoed over to the window. She knelt close to the ground so just her eyes and the bridge of her nose butted up against the slate gray window trim. Lore knitted her brow as she watched the animals in trench coats, odd hats, and billowing white sleeves of cotton filed together. She could imagine the townsfolk whispering, gossiping about the what-ifs regarding whatever it was they were going to see.

From under the front porch's roof, made of dark slabs of wood, she saw the mice shuffle out to meet the crowd gathering farther up the path.

Lore spotted a creature that stood out against the crowd, mainly because they were walking against it, unnoticed by anyone else. Lore watched the figure. *A rabbit? No, not quite.* She couldn't put a finger on it. Something about this entire scenario felt familiar but when would she have seen such a thing before? Then, for a moment, it looked up to the window and Lore felt the persistence of golden eyes pressing against her through the glass.

Her face went red, and she quickly backed away from the window. The pink petals on the wallpaper still seemed to blow in a gentle breeze. Lore swallowed the rock in her throat and crawled back over to the window to see if the golden-eyed animal left.

Sure enough, the figure had vanished, and Lore felt the weight of uncertainty on her shoulders. Mathilde's words echoed in the room. "You're safe within the walls of this house."

Lore raised a single brow. *If I'm bound to the boards of this house, then I might as well get better acquainted with it.*

TWELVE

She stood at the bottom of the stairwell, her hand still gripping the wooden railing tight. *Holy Mary, mother of Joseph.* There had only been one time that Lore had experimented with psychedelic drugs, and even that didn't cause this much of a trip.

Her eyes danced over the bright green wallpaper, the white flowers frantically searched for a single drop of sunlight. The deep plum curtains pulled tightly shut gave the room a sort of eerie purple glow. Lore drew closer to the hearth, where tiny figurines rested on the mantle. They were little porcelain mushrooms, each had a different colored cap. She approached the bright, golden flames and let them warm her.

As she reached a hand up to the small hand-painted figurines, a ghostly voice called out. "Look with your eyes, not your hands."

She whirled around, expecting to see a mouse sporting some sort of vintage dress. But there was nothing. Just her alone with the house and the items it held within it. She shook out the eerie feeling that she was being watched and directed her gaze back to the mantle. Her favorite was the teal-capped fungi. They were the smallest items lining the shelf tucked away in boughs of evergreen and elderberries.

Looking with her eyes and not her hands went out the door, as if the idea itself were trailing the mice sisters to the town square. Lore gingerly ran a finger over the glossy paint. Then she gently cupped the porcelain figurine in her palm. The golden flecks in the teal cap glimmered in the dim lighting. She held it close to her face and saw little painted nubs resembling hands, and small onyx eyes. *Whoever did this really had an eye for detail. They looked great.*

Then the itty-bitty eyes blinked.

Lore dropped the ceramic figurine. She winced, covering her reddened face, and held her breath, expecting to hear the shattering of porcelain. *How will I explain this to Mathilde? Hey, sorry I broke your little, living mushroom statue.* That didn't seem like it'd be effective.

After a few passing moments of still silence, she peeked through one eye to find the figurine dusting its stipe on a pile of throw pillows lazily thrown about on the floor. It looked up at her and shook a scolding nub followed by shrill, knife-life cheeps.

Lore knelt down so she could be eye-level with the creature. "Uh, sorry," she whispered. Then she felt gentle blows against her back.

She turned and saw it was the other mushrooms atop the mantle, hurling beady berries, random rocks, and stray pinecones at her.

"Okay! Okay!" She shuffled backward and felt her butt bump the table that sat between the living room and kitchen. She whirled around to see a pack of stray playing cards spread out flat on the table.

"The girl is lost," the Queen of Spades whispered to the King beside her.

"I'm not lost," Lore forced out.

"The girl is in denial," the Joker blurted out.

"Well, you're just a bunch of cards." She huffed and crossed her arms. "What do you know?"

The cards stood up on the oak table and shuffled themselves. "We know many things," the Queen of Hearts snidely remarked, before a Seven of Spades stood in front of her, then a Jack of Spades in front of it. "The Past—"

The Queen of Diamonds eclipsed the Jack as it—she?—moved to stand in front of the other card. "The present—"

And last, the King of Clubs stepped forward, now the front of the stack. "The future."

Lore's finger lingered on her chin as she watched the red backs of the cards dance on the table. "Can you read my fortune?"

Down The Well

The Joker jumped from the deck and jeered, "The human girl wants her fortune!" His words were interlaced with laughter.

Lore sucked on the inside of her cheek, waiting to see what would happen next. After the cards finished their dance, they all laid flat, only showing the ornate sloping and swirling designs of their back. The Joker paced back and forth in front of the card line. "Alright, human. Pay attention."

Lore pulled out the chair and sat down, her arms crossed, "Okay, you've got my attention."

The card stopped in front of her. "It's no mere coincidence you've arrived here, but let's see why. Instead of past, present, and future, we will lay a spread a bit more focus on your unique…" he paused, rubbed his chin, and did little air quotes with painted hands, "circumstances."

Lore rolled her eyes. "M'kay."

The Joker flipped inside the confines of the card so his bottom side was up and his front side was down. "Now, pick three cards."

"Doesn't matter the three, just pick whatever calls to you," the now-bottom side of the card added. Its tone made them seem a bit displeased about the new placement.

Lore pursed her lips and slid out her first card. She then went to flip it, but the Joker tossed a napkin ring at her hand. "Ah ah." They waved their four index fingers at her. "Two more!" they announced.

Lore's face scrunched as she slid two more cards that seemed to giggle at her previous misstep.

"Position!" the Joker called.

The first card flipped itself over. "Three of Hearts!" the card shouted, announcing itself, and toasted an imaginary glass to Lore. "It appears you're in the position to connect some things and come together with those around you and share."

"Share what?" She folded her hands together. "I got nothing to share."

"But you do. You have your perspective," the Three of Hearts retorted. "And your experience."

She had more questions but, wasting no time, the card beside it began folding up its edges.

The Joker announced. "Obstacle!"

The second card flipped. "'Tis I! Jack of Spades with a message!"

Oh boy, here we go. Lore rested her folded hands in her lap, twiddling her thumbs, and listened to what this one had to say.

"You, a powerful stranger, find yourself in a most mysterious place." The Jack leaned on the black symbol of his suit for some support as it continued its delivery. "As tempting as it may be to detach, it's more important to keep your thoughts and wits sharp."

Lore nodded, taking in what the Jack had to say. Then her eyes followed the Joker card, who was waddling over to the last card. It loudly prompted, "Advice!"

The last card flipped. An Ace.

"Ace of Clubs!" it proclaimed. "To survive this world, you'll need to be creative when problem-solving because you will face many dilemmas," the card stated. "But when the opportunity arises, listen to the call to action."

Lore leaned back on the wooden chair, rocking it a bit. Action, huh? She folded her hands behind her head. Her fingers grazed over a bit of a goose egg and that make her flinch from her own touch. *Ouch.*

Lore took another look at the cards. "Thank you. This was fun!"

The Joker raised a brow as the other cards shuffled again, waiting for someone else to sit at the kitchen table.

Lore went to the window and pulled back the plum-colored curtain. She watched the animals of the little town file down the cobblestone road in the direction the sisters went.

When the opportunity arises, take action. She gave herself an encouraging 'I got this.' She nodded in agreement with herself, lifted the window, and slid into the rose bushes that kissed the side of the Victorian-style house. *They'd look better if they were painted white.*

She felt a prick or two as she crawled under the rich red roses. She grimaced as she brought her finger to her mouth. The metallic, bitter taste immediately registered on her tongue.

She lay there looking for something else that could conceal her as the animals stood still and silent. That was something else Lore couldn't quite place. There was a mystery smell floating in the air. Not even the pleasant perfume of the roses could cover up the smell of rotting cabbage, let alone whatever the mysterious odor was.

She quickly slunk behind some trash bins and she overheard some animals that passed by.

"Damn shame."

"It is. Who knows what will happen to Charmsend now?"

Whatever it was, it didn't sound like a good time.

Lore slipped between shrubs along the walkway and behind trash cans. Each time her heart raced a little faster like a hamster running on a wheel desperate to reach a piece of snack hanging from a string. Then, as quick as her feet and hands would take her, she made her way under a large blooming hydrangea bush. She concealed herself beneath the bright green and pink speckled flowers.

The animals were all huddled tightly together, not a sound but the occasional wind flapping someone's jacket or scarf.

Lore leaned forward and noticed in the dirt beneath the shrub were paw prints. She tilted her head so she could get a better look. *I wonder who did this? Maybe a young animal playing hide-n-go seek with their friends?* She ran her fingers along the cool dirt, and the smell of rot loomed around her nose.

As Lore frolicked through the field of innocent thoughts, she didn't notice a pair of orange furry hands reaching out. The pair of orange paws barely reached past Lore's ears when a twig snapped.

She looked up, her breath trapped in her lungs, thinking someone had found her out.

The orange hands quickly pulled back before she could see them.

Lore saw a large skunk muttering something as he walked away. And then, for the shortest moment, there was a gap large enough that Lore could finally place what the smell was.

Emerald green scales were faint against the pool of thick blood beneath the body. Sharp teeth were plucked from the mouth of the stiffening corpse, and they were so pearly white that they sparkled like stars speckled against a red sky. A single eye had been pulled from its socket, still dangling by a pink vein that looks like a brittle thread.

Lore saw a familiar top hat, and when she looked at the animals at the frontmost ring of the circle, she saw the five mice sisters, frozen with agony painted on their faces like they just walked upon their worst nightmare.

Blood began to run off in little streams as the sky broke with tears of its own.

THIRTEEN

Lore's heart ached. But as much she felt pulled towards Mathilde, she couldn't move. Another scent clung to the wet air. *Smoke.*

Through the crowded cobblestone streets, a tall, thin opossum appeared. Its boney hand resting atop a jeweled cane in hand. "What in the three realities is everyone so concerned about?" he demanded before his beady, dark eyes bolted to the lifeless body. His yellow-stained eyebrows softened as he went to kneel by the dead alligator. "Oh, my old friend. What could have done this to you?" He adjusted the sleeves of his black tailored suit before picking up the alligator's teeth. Droplets of blood clung to the plucked bones and collected into a small puddle in his palm.

Murmurs broke through the crowd as the opossum slowly rose to his feet, that were in well-polished shoes. "Folks of Charmsend, we truly have a tragedy on our hands." His voice had a familiar theatrical tone.

Her brow furrowed as she tried to think of who the voice belonged to, but all that came to mind were distant shadows.

"Are the Grayshade breaking through the barrier, Sir Crinkle?" a shrill voice called from the crowd.

"No. The barrier is so strong. We've got a murderer in town," another animal added.

The last statement caused an uproar and the opossum—Sir Crinkle— whipped his thick hairless tail around, a bit impatient.

Lore's breath hitched, and the sound of the metal staff striking the stones echoed over the crowd and their accusations.

"Folks," the animal called as he gestured to the others, "we are a but a civil community here. There has to be a reasonable explanation." He tilted his head to the hydrangea bush.

Lore felt as if her heart has frost lacing over it, sending the rest of her body into a rigid stance. It felt like those two beady eyes were boring under her skin. She couldn't breathe.

"I fear," the tall shadow of the opossum began as he stalked over to the bush, "that we may have an outsider among us."

The ice blanketing her heart slid down the length of her spine.

As Sir Crinkle knelt down in front of the bush, the crowd of animals grumbled. The glimmering stone that looked like it held the ocean lifted a branch. His black button nose was mere inches from Lore's face, and she could feel his warm breath on her face. The animal's sparkling obsidian eyes looked past her.

And that's when Lore felt a sudden thud on her back. She winced and was sent tumbling out of the bush. The pink and green flowers scattered in the air. The combined scent of musk and smoke engulfed Lore like the thick green smoke from her dream the night before.

Sir Crinkle's staff skidded across the ground like a smooth rock skipping across still water.

Lore steadied herself, the feeling pressed silk between her fingers. When she peeked an eye open, she saw with the displeased creature clearly.

The horde of animals now stared at her. Some covered their gaping mouths, others gasped in fear.

"A *human*!" one cried from the group.

"A *murderous* human," a whisper began.

"But they were all supposed to be dead," another whisper roamed from loose lips.

Dead? In that moment, Lore felt like they gutted her like a fish. *All dead?* In that moment, her hopes of finding more humans like her died. But the mice *had* thought she was an extinct species, so she shouldn't have been surprised.

Sir Crinkle let out an exhausted sigh as he rubbed his temples. "Human, would you be so kind as to remove your weight from me? It's rather hard to take a breath of air with you on my chest."

Lore slid off, her hands still shaking. Her legs felt like jello, too.

The opossum stood again.

Mathilde brought him his metal staff.

"Ahem," he cleared his throat. The murmuring almost stopped, but not quite.

"Everyone calm down," he hissed. "This human isn't a threat, and couldn't have killed our beloved Gannon last night as it was in my care."

The crowd choked aloud in their shock.

His onyx eyes drilled into the townsfolk. "This human isn't a threat. A stranger, maybe, but not a threat."

Lore saw his gaze fall on her again. She couldn't even bring herself to stand up, so she looked back down at her hands on the wet ground. Letting the rainwater run down and soak her hair.

"Hardly."

For some reason, the word stung Lore. *I know what he's doing, but isn't this a little much?*

She felt a hand on her back, and a bold voice spoke.

"This human is under my protection."

She looked to see Mathilde sniffling back tears and snot, moving to stand between Lore and the crowd that appeared like they'd gladly see the human laying next to the alligator, equally dead.

Sir Crinkle commanded the crowd as he waved his staff in the air. "It's clear to me we have some investigating to do." His voice softened as he looked down again at Lore. "And it appears there is more than one stranger in Charmsend." His voice felt like little frost-tipped fangs dancing along her skin.

When no one left, he bellowed, "Go ahead. Leave, the lot of you!"

Thunder cracked across the sky as if to emphasize his point.

As the onlookers cleared out, Lore noticed the vivid orange bricks of the well about seven or so feet away also had a fresh red splatter across them. Her brow pulled tight, and she mustered enough strength to gain her feet.

Mathilde was still by her side, and the other mice sisters gathered close by.

Crinkle looked over at them. "Girls, feel free to head home. Lyudmilla and I can handle the funeral preparations from here."

A wolf Lore hadn't noticed before peeked out from behind the towering opossum. The wolf had long, snowy fur that fell in front of her pale pink eyes.

The four sisters didn't need to hear much else and quickly turned, heading back home with their heads hanging and tears flowing. All but Mathilde.

The self-proclaimed adventurer stood her ground, her face like a stoic statue. "No. We need to focus on who did this."

As the wolf that Crinkle called Lyudmilla began picking up pieces of the dismembered body, a smile twisted along the opossum's snout, making his whiskers twitch. "You're right. We do need to find out who did this," he agreed.

"We can't waste time either," Mathilde began drumming her fingers against her fuzzy chin.

"You know," Sir Crinkle purred, "what better way to win the townsfolk over with the human's innocence than the two of you launching a novice investigation?"

Mathilde's eyes narrowed. "*Novice?*" Her voice was flat and obviously displeased by the unkind and condescending adjective.

"Precisely, my dear." He placed a hand on her and Lore's backs to move them along. "Lyudmilla and I will do all the heavy lifting."

"Where do we even start?" Lore heard the words fall from her lips before she even had a chance to think about saying them.

The opossum hummed and leaned forward on his cane. "Everyone is a suspect."

Mathilde whipped around and gave the scene one last look before scampering over to the fallen top hat. The small creature stood there, heavy silence weighing on those left in the square. Then she knelt down to pick it up. "Come on, Human." Her fingers gripped the now blood-stained accessory in her hands tightly as she walked past Lore. "We have work to do."

Lore didn't wait to catch up with her. She looked back over her shoulder while her feet took her after Mathilde, taking in everything she could. Lyudmilla's sad pink eyes as she picked up the body, the blood on the well. The footprints under the bush. All these things rushed around her head as the well-dressed opossum gave her a gentle wave. She turned forward, but could still feel them both watching her until they disappeared from sight.

FOURTEEN

As she followed the red-clad mouse through the streets of the dreary Charmsend, Lore's stomach did flips and stunts like a trapeze artist. Any animal they came across steered so clear of her as though she had a giant, cartoonish cloud of green smelly smog around her.

"Mathilde?" she whispered.

"Hm?"

"I know I'm sort of an outsider, but why are they being so weird?" She tried to keep her voice low and smile at anyone who would keep eye contact with her—not that there were many. They kept dashing to the opposite side of the road every time they spotted her.

The mouse's fingers tightened on the brim of the large top hat. "It's not *just* because you're an outsider. It's because you and your kind have been long-thought to be extinct."

There was that word again. Extinct.

Mathilde's nose twitched as she looked at her kindly. "Did you really not hear them say that, human?"

At this point, Lore had felt like Death was harassing her—stalking her. It seemed everywhere she turned, the word was there lying in wait for her.

"Many," Mathilde continued speaking freely, leading Lore through the puddled streets, "most likely see your very existence as a bad omen."

DOWN THE WELL

Lore swallowed hard. Her throat felt dry despite all the dampness coating the air. "Oh."

Her companion's green eyes met hers. "But, don't worry. I know you aren't." She also gave a reassuring smile that put Lore's twisting nerves at ease.

"So, they believe me to be the killer? They must think a lot of me." Lore tried to force a casual tone, but the words still stumbled out a bit awkward. "That gator was as thick as an oak tree and maybe as tall as one too. How do they think I managed to take him down?"

Mathilde scoffed, still hugging the top hat. "That *gator*'s name is — was — Gannon. And he was nothing but a gentle giant."

Lore looked ahead. "So, how do five *mice* come to live under the same roof as a reptilian gentle giant?"

The mouse pinched the fur on her snout. "We don't have the luxury for the long version, but he adopted us."

Lore said nothing. *How does an alligator raise mice?*

Of all the charming buildings in town, seemingly to sprung from a pop-up fairytale book, Lore was not expecting to be standing in front of one so run down.

She scratched where her dampened hairline met the nape of her neck. "What is this place?"

"An important one," Mathilde answered, pushing the battered door open.

Lore chewed her bottom lip, not sure what dive bar they were about to walk into. As she stepped over the threshold, a strange sensation lingered over her body. As if she had stepped through a block of jelly.

Firelight danced, seeming to have minds of their own. The soft glow eliminated the darkness inside the building and made it easy for Lore to regain her senses. Soon, she felt her jaw softly drop as she saw rows and rows of bookshelves. There was also an open second floor that hugged the walls of the building, with even more bookshelves and artifacts encased in glass above them.

The only things that followed them were the twirling flames above their heads and the ghostly murmurs that sounded close enough for Lore to reach out and grab them. *What would a murmur even look like? Would it be slimy in my palm, or would the murmurs form solidly like a smooth river stone in my hand?*

"A library?" Lore said, as she slowly spun around, watching books flutter back to their shelf like butterflies. The inside was so immaculate and yet the only turning heads were those of stone busts and animal heads mounted to the walls. Every so often, a shelf of the wooden bookcase would turn like an invisible someone was spinning it in their search for whatever knowledge that brought them here.

Faint whispers landed in her ear, telling Lore that she and Mathilde weren't alone. Yet her eyes told her they were completely alone.

"Well, would you look at that," a stone bust of a bowtie-wearing badger said, squinting at Lore.

A moose head on the opposite wall, wearing a monocle, gave a nod. "I never thought I'd lay eyes on their kind again."

"Not just a library," Mathilde grinned as she took Lore's hand and led her down a curved staircase to a bottom floor.

Away from the speaking stone statues with bow ties, away from spinning bookshelves, away from mounted animals wearing monocles. With each step, Lore heard the echoes of the metal bounce off the brick walls, and at the bottom of the stairwell, displayed above a rather-long fireplace, stood a massive circular stone.

"This is where Gannon would hold important CHS meetings," the mouse explained. She walked over to one of the many bookshelves.

Lore felt like a rope was pulling her closer and closer to the stone circle, tugging her forward from its anchor around her waist.

With a closer look, Lore noticed that the stone was being held up with the help of sturdy iron spikes striking through pre-made holes. *At least they had to be pre-made. Otherwise, the impact would have caused splits and cracks to erupt.* She paused and furrowed her brows. *How would I have known that?*

Lore folded her arms over each other, as she ignored her passing question, and admired the craftsmanship. The rough surface of the stone had faint carvings. A plus sign divided the stone, and each section featured an engraving of an animal's silhouette. Behind the animal, little embossed leaves fluttered, each segment their own hue of peeling paint. "What is this?" Lore called to Mathilde, who was carrying a stack of books taller than her back to a table in the center of the room.

"Shhh," an unseen individual insisted.

It sent a shudder down Lore's spine as she pulled a seat out next to Mathilde. "What's the thing with that rock?" se whispered.

Her companion began sorting the stacks of books into two piles. "It's the wheel of seasons," she said flatly as she flipped through the pages of a worn purple leather book. "The plus sign is supposed to represent the beginning of the Mothertree's roots, and the animals on the stone are those who were chosen to protect the sacred tree."

Lore sat on her hands and looked around at the floating books and her eyes followed the curved metal staircase they came down on. She could still hear the laughter between the statue and the wall mount echoing.

"Why are we the only ones here?" Lore asked, then quickly added, "I mean this place is so…" She tried really hard to muster a word appropriate to describe the magic she was witnessing, but all that came out was, "cool."

Mathilde stopped flipping through the pages and a grin lifted her round rosy cheek. "We aren't the only ones here."

Lore furrowed her brow. She blinked in disbelief. "I'm sorry, *what?*"

Mathilde chuckled a bit and laid the open book in front of Lore. "So, since you are gonna be stuck here for a bit of time—"

"Wait, you can't just say that so damn casually. Who else is here?" Lore pleaded, looking around the room.

Mathilde let out a sigh, bringing her tiny hands and rubbing her temples. "Oh, right. I'm sorry. Don't know where my manners went. I shouldn't have cursed in front of you." Lore picked at the skin around her nails.

Mathilde's weary expression shifted as she started laughing so hard that she held her gut to keep from bursting.

"What's so funny?!" Lore demanded.

"Shhh…"

Another spine-chilling reminder for Lore to mind her tone.

Lore shot up, sending the chair scratching hard across the wooden floor. "What's so funny?" she whispered through gritted teeth.

"You," Mathilde admitted as she wiped away a single tear from the corner of her eye. The mouse then hopped atop the table and leaned on the split stack of books. "Human, I am this size because I am a mouse, not because I am a child."

Lore sucked on the inside of her cheek and quietly sat back down. "You could have just led with that, you know," she grumbled, pulling herself closer to the table and the book Mathilde had laid out for her.

Mathilde rolled her eyes. "Are all your kind so sensitive?"

Lore said nothing but tried to give it a good thought. *Her kind. My kind?* Shadowy figures formed in her head, but she couldn't see their faces. *Were we all as sensitive?* She couldn't answer. The unanswered question left a pit in her stomach.

"So, as I was saying," Mathilde began, still standing on the table, "you're stuck here for a while. Whatever gods you believe in, or don't believe in, something brought you here, Human."

Another shadowy figure flashed in Lore's mind. This one had large, piercing golden eyes. Tall ears atop its head and waved a bracelet at her. *Who was that? Because whoever that is who brought her here.* "If you must know, a less divine being brought me here," she said, the bitterness leaving a bad taste in her mouth.

Mathilde cocked her head to the side. "Human, do you know how you got here?"

Lore's palms felt sweaty. She looked away from Mathilde to the black and white sketch on the pages of the book in front of her. "All I remember is a shadow with big ears and gilded golden eyes."

Mathilde smacked her lips together. "Odd choice of words, but okay." Her hand drifted to the image Lore had just been looking at. "This is what we're taught about your kind."

The image didn't make her feel better. It didn't look like a human at all. The creature drawn stood hunched over a dead rabbit who wore a tattered suit. The supposed human had long, dark, stringy hair, and bright glowing eyes that looked like fire lit from brimstone. It had fangs poking upwards from a prominent underbite. It also had absurdly long dark talons that appeared to be its primary way of attack, likely used to cut open the rabbit's soft belly.

"This is awful," Lore muttered.

Mathilde sat on the edge of the table, her legs swinging back and forth. She grabbed Lore's hands. "I know, but it seems your obsidian claws have been filed down to just nubs."

Lore yanked her hand from Mathilde's furry hands. "Rude." She rubbed the tips of her chewed fingernails.

Mathilde flipped the page. "Well, now that you got a good hard look at how the townsfolk see you, let's look at something less depressing, shall we?"

Lore shuddered. The drawing's gleaming eyes were already burned into her brain.

"Shhhhhhh!" The annoyed shushing had become a part of the ambiance at this point.

Lore let out a sigh. "What else is there to know?" she asked.

Mathilde scoffed. "You've been dropped into a strange and mysterious otherland, and you ask, 'what else is there to know?'" The mouse clicked her tongue and shook a finger. "You're lucky you have me. I'd hate to think about how lost you'd be on your own right now."

Then Mathilde took a book off the stack closest to Lore and began flipping through the pages. "Something else you need to know is that there are folks who can control magic, called Wielders, and those who can't."

Lore wanted to bang her head against the table. *For fuck's sake, this was about to be such a boring history lesson.* "Why is it those with powers always get some sort of badass name, but the normal folks are defined by their lack of kick-ass-ness?"

Mathilde snapped the book shut, its blue cover staring back up at them, and ran her fingers through tufts of her gray fur. "Listen, Human."

"*Shhh.*" This time, it hissed louder than the dancing fire in the hearth behind the two.

Lore looked to the rafters of the ceiling and saw an enormous shadow clinging to the wooden trusses.

Mathilde didn't notice, or just didn't care, as she slammed the book on the table and pointed an angry finger at Lore's face. "I just saw the dead body of the alligator who raised me, shredded to ribbons in the town's market square. In his death, I am tethered to you, and I made a promise to keep you alive!" Her whiskers twitched in agitation—or was it frustration? "While I know this may seem tedious and useless information," she leaned closer, "it could save your life."

Lore gulped as the stinging sensation pricked the back of her throat, and her heart softened as she saw the mouse fighting hard against welling tears in the corner of her green eyes.

"Mathilde—"

Suddenly, a deafening thud hit the ground and shook the walls of the library.

Lore's eyes darted to the other side of the room and saw a large, legless body coiled around itself. Inky scales glistened in the soft light of the free-dancing flames. A snake's head rose, and bright orange eyes fixated on Lore and Mathilde.

"Ssso," the snake said with a flickering tongue, "the fear-filled murmursss are true after all."

FIFTEEN

Without missing a beat, Mathilde leaped off the table with her hands stuffed in the pockets of her bright red jacket. "Hello, Petra. I was curious when you'd show yourself." Her voice was still shaking off the heat of the previous moment between her and Lore.

The snake's body flowed like a rushing black river as Petra positioned herself in front of the mouse. The rest of the thick, scaly body lay in a mountain-sized pile where it had landed from the rafters.

Lore's heart felt like it had turned to stone and she stood frozen while the animals continued their conversation.

"Your father will be misssed. But we should celebrate asss he sssstarts the next journey," Petra said. Her voice sounded like it slipped in sweet syrup, yet the coldness of her tone still rang sharply in the room.

Mathilde said nothing at first, her back still facing Lore, but she could imagine the mouse biting a lip as she nodded her head. "While he's busy on his next big adventure," Mathilde's voice faltered, "I'm afraid that I'm left with a bunch of puzzle pieces that don't seem like they fit together."

"My condolencesss." The pumpkin-eyed snake's tongue flickered around Mathilde. "You know, I consssidered him a dear friend after all thossse yearsss he ssspent in these wallsss during sssleepless nightsss."

"Which is why I'm hoping you can help me." Mathilde looked over her shoulder at the tattered top hat sitting on the table beside the stacks of books.

The shimmering firelight caught a glimmer of silver around the snake's thick neck. It was a charm hanging off of a band of simple leather. The charm looked like four circles overlapping one another. *Some sort of knot?* Lore squinted with hopes of getting a better look, but as Mathilde turned to sit at the table again, Petra's mighty body shifted, rattling the ground beneath.

"What do you have in mind?" the snake's voice sounded as gentle as soft snowfall. "Mind you, my reach isss limited."

Mathilde's eyes glazed over. "The archives?" she asked, her gaze still fixated on the top hat, its golden band now stained with blood splatter.

Petra looked at Lore and then back to the hat on the table, her flat head bobbing as she did so. "There are lotsss of archivesss under my care. I'll need ssspecificsss."

Lore's lips puckered like the thoughts that rippled in her head were as sour as a lemon drop. *Archives?* The sensation of thudding against a sturdy back floated to the forefront of Lore's mind. *That night, it was Mathilde and the alligator—Gannon. They were talking about something. Some group.*

"You know the ones," Mathilde said with faint laughter. "The ones he was always so hard at work on."

Petra's head bobbed up and down. "Ah, thossse." Her eyes fixated on Lore. "Of all the beastsss in Thimbleton that could have broken through Sssir Crinkle's fancy cage…" The towering snake's alluring laugh filled the air. "I would not have guesssed a human."

Mathilde huffed, and Lore leaned back on the legs of her chair as if that would help her escape the intensity of the giant librarian.

"I sssaw the lassst onesss off, you know," Petra added in almost a whisper, her forked tongue fluttering out between words.

"The archives?" Mathilde's voice pulled the snake from her brief stroll down the lane of days passed.

Their host bowed her head to Mathilde. "Of courssse. One moment, pleassse." Her body twisted and twirled, stacking itself up, and up, and up. *No wonder the ceilings were so tall in this place.*

Lore's eyes watched the glimmering scales of the snake's body as it slithered up to the floor above them. *Like polished obsidian.* The shadow of Petra's flat, colossal head shaded over them as she stretched to the third level.

"Human, there's more you'll have to look through within the pages of those books." Mathilde gestured towards the two piles with a head nod. "A bit of town history, customs, and a sprinkle of folklore."

Lore's lips pulled into a thin line. "Never been a fan of reading," she admitted with an awkward chuckle.

Mathilde's tongue smacked against her teeth. "That's unfortunate for you."

She groaned, causing Mathilde's ears to twitch irritably.

The mouse's gaze softened. "Human, are you not able to read?" Her voice was as delicate as the black lace on Lore's dress.

"I can read just fine," she snapped, her words filled with scorn. She picked up the blue leather-bound book her companion had snapped shut. "I'll start here," Lore huffed.

Mathilde didn't push further, but a tender smile spread across her furry cheeks.

Lore brushed her fingertips against the golden embedded letters of the title. THE GREAT WIELDERS OF THIMBLETON. She inhaled deeply, and as she flipped through the first few chapters, skimming chapter titles, and paragraphs, she noticed a trend.

SABINA THE SINCERE

"Sabina is a beautiful name," Lore muttered to herself while looking at the portrait.

The image was of a dark brown hedgehog that had a thin white collar under her narrow nose that dripped down to a point. Her long, slender ears came to a point at the top of her head.

Mathilde's ears pricked up a bit while she looked at Petra's figure moving above. Still watching the snake, she replied, "Ah, Sabina, another of the many great Wielders Thimbleton had the honor of cherishing. She came from the noble N.O.T.'s."

Lore smiled. "N.O.T.'s?" What a funny word.

"Nomads of Thimbleton." Mathilde hummed, her eyes still fixated on the rafters.

Lore nodded even though no one saw, and continued reading.

This powerful Wielder held the title of Grand Caster for twenty years, where she led the folk of Thimbleton out of the shadows of a shattering depression that plagued the land from the icy north to the warm lands of the south. She led with compassion and patience. Her home atop Grand Caster Hill, a sanctuary for the lost, hungry, and weary. The end of her reign marked the end of the Umbra Age, and forward to the age of Kindling.

The ground shook again, bringing Lore away from the words to her thoughts. *Just how many Grand Casters are there? Where is this hill? What's the age of Kindling? Is Thimbleton still in this era? Or a new one?* The vibrations of the ground grew, and Lore's eyes peered over the blue book in her hands to the sight of Petra returning with a single book being held carefully in her mouth.

The scaly librarian lowered her head to the table, tenderly placing the tome in front of Mathilde. There was nothing inherently special about the book. In fact, the only thing that stuck out from its rusty red binding was the fact that the pages were so mismatched. Lore raised a brow as Mathilde flipped it open.

Then the mouse's face was a contradiction of wonder and sorrow as she skimmed the contents. Then her eyes angrily snapped to Petra. "What kind of a joke is this?" Mathilde's voice trembled, though Lore couldn't tell if it was with desperation or anger.

"As sssomeone with no official memberssship in the CHS, that isss all I can give you," Petra assured.

"There's nothing written in this book!" Mathilde's grip tightened on the pages.

Petra's head dipped, and her orange eyes scanned the tea-stained paper as Mathilde flipped through them. "How wily of him." The snake's tongue fluttered. It was the only sound among the ghostly whispers and flying books. "I exxxpected nothing less of him, though. If an outsssider wanted insssight, they'd have to work to uncover the sssecrets of reading the hidden wordss."

Mathilde glowered at the empty book. "He left me with a human to watch out for, and a trail that ended with him shredded to ribbons." She wiped her face with the cuff of her red jacket. "Such a cruel parting gift, Gannon." She uttered the words as if the alligator were there to hear, tears again welling in her eyes. The mouse shoved the book under her arm. "You can't let me see the other archives?"

Petra's orange eyes seemed to glow. "I am not the initiator, only the keeper, and you've no clearance for thossse documentsss."

Lore gulped and swallowed the metaphorical frog in her throat. "You know, there was something odd that stuck out to me."

Mathilde looked up, holding Lore's gaze despite the pain she was clearly in. "What, Human?"

"That bush I was hiding in," she began. "Well, there were footprints there. And there was a splatter of blood on the well, but Gannon's body was moved at least seven or eight feet away from it."

"Footprints?" Mathilde's ears perked up, and she slid from her chair. "We need to go look at them now — before the rain washes them away. If it hasn't already."

Lore nodded and kept the blue book in her hand as she pushed the wooden chair in.

The librarian's head swayed back and forth as they took turns speaking.

"Petra," Mathilde called, as she placed the top hat on her head, engulfing her with how oversized it was. "We will be taking these books —"

The reptile walled off the stairwell with her massive body. "Ssssory, but I made a vow to Gannon that nothing of the Charmsssend Hissstorical Sssociety archivesss would ever leave thisss thressshold." Whatever warmth the snake possessed before was no longer there.

Mathilde swallowed hard as she gripped the rusty red book close to her chest.

"I'll keep it ssssafe. You can return and sssee it when you figure out the key to reading it," Petra said before softly and expectantly opening her mouth in front of Mathilde.

Lore's eyes shot wide. The snake could have Mathilde in one bite if she wished for it.

Mathilde carefully placed the book in the enormous mouth.

The snake held it on her tongue. Then the coiled-up end of Petra unraveled bit by bit. The tip of her tail waved a librarian's stamp, just outside Lore's personal bubble.

Mathilde turned and flipped the front page open and pulled out a card from its pocket.

In a fluid motion, Petra stamped it. Then her body raced back to whatever secret hiding place she had for the Charmsend Historical Society's archives. The ground and walls trembled and gradually steadied until the vibrations completely halted.

Mathilde led Lore back up the curved metal staircase.

"Let's hope the prints are still there," the mouse said.

Their feet pounded against the metal steps. As they ascended to the entry-level floor, the irrefutable sound of rain thrashed against the roof and windows. The badger bust whistled when he saw them again.

"Not now, Sir Bernard," Mathilde said, rushing past the stone bust.

As Lore went to pass by him, he quickly spilled out a message. "He came in last night, you know. He was in quite a hurry. All a flutter. And Petra. Well, she and he had a bit of a disagreement." The stone badger's message was quick and quiet. As if the snake would hear his faint warning and punish him for sharing it.

The words landed hard, making Lore breathless as the tingling sensation of adrenaline rushed from her neck, down her arms, and to her fingertips.

"Go, go quickly." He turned his stone head toward the door where Mathilde had already disappeared.

"Thank you, Sir Bernie," Lore muttered as she darted for the exit.

"It's Bernard!" She heard the badger's voice call behind her.

SIXTEEN

The door slammed shut behind Lore, like the building itself was happy to be rid of a human intruder. Large droplets of water pelted her hair as she whipped her head back and forth, trying to see any sign of Mathilde. *Which way did we come from again?* As the rain picked up, the accompanying chilled air soaked Lore to the bone. *Well, if I continue standing here like a lost dog, then all I'm gonna do is catch a cold.*

She tightened her jaw and huffed as she started walking in a random direction. Looking for a warm place to rest, or Mathilde. She clutched the blue book close to her chest, under the cover of her green flannel. *I wonder if there is another animal kind here like Sabina the Sincere that would lend me an umbrella at the very least. A warm drink if I were lucky.*

It wasn't long before Lore saw a figure in the gray sheets of rain. *By Lady Luck's good graces, this could be someone to at least point me in the right direction.* As the figure and Lore closed in on each other, Lore felt like the long hairless tail ripped her lungs from her chest.

"Oh. Hello, human," Sir Crinkle purred with amusement, twirling the handle of his hefty umbrella.

Lore took a step back as the tall, slinky opossum stepped towards her. "Hi," she said in a nervous breath.

"Where is Mathilde?" His eyes peered around Lore, feigning a search for the mouse.

"That's a good question," Lore added. "One I am currently trying to figure out myself." Her grip tightened on the book under her flannel.

"Tsk tsk. She shouldn't have run off alone with a murderer on the loose." Sir Crinkle leaned on his staff, his narrow snout curled into a wicked smile. "Why don't you come with me?"

The very offer felt like an icicle had begun drip, drip, dripping its cold water down Lore's spine. *No, thank you.*

Sir Crinkle pointed with the end of his staff at the neon sign that was swaying in the whipping wind. "I'm on my way for a drink and a warm meal."

The crisp air blew again and the thick cloud coverage made it difficult for Lore to guess what time of day it was. The rain seeped through her flannel, and the frigid air nipped at her skin. She gritted her teeth and said, "Sure."

His thick tail seemed to wave at her, beckoning her to share the umbrella with him. "No further reason to weather the storm. The umbrella is big enough for the two of us."

She didn't move. *Mathilde is going to hear all about this.* Maybe then she'll think before taking off, but he *did* help clear the misunderstanding that she was capable of *murder.* Lore tensed as the conflicting thoughts battled.

Taking matters into his own hands, the opossum wrapped his tail around her. The weight of it on her waist made her want to vomit.

Thankfully, the pub wasn't that far of a walk, and when Sir Crinkle opened the door, a bell rang. All drunken cheer and laughter halted as blank stares carefully watched their entrance. The only sound was the sultry voice of the ginger vixen on stage and the keys of a piano. The other patrons watched as a long-haired, green-eyed calico cat wearing a wicked glower approached.

She was clad in a thin-strapped tank top, ripped pants, and thick-heeled black boots that clicked louder and louder against the floor as she approached them. A cigarette hung from her lips. Before Crinkle could request a table, She stepped closer to him and lifted her chin, stared him dead in the eye as she took a long hit off of it and blew the smoke into his face as she spoke. "I see that the only way you can get a plus one is by taking advantage of the human's naivety."

DOWN THE WELL

Lore was too stunned to say anything. Her wide eyes bounced to Sir Crinkle, who casually laughed the insult off as if it were a normal way to greet someone.

He fastened his umbrella closed. "You flatter me, Dina. But, no." Sir Crinkle's eyes sparkled like a freshly polished jet stone. "I'm afraid your wild imagination has once again misinterpreted the circumstances."

Dina raised an eyebrow. "That so?" Her tone invited a retort, and the crowded pub looked on. It appeared no one had let a breath slip since they'd entered.

The opossum didn't press further and merely smiled. He seemed smart enough to know which battles to choose. He tilted his head and let a soft laugh escape. "It'll be my usual booth, Dina."

The calico cat turned her back and picked up two menus from behind the hostess's podium. "Right this way," she said, her voice primed with the appeal of a molded fruit.

As Lore and Crinkle followed the cat to the booth in the farthest back corner of the pub, the conversations of the other animal folk picked up again. As if nothing out of the ordinary had just unfolded before them.

Seems like I'm not alone in my skepticism of the magic-using opossum. Lore noted as she slid against the rubbery cushion of the booth. Crinkle sat across from her, his naked hands folded neatly together. Felicity tossed down both menus, one in front of each of them. Then Lore noticed she had two leather cuffs with a circular metal ring hanging off each one. *Those are cute.*

The calico rested a hand on her hip. "Can I start y'all off with somethin' to drink?"

Lore opened the menu and sat it up, like a little wall between her and Sir Crinkle. "I'd like a water please." Then she watched the cat's stare bore into the opossum, who gave a smile.

"I'll have a coffee, two creams, four sugars, and shaken this time, love—last time I could taste that it was stirred."

Dina rolled her eyes and the sounds of her clicking heels faded away as she went to fetch their drinks.

99

Sir Crinkle rested his head on his folded hands. "You're soaked to the bone and you opt for a water instead of something warm? Like cocoa, coffee, or tea?"

Lore sat with her back flat against the booth. "Water is normally free or relatively cheap. As you could imagine, I don't have any money."

He said nothing at first, mulling over her answer and his next question. "So, how's that head of yours feeling?"

"Fine."

"You remember everything just fine, then?" His eyes narrowed, but he sounded amused.

Lore's forehead wrinkled. Before she could ask anything further, Dina returned.

"Anything look good to ya, human?" she asked, gesturing to the menu.

"Oh, sorry." Lore squinted at Crinkle before turning to the cat. "I didn't get the chance to see what there was."

"Take your time."

"Well, I am ready," Crinkle protested.

"I'll get to you when I get to you," Dina said firmly before disappearing into the smoke-filled bar.

Lore's eyes fluttered over the menu standing between her and Crinkle. *Lamb? Chicken pot pie?* "You're a bunch of cannibals?" she gasped, slightly horrified.

He bellowed out a laugh. "No, human." He adjusted himself as he took a sip of his coffee. "You see, there are some natural predators among us, and it's only just that we also accommodate to their uh…" his mouth cracked into a smile that looked like a spidering fracture in glass, "particular tastes as one might say."

Lore sucked on the inside of her cheek while she thought. "So, you mean to tell me you just pick someone random to slaughter because Frank the bear needs to eat?"

He laughed again. "You're a funny one, human." He took another sip and then smacked his lips together. "Not every rabbit, chicken, or animal has the factor that makes us folk, *us*." He paused, then leaned in like he was sharing some secret with her. "All animals are sacred in Thimbleton." He drummed his fingers against the table before softly adding, "Some are more competent than others, though."

Lore took a sip of her lemon water and digested this information.

He pressed his own questioning again. "So, I'm assuming since you slipped out of the mayor's manor, you didn't have any odd happenings when waking up after that healing spell?"

Lore used her straw to stab the lemon floating in her water. "Not anything that I noticed." *But how would I notice any weird side effects coming off of a healing spell? This whole damn town seemed like some sort of fever dream.*

Crinkle ran a finger around the rim of his coffee cup. "So, what's your name, human?"

Lore's eyes shot to his. She took a sip of water hoping it'd get rid of the sudden dryness coating the back of her throat. "I—uh, my name. Right."

The opossum grinned as he watched Lore silently search the crevices of her mind for something as simple as a name. *Her* name.

Her eyes lost focus, vision blurring and a few wrinkles scrunching on her forehead as her eyebrows pulled tightly together.

"Don't strain yourself," Crinkle's voice mused. "My magic must have been too potent for you, darling. Give it another day or so and you'll get your memories back."

Lore didn't trust the certainty of his voice. She crossed her arms. "How do you know?" *This place may have giant snakes and a talking deck of cards, but I draw the line at all-knowing magical opossums. Of all the animals—an* opossum*? Really?*

The animal in question let out a ghoulish cackle, "I may not be specialized in the healing arts…" He leaned forward over the table, closing what bit of space they had between them. "But I assure you, I am confident in my familiarity and ability with my magic."

Lore leaned against the rubbery back of the booth. She bit her lip and looked out the window at the rain pouring down outside. *There's no way those tracks are still there.* She looked back to Crinkle, who was taking a deep drink of his coffee. *Got to get away from this guy.*

Dina returned with a pad and glittery pink pen. "Y'all ready to order?"

Crinkle nodded. "Ah, yes. I'll have my usual, my dear. You know how I like the fruit cut just so, and the insects in a bowl on the side."

The fluffy calico scribbled down what he said. "How could I forget my pickiest customer's signature order?" she muttered. "How 'bout you, human? Anything catch your eye?"

Lore pursed her lips. "I'll just have what he's having."

The cat tilted her head. "Well, I'll be damned. The human doesn't want the raw meat of children with a side of blood sauce." She gave a teasing pat on Lore's shoulder. "S'pose I owe the cook a few copper taels after all." She laughed playfully.

As Dina turned to go take the order back to the kitchen, Lore reached out and grabbed her arm. Her striking green eyes felt like broken glass pressing into Lore's skin.

"Human, whatever you need, I'm certain you could have used a word," she said with a hiss.

A little gasp escaped Lore's mouth as she let go of the cat's fluffy arm. "Oh, right. Sorry. I was just wondering where your bathrooms were?"

Dina rolled her eyes and pointed with the bubblegum pink pen to a hall on the other side of the large fireplace. "Down that hallway." She looked Lore up and down with a less friendly attitude than earlier, then clicked away to the kitchen.

Crinkle said nothing as Lore slid out of the booth. He just took another drink of his coffee and looked out the window at the somber weather.

She walked as fast as she could, the strangers staring making her stomach uneasy. At the end of the short hallway was a single door with a toilet painted on a little piece of wood that swung when Lore opened the door. Inside were two stalls that almost kissed the top of the ceiling, a pair of sinks, and a mirror. *No window? Are you kidding me?*

One of the stall doors opened and the orange fox, the with the voice of a siren, sauntered out. She washed her paws in the dingy sinks. Then she applied some deep red lipstick and her blue eyes were the color of clear, cerulean waters, drawing Lore in when they made eye contact. "I'm used to the gazes of the folks in town, but the eyes of a human—"

her laugh was coated with a thick layer of sweet honey, "never thought I'd get the honor."

Lore gulped. She didn't realize she was staring. "Sorry." Then she adjusted her focus and scanned the walls for a hidden window.

The singer giggled and walked past Lore. Her sleek black dress glittered like a million stars in the grimy yellow light that flickered above them. "There's one in the second stall, though you may have to climb on the toilet to reach it." Her whisper tickled Lore's ear.

Lore looked over her shoulder. "How did you know?"

The fox smiled. "I can spot someone dying to escape a bad date."

First off, ew. "With all due respect," Lore fidgeted with her braid, "I think you misunderstand my circumstances."

The singing vixen's hand hovered over the doorknob. "Then should I say I know the face of someone who wants to get away from..." she put a claw to her chin, "unpleasant circumstances."

Lore smiled. *This was good. This was someone who wasn't itching to get as far from her like she carried the plague.* "Would you happen to know where the market square is?" Lore added, her voice more desperate than she'd like.

She opened the door, and the smell of fried food and booze-filled Lore's nose. *Wait a minute. How did I not catch it before?* The smell sent her mind tumbling after hearing a swish in the air and being hit over the head. Then the sensation of her weak body thudding against a scaled back sent a ghostly chill down her sprint.

"Human?" the vixen's voice brought Lore away from the foggy thoughts. "If you can fit through the window, the square is south. Just walk round to the front of the building and take a left, and you'll find yourself there." She gave a wink and left Lore alone in the flickering light of the bathroom.

Now alone, Lore looked at the large mirror that spread over both sinks. Her large, round gray eyes stared back at her. *I don't even recognize myself.* Her stomach growled. The temptation to go back and eat was pulling her to the door. *Oh, yes, right back into the hands of some creepy opossum and to be gawked at like some hideous beast? Stupid human.* Now she even sounded like the animals who kept talking down to her. She gripped the doorknob for a moment, her knuckles bright white. Then she shook herself out of whatever dark pit she found herself muddling in. *Come on, get it together. We got a mouse to find and tracks to identify.*

She opened the second stall and, sure enough, there was a long, thin window above the toilet. Already propped open. As Lore popped the screen out, she did her best to suck her stomach in as she climbed through. The metal frame scraped uncomfortably against her ribs. And the lean rectangle squeezed the air out of her. *If there ever comes another time or place that we have to go through a window or tight space, I'm not volunteering.* By some miracle, she actually pulled it off—then fell head-first into a pile of trash bags.

Lore groaned and the smell of rotten food that had sat out in the sun for two weeks forced itself upon her. She sat up and flicked a slimy tomato slice from her cheek. *Fucking gross.* She shot up and wiped off her lace-trimmed black dress and buttoned her dampened flannel.

She ran her hands ran alongside the brick wall, going toward a light poured out in front of her. A window. The same one she had been looking into just the night before. The hair on the back of her neck stood straight and tall like a threatened porcupine. A tingle shot from her neck, down her arms, and danced along her fingertips.

Lore let out a ragged breath. *Gotta find Mathilde. Gotta get back to Mathilde.* She peered in and saw Crinkle enjoying his dinner, admiring the sultry fox's melodic voice on stage. Her meal sat across from him with a to-go box sitting beside her cup of water. Her stomach growled. The fresh fruit looked delicious, and Lore could feel her mouth salivate. *Focus.*

She turned her back pressed against the wet brick and slowly slid down so her knees met her chest. *Find Mathilde, identify whatever is left of the tracks, then go home and eat.* She nodded to herself and peeked out of the alley. With no one around, she did as the singing vixen said. She took a left and stayed straight on that path.

Sure enough, Lore caught sight of the bright, orange well. She felt a spark of joy. She'd found the square. But the spark of joy quickly disappeared when she saw the numb figure of Mathilde standing in the pouring rain looking at the spot where the alligator had been found.

SEVENTEEN

Mathilde turned, peeking over her shoulder, her eyes bloodshot. "Doesn't even look like there was a murder scene anymore. It's all gone." Her laugh was cradled in bereavement.

The mouse's display made Lore feel like her own heart had tumbled from the cupboard, like a teacup and chipped—as if hearts were also made of such fragile materials.

She walked over. "Sorry, I couldn't have gotten here sooner," she murmured, kneeling down to the animal's eye level.

"It's okay, Human." Mathilde wiped her snout. "I shouldn't have left you in such a hurry."

Lore nodded as lighting cracked across the sky. "Did you see any tracks?"

Mathilde shoved her hands in her pockets and walked over to the bush. "No, the spotless scene made me freeze up." Her gaze was downcast as she sheepishly admitted, "Embarrassing, really."

But it isn't. It's totally understandable.

The cloudy sky's large puffs of gray and black blanketed over—not one—but both moons' light.

In the darkness, Lore could now only see the faint figure of her companion peeking under the branches of the hydrangea bush. The mouse turned and shook her head. Lore saw soft shadows on Mathilde's face thanks to the fire beginning to flicker alive behind the glass cages of the street lamps. The mouse's face had melted into an even more disconnected expression. And her ears wilted like sad flower petals on a hot summer's day.

Lore walked over and peeked. The soft silt devoured her fingertips, and the tracks weren't obvious anymore, but she narrowed her gaze and kept looking. The circumference around the bushes was wet, but further back it, seemed dryer. Lore crawled under the cover of the branches of the hydrangea.

"Human, the rain washed them away," Mathilde sighed. "We'll just have to find another lead, or hope one will fall in our laps tomorrow morning."

Lore ignored the words and reached further in toward the center of the bush, where damp dirt covered the area around the shrub's heart-wood. She scanned the ground, but she could hardly see anything. She reached out, frantically searching the ground by touch for any indentation of a print. Then it happened. Her fingertips dipped gently down into the earth. *Yes! Lady Luck is on our side today.*

"Mathilde!" Lore called. "Mathilde, I found them!"

The mouse's hand suddenly lifted the branches. Then she walked under the bush and stood beside her.

"They're here!" Lore cheered. "Can you see them? I'm having a hard time, if I'm honest."

Mathilde gasped. "Human!" She placed a small hand on Lore's shoulder. "That's it!" Relief washed away any previous doubt in the animal's voice. She then peeked out of the shrub and whistled at a streetlamp.

"What are you doing?" Lore asked, resting her dirt-covered hands on her thighs.

"Going to get us a light."

She tilted her head.

Mathilde let out a huff and crossed her arms. "Oh, they're just being shy." She insisted as she parted the branches of the hydrangea bush.

Lore sat there for a moment, and her ears detected Mathilde whispering something like there was something listening to her out in the square.

No. Someone.

Lore crouched and shuffled over to push the branches out of the way, to peek between the parted green and pink hydrangea growth and see what nonsense the mouse had to be up to.

107

There, in the middle of the empty market, only accompanied by closed wooden stands, Mathilde stood. Her hands sat on her hips, her ears flat against her head, and her finger pointed to the iron street lamp. "Come on, now," the mouse prompted. Then she walked behind the lamp and gave a little push. "When did you get so heavy?"

The streetlamp stood solid. Not even the sloping u-shaped metal adorning the iron stem budged.

Lore tilted her head and continued to watch. *She'll never be able to move that.* Her face scrunched as she watched the mouse struggle against the cold slippery alloy base. *Wouldn't it just be easier to open the glass and light a twig on fire or something?*

Mathilde lost her balance against the slick cobblestones beneath her feet. Then gave a scowl to the lamp. "Come on, you! We need a light." Her voice was riddled with cynicism.

Silence.

"How silly of me," the mouse said softly, as if to herself. She adjusted the oversized top hat so it wasn't blocking her vision, and with her hands on her hips, she changed her tone. She clasped her hands in front of her as if she were now as shy as she claimed the lamppost to be. "Grian, will you please come this way? We are in need of assistance." Her voice now sounded like a child asking for a sweet treat just before bedtime.

The street lamp's curved limbs straightened and the iron body bent down to look at Mathilde. The fire behind the glass flickered rapidly.

Was it talking to her?

"Right this way." Mathilde motioned for the street lamp to follow her, and it did.

The lamp left its corner and its metallic feet clinked against the stone path.

Lore stumbled further back into the damp dirt. *What was next? A self-pouring teapot to serve me?*

As Mathilde lifted the branches of the shrub, the streetlamp poked its head under.

Lore did her best not to jump or act startled, but that didn't stop a rush of needle pricks down her spine.

"Human, do you see the prints better? What are they?" Mathilde called.

While it was brighter under the bush, she never really learned animal tracks. *S'pose Mathilde can only lift the branches as high as she was.* Lore crawled through the bush and came out on the other end. *No way I'm crawling past a live fire.*

She walked 'round the bush to Mathilde. "Hey, why don't I hold the branches up? I might be able to lift it high enough so that the street lamp can shimmy under more."

The mouse nodded.

Lore grabbed the bundle of hydrangea growth in her hands, and her friend scampered under the shrub. With a single lift, the street lamp pushed its top half under the growth of the shrub.

"So, what kinda print is it?" Lore asked.

"Fox," Mathilde called back, as she shooed the iron lamp back out to the cobblestone path.

"A fox?" Lore asked aloud, her mind trailing back to the singing vixen from Dina's Pub.

The adventurer tapped her foot and the sound of raindrops thudded against the top hat. "We can think more on this in a dryer spot, and away from any more eyes." She grabbed Lore's wrist and pulled her along.

Lore turned her head and watched as the streetlamp paced back to its corner. The echoes of clinks with each step carried in the air as the two made their way from the square.

What eyes? There was no one else in the market square besides us?

EIGHTEEN

Lore stood in front of the door and watched the mice sisters who were all flocked around the hearth she'd investigated earlier. Minifred was in front of the coffee table, her gaze fixed on the intense golden flames, and the silver-furred twins sat in front of the large rocker.

Lore rocked back and forth on her heels. *A fox was with me in the hydrangea bush. Was the singing vixen from Dina's capable of murder?* She crossed her arms and drummed her fingers against the thick green fabric. *I could hardly picture a dainty fox like her approaching and killing Gannon, especially in such a manner.* Lore heard a teapot scream, and her eyes bounced around the open living area of the grand, yellow manor. *Perhaps not the murderer, but maybe a witness?*

Lore felt velvety fur kiss her forearm.

"Oh, sorry, human," Mildred muttered as she scurried away from Lore, her cinnamon fur sparking with life in front of the warm glow of the fireplace's light. Teacups and teapots rattled against the shining silver tea tray in the mouse's small hands. She set the tray on the dark coffee table and poured steaming liquid into the twins' cups with care.

Then Mathilde took the teapot from her sister with ease and filled the remaining four cups. It went so smoothly, it must be a part of their nighttime ritual.

Lore noticed each cup had its own pattern.

The twins were the only ones with cups that matched. They were taupe with a string of bright white dandelions wrapped just under the rim. Minifred's had a cluster of vivid pink star-shaped flowers. Lore didn't know the plant's name, but the center of the blooms each had about a dozen long thin feelers. Mildred took a deep drink from a cup with lavender strands woven around the circumference. The braided purple flowers really popped against the snow-colored cup.

There were two unclaimed mugs. The left had what seemed to resemble pinkish dragon scales rather than petals to follow the floral theme of the other cups. The center of the plant was a tawny bulb that got darker towards its center. Mathilde picked it up with her left hand and the last with her right.

She offered it to Lore. "Here, Human."

Lore would recognize this bright yellow flower anywhere. *Daffodils.* Dancing in a nonexistent spring breeze.

Just as she felt the warmth of the teacup starting to seep into her fingers, Maybel whimpered, "But—but that's Father's cup."

Mathilde bit her lip, not turning to face her sisters. "And I think he'd want his guest to enjoy a cup of tea." For once, the brash adventurer's voice had no fight in it. Even at the murder scene, her words had determination, but now, no jokes or sass colored the tone. She sounded utterly and completely drained.

Lore watched as Maybel gave a worry-filled look to Minifred.

The oldest sister reluctantly pulled her eyes away from the crackling fire. Her silver eyes made Lore's hair on her arm stand straight up. She began to nod slowly as if Mathilde's words had a delay and had only just now fallen on her ears. The coal-colored mouse's absent gaze bounced between her sisters, then landed on Lore before returning to the hearth. She waved a hand nonchalantly. "Mathilde's right. It would be important to Father that we keep his hospitable spirit alive."

The room was quiet and Lore took a sip of the steaming golden liquid as the mice swam in their thoughts and feelings. Sweet honey kissed her tongue, and the floral notes of chamomile warmed first her chest, then her stomach. She took in a deep breath and thought of her time in Charmsend thus far. *The town is absolutely adorable. The residents are peculiar, but the little details of magic and wonder feel like they're from a dream.*

Mathilde pulled a chair out at the table close to the kitchen and pointed to the seat beside her. "Human?"

Lore didn't take long to settle herself.

The room stayed relatively quiet aside from the whispers of Gannon's tales from around the hearth, and a pattern emerged. The mice would fill their bellies with laughter, then a sudden onslaught of tears would follow.

This is what Death does. Gifts the heavy burden of carrying a legacy to the survivors.

Mathilde rested her head on a hand propped on the table. "Human," she whispered. "Tomorrow is the ceremony where we will celebrate Gannon's life by burying him in the cold dirt." Her eyes looked like delicate green glass that could break at any moment. "It'll be in the morning, but then after we can, uh —" she wiped the tip of her nose with her red sleeve. "We'll go question the orange siren." She waved her fingers to add an air of fun, but it was clear the mouse was feeling everything but.

"We'll see how the day goes," Lore replied gently, then took another sip of tea.

Mathilde gripped her own mug. "No," she said flatly. "We'll question her. I will not rest until I figure out the truth of Gannon's death." Her words were biting.

Lore's forehead wrinkled, but she said nothing. *I guess that's one way to cope.*

Mathilde gulped some tea, then put down her cup. "Don't worry, though, Human." She gave Lore a soft smile. "I'm sure by the time we unmask the culprit, Sir Crinkle will have stirred up a way to get you back where you belong."

Where I belong? Lore looked at the other four siblings then back to Mathilde, who would be alone in her quest if Lore weren't here. *Perhaps, for now, this is where I need to be.* She looked down at her calloused hands. *After all, I can't even remember my name—let alone where I belong. What was home like? Where was home?*

Still, she nodded to Mathilde.

One by one, the mice went up to sleep as the crackling of the fire dwindled down. Mathilde's head kissed the tabletop, and she was asleep when Minifred came over and lifted her up. "Come, human. It's time we all get a little rest."

Lore noticed the strain in the eldest animal's voice as she followed her up the staircase.

"You remember which room is yours?"

Mine?

"The guest room? No, sorry."

Minifred wrapped her tail around the knob of the first door at the top of the staircase. "This is the one," she said with a gentle smile. "Goodnight, human."

"Goodnight," Lore replied, watching the mouse carry her sister away to another room.

Lore's nose twitched as the sweet smell of warm maple syrup aroused her from her sleep. When she brushed the dream from her eyes, she saw the early gentle rays of dawn filtering into the room and Mathilde at the foot of the bed.

The mouse had a plate of pancakes in her lap and, underneath the plate, some folded clothes.

"Well, I s'pose I should get used to you always coming in unannounced in the mornings?" Lore asked with a large stretch.

Mathilde's eyes stayed locked on the door. Not even a grin pricked the corners of her mouth. "Maybel made breakfast." She sat the plate down by Lore's knees and folded her hands atop the clothes. "It's not the way Gannon made them…" Her voice wavered and faded into silence before she continued. "But they're not terrible."

Lore's expression softened. "I'm sure they're delicious." Then her stomach growled. *I forgot just how hungry I was.* It wasn't as if she'd eaten anything at Dina's Pub when she was there with the opossum. The aching for food gnawed at her, so she leaned forward and sat the plate on her lap.

"What else do you have there?" she asked, cutting into the golden stack of pancakes. As the first bite passed her lips, the sweet sticky syrup swept over her pallet. *This has to be the most delicious thing I've ever eaten.* She quickly went for another bite. Lore shoved another perfect piece of pancake down her hatch when she saw bloodshot green eyes fixated on her.

Mathilde's ears curled over, drooping.

Lore sat the plate on the nightstand beside her even as her stomach twisted and begged for just one more bite. She focused on the little mouse at the foot of her bed. *I need to do something. But what?*

The two sat in silence for a few passing moments. The only movement in the room was the flowers searching for light on the tea-stained wallpaper. *What would I want someone to do?*

She leaned forward and Mathilde's breath hitched as Lore placed a hand on her shoulder. "You are not alone," she whispered.

Mathilde gripped the bedding. "Thank you, Human." She wiped her snout. "You know, I don't care what they say." She looked up and locked eyes with Lore. "You're not that bad." There was now a smile under the tear-filled eyes.

Lore nodded and looked over at the shifting vines across the walls. They moved like a snake. *Snake. Oh, that's right!*

"Mathilde!" She grabbed the little mouse's hands in hers with urgency. "I have something I need to tell you."

The mouse's tail seemed to stick straight out as if it were a pair of jeans on a line to dry, suddenly on high alert. "What?"

"When you left me at the library yesterday," Lore got out, trying to recall the exact words the badger said to her.

"Yeah. I said I was sorry about that?" Mathilde tried to chuckle.

"No," she said. "That badger! He told me that Gannon went in there the night he was murdered, and that your father and Petra had some sort of disagreement."

The mouse froze like a deer in headlights. Lore gripped her tiny hands harder—either trying to ground her or prevent her from running off to get revenge—she wasn't sure. "Don't worry. We'll figure this out." *We? But how can I sound so sure when I barely know myself?* Her doubt wrestled with her hunger to see which would win in successfully upsetting her stomach. Through the twinges of uncertainty, Lore loosened her grip and rubbed the back of Mathilde's hands. The motion felt familiar somehow, but she couldn't place it.

Her only friend in this strange world said nothing as she slid off the bed and away from Lore's warm-hearted words. She laid the folded clothes on the bed and quickly scampered to the door. Taking a ragged breath as her hand rested on the knob. "Dina dropped those off for you early this morning. She thought you were about her size. They're for the ceremony today."

The door silently shut and as Lore lifted the dress, she saw the lace trim around the bottom, and cable knit snow white stockings fell from the once folded dress onto her lap. Lore rubbed the soft cotton between her index finger and thumb. *Wait. Why am I a part of this ceremony?* Her brow pulled tight, but the smell of the maple tickled her nose once again, making her refocus on the food.

Another few bites before changing won't hurt. She left the clothes piled at the end of the bed and only glanced at them again on the second or third bite. *Wouldn't want to stain Dina's dress with syrup, after all.*

An icicle melted down her spine as she recalled the intense feline blowing smoke in Crinkle's pointed face.

NINETEEN

Lore ran a finger around the mouth of the stocking against her thigh. It grated against her skin. Whatever type of fabric it was knitted from, it itched and was bound to be bothersome for the rest of the day. She sighed and made her way down the steps. She didn't have to announce that she was coming. The creaking of the old wood had done that for her.

She held her bare arms, her mind drifting back up the stairwell to the green flannel folded neatly on the unmade bed. She couldn't place a finger on why, but wherever—whatever—home was, the flannel felt like it. It smelled of campfire smoke with notes of vanilla, which she hoped meant she had a life of sweetness and adventure to return to.

Her eyes drifted to the hearth that had embers smoldering in the morning sun that snuck around the curtains. The glass mushrooms were silent and still. Lore looked around the room. *No talking deck of cards to be found, either.* She looked back toward the mice huddled together by the door. They were all wearing white, and each clutched a tiny box close to their chest. Mathilde, however, was standing by herself at the window that looked out onto the front porch, her box sat close to her feet.

"They've got the tunnel set up." She turned to her sisters. "Won't be much longer." Her voice was almost a whisper.

Lore moved to the door and saw that a rather large crowd was gathering outside of the yellow manor.

"You said something about a tunnel?" she murmured.

The mouse nodded and fussed with her pleated white skirt. With the look on her face, one would think she had just been dipped in a bucket of slime.

Lore couldn't see the structure in question, but she saw figures and posts. "Just go along with it, okay?" Mathilde urged.

Lore looked down at her, still uncertain as to why she was involved.

Mathilde's shifting green eyes signaled a clear message. *I'll explain later.* *It was becoming quite the trend, really. Later, explanations. Later, a way home. Later. But never a promised time.*

The room was silent, so much so that when Crinkle opened the front door. It wailed as if the bones of its frame were broken.

"It's time." His voice was filled with as much life as Gannon's had in the short and hazy time Lore had heard the alligator speak.

The mice filed into a line. Minifred stood at the front with her head held high, and Mathilde in the back, her spirit fracturing under the weight of Grief's blanket wrapped around her shoulders.

Lore couldn't place it, but a feeling welled from deep within her chest. She, too, felt a gaping hole left unfilled. She stood behind Mathilde, knowing she needed to say something, but struggled to find the words.

Crinkle's beady eyes looked over them as they began to move out the door, boxes in each of the mice's hands.

The morning light blinded Lore, and she shielded her eyes from the rays. *It's beautiful, though.* The watercolor blending of the orange and pink hues painted the clear canvas above Charmsend.

The crowd of townsfolk gathered around a long, winding tunnel. It was made up of a deep red wooden skeleton frame that came to life as white lace was draped meticulously around every wooden support. The ends must have been steeped in some sort of gold, as they reflected the rising sun's light, casting a warm glow onto the town animals that held the pillars.

The mice and she stopped at the edge of the wooden porch, and the opossum's thick hairless tail swayed back and forth as he passed the sisters and Lore. He stood silently on the top step, and the only noise was the rasp of the wood under his weight. The gentle breeze kissed his pristine white coattails, and it was odd not to see the vivid green and purple fabrics draped around the yellow-tinged fur of the opossum.

With a deep exhale, he lit the end of what appeared to be a piece of driftwood with a flutter of his thin fingers and a pass of the hand. Crinkle pursed his lips and blew, a soft whistle escaping his mouth. The gentle breeze suffocated the lit flame. Just as quickly as it had been brought to life, it had died. Broad puffs of somber gray smoke coiled into the beautiful pastel sky.

"Step forward," he said stridently.

Minifred did as instructed, and Crinkle waved the smoking wooden wand around her.

"You may take the first step into the spirit tunnel and may a remnant of Gannon's character embrace you in this mortal form." His words passed over the other four mice and hit Lore right in the chest like a physical blow. Where the gaping hole's screams grew louder and louder. She held her breath and the oldest sister stepped down the stairs and onto the path under the dainty lace.

Some of the animal folk began humming. Others held the red posts of the tunnel's frame, tapping the heavy wood against the ground. Which added an almost rhythmic sound to the ceremony. One by one, the sisters stepped through the smoke and down the path.

Lore was an outsider. She did not know where the lace tunnel would let out, nor did she carry the weight of a small box with her. And some invisible force continued to push against her with each step forward. *Go back into the house,* her thoughts echoed in her otherwise empty head. *No, I need to stay with Mathilde. She asked me to be part of this.* Going back and forth with the conflicting thoughts, she didn't hear Crinkle's voice.

He loudly dropped his tail against the porch to get her attention. The vibration made Lore jolt. Her eyes darted to Crinkle, who was motioning for her.

"Come, human. Step forward." He sounded a bit annoyed with her but she ignored his tone. But she didn't care if he was frustrated with her for her hesitation or because she was included in this ceremony at all.

DOWN THE WELL

Her legs trembled as she stepped forward. But she didn't look at him. Instead, she watched Mathilde walk atop a mix of white petals and the natural path of the town. Between the flickering lanterns, her main companion's figure was slow, and it was with apparent care each step was taken. The smoke swirled around Lore, and the cedar smell made her nose itch and her lungs sting. She coughed and finally turned back to the opossum.

Crinkle's pensive eyes bored into her. "You may take the last step into the spirit tunnel and may a fragment of your character be used to close this sacred tunnel," he said with a tightened jaw.

Lore stepped down and into the tunnel. The sun's light kissed her skin with shapes of flowered designs between the airy lace. The eyes of the animal folk of Charmsend surrounded her. She could feel their thoughts like rocks being hurled at her.

"Why does the filthy human get such an honor?"

Murderer.

"Does the human even comprehend how important this is?"

Murderer.

"Why did they choose a human to take the last step?"

Murderer.

Lore's gaze stayed on the ground, but then the lanterns caught her eye. Pink fire danced behind metal animal silhouettes, creating quite an unusual dance for the shadows cast by the candlelight. *Firelight though it's early in the morning? And pink at that, how curious.* Lore noticed a pattern rather quickly. A hare, a lizard, an owl, and, lastly, a stag. They seemed to go in this repeating pattern as far as she could see. And the same blush pink fire burned the whole way down.

Lore heard a hefty something dragging along the ground behind her. She steadied her breathing and focused on Mathilde's figure, which was about five feet or so in front of her. The melodic thudding of the posts holding up the lace tunnel continued, and the chilling stares made the hairs on Lore's neck prick up. Yet, despite the distance the townsfolk wanted to keep from her, she found this ceremony quite beautiful. The twirling pink flames beckoned her to join them in an ancient dance.

It was moving and seemingly alive as Crinkle continued gripping the white material with one hand as he followed Lore. His staff thudded against the ground with each step. And each time, Lore swore a goose-bump appeared on her arm. As the suited opossum continued to fold the fabric, the animals holding the red posts would run to the front once they handed them over to him.

Lore dared look up, between the delicate spaces of woven white thread. Past the figures of strangers, she saw rolling fields of wheat in the distance. *Outside of town?*

The dragging sound continued to grate against her ears and she peeked over her shoulder to see Crinkle on the other side of the worldly tunnel. His grim gaze fixed on something past her. She noticed there appeared to be a pink ribbon woven in the fabric, keeping the 'door' closed.

She whipped her head back 'round and ran a finger around the mouth of her itchy stockings. Mathilde had stopped moving, and Lore wasted no time quickening her pace to stand by the mouse. The sun was high in the sky now, and as she stepped beside her friend, the two began walking together.

Mathilde pointed to the dancing flames. "The season of his birth."

Lore nodded, and her eyes brushed past the stone walls surrounding the graveyard.

The mouse's hands trembled, rattling something inside the box she held. It had a Hare carved into the top along with the letter 'G'.

At the end of this tunnel, a waterfall of more white lace cascaded around a stone grave marker paired with a giant deep hole that looked like it could cover an old thick oak log without a trace. Lore swallowed hard.

Crinkle walked around the outside of the now shrunken tunnel. He stood behind the grave marker that read, GANNON A. FITZGERALD: FOUNDER, FATHER, BELOVED MAYOR.

Lore felt the town circle around her and the sisters, the delicate fabric the only barrier between them.

Sir Crinkle cleared his throat and blotted away where tears *should* have been falling with a hanky. "We are gathered to mourn the loss of our town's mayor, but he was more than that title alone. He carried many.

DOWN THE WELL

Gannon was a father, he was an elder of the Charmsend Historical Society, and I had the privilege to call him my dear friend." He gestured to the mice sisters. "Minifred, please share what is in your box, then put it in his final resting place."

The white dress she wore made her coal fur shine, and she composed herself with the most poise of the group of sisters. "I brought my father a pocket knife he gifted me and a piece of wood perfect to whittle. When I lost my temper, he always said I made the most beautiful carvings, and that was a better use of my anger than lashing out…"

Lore felt her lips purse. *I can't imagine Minifred lashing out. She's so together. It's clear she cares deeply about her younger sisters.* Lore shifted her weight a bit. *Her eyes have felt like silver bullets before, though.*

The next one was Mildred, the cinnamon-colored mouse. She had a hard time revealing her item because it got stuck in her box. She kept choking on her tears, but eventually she explained, with the help of her older sister, that she'd brought a family photo so even in the next life, Gannon knew he still had loved ones who would carry on his good name and values.

Maybel stepped up next. "I brought my father the recipe book we put together for my fifteenth birthday." She lowered her box into the hole and stepped back. "I hope the next life is just as sweet as your custard donuts," she murmured. She hugged her twin, who let out a sigh as her grip on the wrapped item started to shake.

Mayberry held her chin high and leaned down to lower her gift. "I brought playing cards so that you aren't bored and can teach others how to play, just like you taught me." As the box disappeared into the grave, Mayberry grinned. "Maybe you'll school Death in a game." She stepped back and resumed hugging her twin.

Then Mathilde stepped past them all, wiping away her tears. None of her sisters stepped up to console her, and Sir Crinkle didn't give her any sort of understanding nod or gesture.

121

Lore swallowed the rock in her throat at the sight of her friend standing without any support.

"For Gannon, I brought a storybook he wrote himself for me shortly after arriving here at the cost of my biological parents' lives." She looked back at her sisters, her eyes begging for one of them to join her. But Minifred was too busy consoling the others to notice, and the remaining sisters were too distracted by their own pain to help their youngest sibling.

Lore felt her legs pull her toward the grave and Mathilde. She knelt down and rubbed her hand along the mouse's back.

Mathilde continued speaking through ragged breaths. "It has brought me comfort through the years, and comfort is what I want Gannon to have in his next life." She slowly lowered her box into the grave before promptly joining her sisters, hand in hand, as Crinkle closed out the ceremony.

"Per tradition, the one who closed the sacred tunnel shall be the one to cover the soul's shell with earth."

Before Lore could put two and two together, a snap of Crinkle's fingers made the weight of a shovel's shaft drop in her hands. A fresh pile of dirt erupted from the ground beside the open grave.

Her gaze met Crinkle's through the fluttering lace between them, then drifted back to the mice sisters. *I shouldn't be doing this.* "I can't," she mouthed.

Mathilde's voice cracked through the air. "You can, and you will."

Her fingers gripped the shovel on instinct, though her legs shuddered. The first heap of dirt felt like mountains weighing her arms down. Following that, she tried to move as quickly as she could. Partially to get the glaring eyes of the townsfolk off of her, partially to end this drawn-out funeral for the hospitable sisters, and partially to get away from Crinkle. When the last bit of earth was smoothed over the grave, the lace circle was lifted, and the animal folk rushed forward to embrace the grieving family.

Lore watched from the side.

Crinkle's figure loomed close by. "It's over now. He is free to begin the next part of the cycle."

She furrowed a brow and stabbed the shovel into the ground between her and the well-dressed opossum.

But it isn't over. His murderer still roams free.

The setting sun cast an amber glow on the fields of the valley. In the distance, nestled amidst the hills, Lore could see the lights of the town aglow. *Pink fire.*

"Mathilde." Her voice sounded like that of a stranger. Certainly not her own. Her hand muscles throbbed, still feeling the strain of shoveling from earlier in the afternoon.

The mouse in question was sitting in silence beside the stone grave marker, her head leaning on it. She had been this way since the crowd retreated back to the safety of the town.

Lore could still hear Lyudmilla's gentle warning before she, too, had left them.

"Crinkle didn't want to frighten the town," the wolf had said, "but a Grayshade very well could have broken through. I've seen them in action. Please don't dwell here long after dark."

"Mathilde," she repeated. Her pleas were tight as the sun sank behind the twisted, mangled tree line that cradled the valley.

Large green eyes met hers. "Just a little longer, Human." Mathilde's voice faltered at the end.

"We don't have much longer. You heard Lydumilla."

Mathilde folded her hands atop the cold stone and tilted her head toward the forest line. "I'm not ready," she insisted through bitter tears.

Lore's knees hit the soft earth beside the mouse. "And you may never be."

"He was there as I watched my parents torn limb from limb, you know."

Lore's jaw tightened. *Not the time or place I was expecting this story.*

"I watched as he and Lyudmilla fought back the altered spirits."

If Lore squinted hard enough, she swore she could see the memory playing out on the glassy surface of Mathilde's bloodshot eyes.

"My parents assured us before we left Taper all those years ago that the rumors were just that. *Rumors.* And that this was a new start for us. For our family."

"I'm so sorry." Lore leaned closer. If Mathilde decided she wanted a hug, she was there.

The mouse wiped her snout, and as her mouth opened, a guttural wail erupted from beyond the iron gates of the graveyard.

As bad as she felt about rushing her friend, she had to. "It's time, Mathilde," Lore insisted. "We *have* to go."

For the first and only time during their acquaintance and unlikely friendship, the mouse's face scrunched with panic as she grabbed Lore's hand.

Without further delay, they rushed back to the enchanted pink fire dancing in the lanterns of Charmsend just beyond the hills.

TWENTY

Mathilde and Lore watched the stretching and shrinking shadows of the animal folk that moved along the stone ground. The market square was alive with dancing bodies and a blazing fire in the center of the square. The lanterns were even swaying from side to side where they stood.

"Celebration of his life," the mouse uttered amidst the deafening music.

A smoky scent filled the air, carrying a hint of pepper and garlic. Lore scanned the crowd to find the source, and she saw a spitfire roaring with about a dozen chickens being roasted. Her stomach growled.

The mouse's stomach echoed the sound. Mathilde looked at her and grinned, scratching behind her ear. "I s'pose Gannon would want me to eat." She led Lore to the wooden stalls displaying pre-plated food. They each took a serving and found somewhere quiet to sit, though the music could still be faintly heard.

"I don't think I see your sisters here," Lore said before she took a bite out of her juicy drumstick.

Mathilde shook her head as she picked at an apple dumpling. "They are probably at home. Trying to make the night as routine as possible."

Lore pursed her lips, then quietly asked, "Do you want to turn in for the night, too?"

Her companion took a large bite, tapping the fork to her lips as she chewed and considered her options. "No, I don't think we will." The flat reply was thoughtful, almost dreamy, but didn't leave room for argument.

Lore was too busy gnawing a corn cob to reply immediately.

Mathilde's eyes drifted to the hydrangea bush they crawled under just last night.

"Fox prints, right?" she asked, as if they both hadn't burned the knowledge in their minds the moment the mouse identified them.

Lore nodded. "Yup."

Mathilde took the last bite of her dumpling. "Let's go tangle with a certain auburn siren."

Lore sighed, quickly got up to toss her paper plate in the trash, and followed behind Mathilde, who was already making her way down the path to the north side of the town. "Wait for me!" she called, then took a rather large bite of the sprinkled donut she'd saved for last.

Mathilde's figure halted on the road, now devoured by murk and gloom. A crisp breeze blew, and the more north they walked, the quieter the music and banter became. This end of the city was dull and gray compared to the vivid colors of the market square. The only flash of color was the flickering hot pink neon sign that drew them in like a pair of moths.

As the door groaned open, a familiar hypnotizing voice fluttered in the air like monarch butterflies floating on a warm breeze at the start of summer.

> "Of all the money that e'er I had, I
> spent it in good company.
> And all the harm I've ever done, alas, it
> was to none but me."

Lore followed behind Mathilde as she wove between the empty seats and tables of the pub. They could hear the murmurs of the other waitresses sitting at the booths counting their tips from the night.

> "And all I've done for want of wit.
> To memory, now, I can't recall."

The vixen's hands gripped the mic from both sides, held together between her paws. Her eyes closed, probably mentally singing for no crowd, but Lore and Mathilde watched.

> "So, fill to me the parting glass.
> Good night and joy be to you all."

The fox's voice rang low like a deep toll of a bell.

Down The Well

The sound of heels against the aged wood floor sent a shiver down Lore's back. She peeked over her shoulder and saw Dina linger around the door. With a flip of a switch, the pink neon glow dissipated from the window behind them, leaving only darkened streets before Lore.

> "So, fill to me the parting glass,
> And drink a health whate'er befalls.
> Then gently rise and softly call."

Mathilde whispered the lyrics along with the sultry voice of the fox filling the empty pub.

> "Good night and joy be to you all."

Lore looked to the back corner where Crinkle and she had sat. The booth was empty, but just looking in that direction gave Lore the hee-bie-jeebies.

The singer took the mic from the stand and put it close to her ruby-painted lips.

> "Of all the comrades that e'er I had,
> they're sorry for my going away.
> "And all the sweethearts that e'er I had,
> they'd wish me one more day to stay."

Mathilde slowly clapped.

The vixen's eyes shot open, and she stood like a deer in headlights on the stage.

"Lovely as always, Tansy," Mathilde commented.

The fox placed the mic back on its stand. "It wasn't the end, you know," she said, yearning chiming clear.

"Well," Mathilde's eyes drifted down to the grain of the round pine table. "We were hoping to have a word with ya."

The singer's ears flattened.

In fear or aggression?

"Regarding?" the performer asked.

"Some tracks we found the other night," Mathilde said.

Tansy's fluffy, white-tipped tail flicked from side to side like an agitated cat, though her eyes still sparkled. "And what's that have to do with me?"

"Hopefully nothing." Mathilde's voice still carried a ball and chain.

Lore's ears heard thick-heeled black boots clicking on the floor, getting closer with each step.

Dina pulled out a chair and rummaged around in her pockets for her pack of smokes. As she lit a cigarette, she took a long hit and plopped down in the chair beside her. "Hey, human." She tilted her head back and blew a drag of gray smoke upwards. Then her feline eyes locked with Lore's. "Didn't think I'd see you again so soon."

Mathilde's ears twitched. *She heard that comment.* But her gaze remained on the stage.

"Fox tracks," Mathilde divulged. "In a bush with a perfect view of the murder scene."

The singer's head tilted. "How peculiar." Tansy sat on the edge of the rounded stage. Her shimmering sapphire dress washed over her legs that dangled, barely touching the floor.

The waitresses paused counting their money—no, taels, Dina had called them—from a hard night's work. Listening to what would surely be spread as town gossip the following day or so.

"Tansy?" Lore asked, drawing the fox's attention away from Mathilde. "Did you see who killed Gannon?" *Maybe if we frame her as being a witness instead of a suspect, she'll be more willing to cooperate.*

Her companion's tail brushed against Lore's leg as if to say, well done.

The fox leaned back, resting her body's weight on her arms as she stared up at the pale glint of yellow lights hanging above. "How I wish I had." Tansy's head shot back to the table. Cerulean eyes burned brightly. A deep-seated rage that not even the most adept blacksmith would be able to hammer out. "I'd make sure they'd pay for the atrocity that invited Grief to all of our doorsteps."

Mathilde's hand was steady on the round pine table as she let out an exhausted groan. She wiped her other hand down her face. "You're the only fox in town." Her words were true, but bobbed around like a fishing lure atop still water. "No one is feeling Grief's greedy hold like my sisters and me." Mathilde was pleading at this point. "Tansy, please."

Dina snuffed out the butt of her cigarette in the orange glass ashtray. "How do you know the tracks were made the night of the murder?"

Mathilde clicked her tongue against her teeth.

Lore shrugged, then spoke. "We don't, but the day the body was found, I was in that bush and with what Crinkle alluded to, I wasn't alone in there."

Dina cackled, but Mathilde's eyes were still fixated on the fox sitting on the stage.

"So, what you're saying is the human was in the bush with the killer and didn't know it?!" She flipped her lighter open. "And Crinkle saw the killer, but didn't pull them out of the bush to let us townsfolk have our way with 'em?"

Mathilde hung her head. "This was pointless."

"It's pointless because you've no direction, and no knowin'," Dina said.

"Yeah." Mathilde's ears drooped. "Gannon didn't leave behind much for me to follow."

The calico cat slid her lighter across the table to the mouse. "You know what I know, though?"

"Hm?" Mathilde picked up the lighter, examining it.

"Tansy worked her entire shift that night, not once leaving the stage. Not for food or even for a bathroom break."

Lore leaned in as Dina's voice lowered. "And besides, she came home with me."

Mathilde flicked the lighter. The lid popped up, and a yellow flame danced. Then the mouse closed the steel lighter and her palm around it as she leaped from the chair. "I think we have all we need from here. Let's go, Human."

Lore hesitated to stand up, the glowering green eyes of the calico cat following her as she followed Mathilde. She pulled the door closed behind her, and she watched as Mathilde paced back and forth, flicking the lighter open and closed.

"What is it?" She hoped the question would make Mathilde stop.

"Dina was telling the truth."

"How can you be certain?" Lore found the thought escaped her mouth before she could really ask herself if she wanted to ask it or not.

Mathilde held up the lighter with a grin. "This symbol is painted on the lighter." The mouse tried as best she could to shove it in Lore's face, though their height difference made that a little tough. Still, she showed off the overlapping circles of the infinity knot from the library. "It's the mark of the Charmsend Historical Society." Then she shoved the lighter into a pocket of her pleated skirt.

Charmsend Historical Society. The words sent Lore back to the night she came here. Not entirely sure how or why. But the imagery of a small shadow, a reflection in the window of Dina's, stuck in her mind. *Where do I fit in all this? Do I even fit?*

"So," Lore whispered as she followed Mathilde in the dreary grey streets. "From what I gather, the CHS is an anonymous group of villagers? What do they do?"

Mathilde didn't look over her shoulder as she responded. "They gather and share the truths of the town. In the Charmsend Compendium." Her voice was as stale as Crinkle's green and purple suit. "And it appears we now know who the initiator is." Each word dripped with an early sense of victory as they fell from Mathilde's mouth. Lore only hoped she wasn't getting too far ahead of herself.

The two stopped in front of the frail exterior of the town's library.

Lore's stomach churned as the image of the herculean snake slithered to the front of her mind. "Mathilde. Do we have a plan?"

The mouse's brow furrowed. "Human, by now I thought you knew I don't plan." She forced a laugh.

Lore tried to stifle the fear crawling its way up her throat. "Right."

Her companion opened the door, and silence fell on them, worse than before. No ghostly murmurs were heard this time. Not even their footsteps made a sound as they walked between bookshelves.

Lore's heartbeat was the only sound that echoed in her ears. *Mathilde might not have a plan, but if things go wrong, we may need one.* She nodded, agreeing with herself, as she followed the mouse down to the bottom level. Her eyes scanned the walls as they walked down the sloped stairwell. There was a whaling harpoon she didn't notice before. *That could work. But how would we get to it? Let alone get it off the wall mount?*

Her jaw tightened. The questions and possibilities raced in around her head. Fighting for which worry was dreadful enough to be worthy of taking center stage.

Mathilde sat down in a seat facing the hearth that always seemed to be just the right amount of warmth. Instinctively, Lore sat across from her, her back being soothed by the golden heat.

The mouse took Dina's lighter out and flicked it open. The flame swayed back and forth. Mathilde repeated this a handful of times and, sure enough, a groan escaped from the thick rafters above.

Chills like the first crisp wind of autumn tingled down Lore's arm, leaving goosebumps in its wake. *Petra.*

Mathilde's eyes did not waver. They held firm on the burning fire sitting in the hearth.

The snake's enormous body lowered, and she hung that way, looking down at the two of them. "What bringsss you in tonight?" she asked with her head tilted in curiosity.

Mathilde, not one to waste time, flipped the lid of the lighter shut. "Just need to ask you a few questions."

Lore's eyes darted between both animals.

Petra's tongue flickered. "What quessstions would thossse be?"

Lore thought the librarian said the question more as a dare than genuine curiosity.

"What were you and Gannon arguing about the night of his murder?" Mathilde's eyes stayed forward, not glancing once at the large reptile. Her hand continued mindlessly opening and closing the lighter.

Petra's laugh was cool like a burst of air from a deep freeze. "Where did you hear such a thing?"

Though Mathilde was maybe the height of a human toddler, Lore felt like she had shrunken down to the size of a dwarf hamster next to Petra. *Get it together. Come on.* But every muscle in her body felt frozen by the snake's chilly laughter.

The mouse climbed atop the table and looked the snake directly in her keenly observant orange eyes. "Today is not the day to mess with me, and *I'm* not the one being interrogated," she spat, gripping the lighter in her palm.

"Sssuch big wordsss for sssomeone sso sssmall."

Mathilde's eyes narrowed like polished emerald daggers, but she uttered nothing else. Just held the reptile's piercing gaze.

"I sssee you've nailed down your father's no-nonsenssse look." Petra's glistening scaled body slid gently from above, piling into what looked like a mountain of pristine polished obsidian. "Sssecret isss out then." The snake's tongue flickered out once more.

Mathilde's stance didn't break, nor did her silence.

"If you mussst know, yesss. We had a bit of a disssagreement." Petra moved slowly, dragging her body against the ground. "But what friendsss don't?"

"What were you two *disagreeing* about?" Mathilde's words shot out.

Lore stiffened when she felt the tickle of the snake's tongue on the back of her neck. Petra was behind her. Was she about to be eaten?

"You know I can't tell you," the librarian said.

"Can't or won't?" Mathilde demanded.

Lore felt like a chilled dagger was being dragged against her spine. *A sensation I think I've felt before?* Lore's eyes bounced again from Mathilde and the reptile that was now peering out from behind her chair.

"Both."

Lore sat there frozen as Mathilde's scrunched forehead gave away. The mouse now lost deep in thought.

How to get Petra to talk... Would anything make her talk?

The librarian moved again, returning to the spot where she had originally landed from the rafters.

"You weren't at the ceremony. Why?" Without giving it a second thought, the words fell quickly from Lore's mouth.

The bold question even made Mathilde's tail twitch.

Another burst of cold laughter erupted from Petra. "Human, hasss no one told you the ssstory of the cursssed Librarian?"

Lore looked at Mathilde, whose ears furled over.

"No, I didn't think to share it," she whispered.

Lore looked back to the illuminated orange eyes of Petra, now gleaming with a dangerous amusement.

"I am confined within the walls of this building. Forever bound to the building like pages bound to the spine of a book." Her voice was laced with clear bitterness.

"Wh-what?" Lore's forehead wrinkled. "Why?"

"To be a caretaker," Mathilde interrupted quickly.

Petra didn't protest the answer, but the glare that burned brightly told Lore all she needed to know. *Later. I would find out why later. Like everything else.* Lore sighed and went began fidgeting with the lace trim of the dress.

"I think you'll see I *do* have a reason to know what you both were talking about, as I am now in," Mathilde announced.

Petra's smile split like a fracturing crack through glass. "Isss that ssso? Your father never gave you the sssymbol. I'm calling your bluff."

Mathilde held the metal lighter flat in her hand. The warm glow of the fire made the silver of the infinity knot shimmer. "My father was never the initiator."

Petra flicked her tail in annoyance. "Fine."

Mathilde smiled and climbed off the table. When she sat down, it was clear relief had washed over her.

Petra moved again. "He ssslithered behind my back."

Lore looked at the mouse. Was Mathilde really as calm as she looked? Or was she just a remarkably good actress?

"Betraying my trussst," Petra's body continued to move around the table, piling on top of itself, creating a scaly wall that would be hard to climb.

Lore's heart skipped a beat. *She's trapping us.* Her eyes flicked over to her friend who either did not see the danger or simply chose to ignore it.

"He ssswitched out the Compendium with a fake. A ssslap in the face really after trapping me here to guard the carefully written wordsss immortalized between the pagesss for all eternity." The snake's words seethed with anger.

Mathilde's snout twitched. "And when this role was given to you, he made you immortal as well."

"Forced upon me." Petra's tone flipped between ice and fire. Bitter coldness and fiery passion from years of being trapped in a box—even if said cage was a whole building. "My life'sss forced purpossse rendered uselesss in one sssneaky move."

"Did he say why he switched them?" Mathilde pressed.

"No. He liked to keep sssecrets." Petra now paused where the start of her circle began.

"There has to be a reason," Mathilde said aloud, drumming her fingers against the table.

"A reassson he didn't give," Petra chimed, enclosing the table once more.

Lore watched carefully as the snake reared up behind Mathilde.

"I didn't want him to die. But I'd be lying if I thought hisss death would mean my freedom." Her tongue flickered around Mathilde, who finally glanced up at Lore.

Lore's muscles tensed, the librarian's mouth was open wide and, in the same beat, she didn't hesitate. She leaped over the table, knocking her and Mathilde to the wooden floor just in time for Petra's mighty jaw to snap the oak table in half.

"Ssssorry. You mussst understand." The snake's body quickly closed the space between them. "A powerful ssstranger told me my freedom could not be mine until the entire bloodline of the one who cursssed me wasss no more." Her words were a riddle of a sweet and sour contradiction.

Mathilde's hair was now sticking up like she had stuck her finger in an outlet. "Are you *crazy*?!" she shrieked, still in disbelief that someone she had seen as a friend would do such a thing.

Being forced into a box and stuck inside a box for years could actually do that. But Lore knew this was not the time to let that thought slip through.

"Besides, I'm *adopted*!" the mouse added. "How does that make sense?"

Lore grabbed her friend's hand, and they tried to climb out of danger.

DOWN THE WELL

They didn't have time to argue over details with the giant snake trying to murder them. But her hands slid against the slick, shining scales. Nothing to grip. She looked back toward Mathilde, who seemed to be racking her brain for a backup plan.

"You mussst undersssstand," Petra desperately pleaded once more before darting to take another bite at the mouse.

With a quick roll, they were able to dodge. Lore's heart was thudding hard against her ribs.

The snake's head hit the wall of her own body with the sound and force of a giant, smooth river stone thudding against the water before it sinks. Her powerful body moved inward, tightening around them and crushing the wooden furniture.

The mouse quickly ran toward the wreckage and gestured for Lore to stand by her.

"Ssstand ssstill," Petra hissed with a flicker of her tongue.

The fractured wood rubbed against Lore's legs and arms as the scaled body tightened the circle once more.

Mathilde grinned and grabbed Lore's hand.

When Petra's mighty mouth opened again, Lore felt the floor shift beneath her as the snake's body contracted, pushing them and the pile of broken wood toward her mouth.

The snake's gaping jaws forced a flash of memory over Lore. A figure she was chasing, down, down a blue well—not orange like in the town square. Gentle petals of daffodils in the spring breeze. A sense of urgency flowed through her veins. But as the wall of Petra's body pushed against her back, she stood frozen. Her feet dragged along the floorboards. Panic pulsed through her blood so loudly, she was convinced she heard it in her ears. *Is this where I die?* And why did it feel like she'd had that thought before?

"Do you trust me?" Mathilde called out.

The question snapped her out of the swirling thoughts that pulled her down like a riptide in the water. She hesitated in her answer, looking at Mathilde. *Did she trust her? Honestly, no. Especially when it came to safety concerns.*

She had a hard time trusting anyone here, but she did trust the mouse's tenacity. "Yes!" she finally shouted.

Mathilde nodded and shoved Lore hard towards Petra as the snake shot forward.

A sense of doubt and fear whirled in Lore's gut, but instead of falling victim to a quick bite that would end her, she rolled against the ground under the serpent's massive head.

She heaved a breath, relieved she'd survived, only to realize Mathilde had disappeared into Petra's mouth. Lore's heart felt like it had turned to stone and smashed on the ground.

Then it happened.

Just as quickly as the mouse had been swallowed up, a spiked end of a broken chair leg pierced through the bottom of the giant snake's jaw. Blood trickled from the broken wood, like water running off an icicle when it warms.

Petra's body jerked and pulled, giving Lore an opening to slide out, but she couldn't. Not yet. Not until Mathilde was safe.

The walls of the library trembled, and another piece of sharp wood pierced the reptile. The librarian's mouth gaped open, dropping Mathilde to the floor as she wailed in agony.

Lore bolted over to the mouse's side, lifting her in her arms. The small adventurer was shaking against Lore's chest. "Don't worry," she assured as she swallowed the frog of anxiety forming in her throat.

Petra's body was still jolting with pain. Lore's eyes watched as the massive body rose and fell against the ground, each time causing her entire being to jump. *Okay, just have to time this right. Best case, we get out and have to run for our lives.* She nodded, giving herself the benefit of the doubt. After all, Mathilde needed her right now.

As Petra's mighty body raised again to strike, Lore bit her lip and darted under. *Worst case scenario, we're flattened and die.*

The library's walls continued to tremble and the large stone over the fireplace even shook against the iron stakes holding it in place.

"We need to get out of here," Mathilde panted.

Down The Well

She nodded, drew a breath, and darted up the metal curved staircase.

A sudden blow to the steps made her stumble, falling down two.

Her shin cried out as warmth trickled down her leg. She looked behind her to see a feral Petra attempting to make her way up after them. Lore felt lighting surge through her body as she huffed it up the rest of the stairs with the snake right on their heels, predatory breath against her back. Her legs begged to stop, but she kept going.

Past the bookshelves that Petra's massive body demolished, her destruction sending papers, book covers, and wood into the air. Past the mounted animals. And past Sir Bernard, the badger, who hurled himself between them and the infuriated librarian in a self-sacrificing move.

As Lore looked over her shoulder, she saw Petra's jaws crush the stone as easily as a toothpick.

She jerked her head forward. The door was open but was slowly closing with each shake of the building. Her body felt like collapsing, a n d the sounds of destruction engulfed her senses, but with a final push forward, she tumbled through to safety with Mathilde in her arms.

The two sat there on the cobblestone street as the wooden door—as if pushed by a magical wind instead of physics—slammed shut on Petra's final strike. A four-leaf symbol glowed, practically burning in the door's center, sealing in the snake librarian.

Then the building collapsed in on itself.

And when the dust finally settled, nothing remained but small fragments of wood, paper, and ash.

Mathilde wiggled out of Lore's arms and stood up, offering a hand. Her voice was shaky as she said, "We need to go somewhere I can think."

TWENTY-ONE

Lore and Mathilde made their way back to the large, yellow mayor-al manor. The music and delight that echoed down the empty gray streets behind them left a ghostly bite on the back of Lore's neck.

Her eyes returned to looking through the window. Inside, Minifred carefully picked the sleeping twins up in her arms and headed up the stairs. The set of mismatched tea cups all sat out on the table. Lore could taste the honeyed herbs on the tip of her tongue. *Maybe when we go in, I can sneak a sip.*

The red glowing embers of the fire brought the memory of a pur-plish red stone rolling around in her hand. A faint voice of an old woman spoke. "Garnet."

Her heart stopped. *I know that voice. I don't know who, but I know her.*

Lore shifted her weight from side to side. *Maybe this familiarity could help me go home.* Her hands clammed up. *Do I share this with Mathilde now or later?*

"We should be good to go in when she takes Mildred up," Mathilde whispered, bringing thin fingers to her chin. "We just need to make it into Gannon's room without her knowing."

Lore nodded. "What's in his room that'll help, you think?"

Her companion's face beamed a smile, one that challenged the warmth of a summer sun. "His thinking chair. It's where he did all of his prob-lem-solving." There was a brief pause before Mathilde stammered out, "It's like magic or something."

Lore nodded again, then glanced over her shoulder. Her gaze trailed back to the dancing pink light in the distance. Shadows of animals, stretched against the smooth gray stone path, dancing 'round a fire, certainly enjoying themselves. It made her gut clench.

Her gaze fell on the wooden knick-knacks, glass collectibles, and oil-painted pictures Gannon had left behind. *They had lost a mayor, a leader—a friendly face that they no longer have the pleasure of greeting or laughing with.* Her eyes peered back at the far-off celebrations. They could return to the day-to-day, but it would still be hard. Her expression softened as she looked at Mathilde, who was trying to time how long it took her eldest sister to walk up and down the staircase. *Mathilde and her sisters will have to learn to move through life without the one who comforted their tears and showed them how to slay their fears. The one who guided them through the years.*

"Okay. Let's go, Human." Mathilde grabbed Lore's forearm as she passed her. "I wanna change first, then we can go to the thinking chair," she said before she quietly scampered to the great oak door and opened it without a sound.

Lore ran a hand down the white lace dress that Dina had been so kind to drop off that morning. *It would be smart.* Her stained fingertips looked as if she had just pitted five buckets of cherries by the spilled life that speckled the dress as if watercolor on a canvas. *To distance themselves far from the slaughter that just occurred.* Yet another death brought to Charmsend. Lore's eyes drifted down to the mouse, who reeked of snake saliva and drying blood. *Wouldn't want to soil Gannon's magic thinking chair.*

Lore followed close behind. There wasn't much of a choice with the mouse, holding her hand tightly.

Mathilde released Lore once they crossed the threshold of the old yellow manor. She then pressed herself against the wall in the nook under the stairwell. It was near the same window Lore had snuck through when all the animals were surrounding Gannon's body in the town square.

The memory of her body brushing through the rose shrubs forced the faint scent of the flower to flurry around her. Not my favorite smell. *I almost prefer Death's lingering stiff scent.*

Mathilde motioned for Lore to stand beside her. The hardest part of this super stealth mission was going to be the old, worn, creaky, staircase that was most certainly overdue for a few board replacements.

Mathilde held her breath as her foot pressed down onto the first step. Then released a sigh of relief when the board didn't squeak. The small adventurer's head whirled around to Lore with sparkles of excitement shining like the stars outside in the night sky. *Like they didn't just murder Petra and demolish the town's library.*

Lore followed the exact path Mathilde took up the steps. The end was just a hop, skip, and a jump away. It was silent. It was going well.

Until it wasn't.

Mathilde moved a bit too quickly and Lore didn't see where her foot had landed.

When her heavy, human foot pressed down against the wood, it sounded like a deep groan from a hungry cow.

The two froze quicker than an orange troll caught in a lie.

Did they backtrack? Did they press on? They stood there like two terribly-sculpted park statues, holding their breath.

Eventually, Mathilde broke her pose and then slowly made her way down the narrow hall. It ended what felt like the longest, most agonizing, three minutes of Lore's existence so far in Charmsend—maybe of all time.

Lore let out a breath of relief when the mouse motioned for her to follow. As she walked closely behind her companion, she examined the doors. Each one unique. The guest room's was plain pine wood. But the one next to it was a brilliant bright burnt orange, a cinnamon and caramel candle's scent seeping from under its base. On the right wall, one was half-red and half-white with a pink stripe down the center. Lore could hear the chimes of a music box being played on the other side. Then they passed a door painted a glossy green with a peculiar purple gemstone in place of the doorknob.

Lore paused, staring at how it caught the dim light in the hallway.

"Ahem," Mathilde scoffed, pointing a hand to the last room at the end of the hall, the door standing wide open. *Her room.*

As Lore stepped into the mouse's room, she noticed that Mathilde's door wasn't painted a vibrant color, and it also lacked a special design. The grain of the wood was dull, not even enhanced by a stain. The only thing that hung on her door was a tattered piece of parchment.

She squinted. "Is that a map?" she whispered.

Mathilde grinned. "That's the world of Thimbleton," she said with a wave of her hands, as if performing a magic trick.

Lore smiled and once they were both safely inside, the door suddenly slammed shut behind them.

Mathilde whirled around. "I can explain!" she declared quickly, the words sounding practiced. As if this was a normal occurrence for her to find herself in. Though Lore wouldn't be surprised if it was.

"Don't bother," Minifred's controlled voice carried, tumbling into Lore and Mathilde like a boulder that had launched from a booby trap. The larger mouse was silent for a moment, her brows knitting together as she searched for the right words to say.

Lore could see Mathilde brace for some sort of *talk*, but it didn't come.

"I brought these for you. Here." The older sibling passed the folded clothes that were draped over her crossed arms, including a green flannel, to her adventuring sibling.

"How'd you know?" Mathilde's voice was hushed, diminished after being caught.

"What?" Her gaze narrowed on her sister. "That you and your little human friend were outside on the porch peering in like a pair of weirdos?" Minifred looked at Lore, silver eyes cutting against her skin. Then her gaze shifted again to her youngest sister. "Call it a gut feeling." Silence hung like a heavy fog as Minifred paused. "We need to talk, though. Someone dropped a letter off for you today."

"What?" Mathilde handed the green flannel to Lore, then faced her sister once again. "Who?"

Minifred chewed on the inside of her furry cheek.

Mathilde ignored this and pushed both Lore and her sister out of her small room.

"I'll meet you downstairs, Human. Going to change."

Lore followed behind a silent Minifred. She rubbed the black fabric of the dress she came in between an index finger and thumb. The door latched behind her and Minifred. She had come in this dress, though it didn't feel like something she actually wore on a casual day. Why did she know that? And why had she been wearing that?

But the cream dress the mice were wearing today matched hers down to the lace trim. *Coincidence?* Who knew at this point? She was trapped in a world of talking animals, so it seemed possible.

Once they reached the ground floor, Minifred quickly went over to collect the mismatched teacups.

"It's a nice set," Lore muttered as she walked over to the oversized rocker.

The mouse's stern gaze remained fixed on the porcelain. "They're not a set."

Lore tilted her head as she lay the black dress on the arm of the rocker. "They are though." The air between the two felt like it was thick with some invisible smog. Lore's eyes softened as she continued to speak, "Even if they don't look the same and were meant to be among other groups, they are better together because their differences complement each other."

Minifred silently sat the tea tray on the kitchen table where Lore had once listened to the talking cards. The mouse didn't turn to face her, just forced a laugh and let her shoulders drop. "S'pose that's why my sister looks fondly on you, human."

Before Lore could ask her to elaborate, the sound of the stairs groaning meant a certain squirrelly gray mouse was amidst the conversation now.

"Fond of what?" Mathilde demanded.

The older mouse's hand spread out on the table, her head hung low between her arms. She gripped the piece of paper so tight that it crumpled around her fingers. "Nothing." Her voice was as pulled tightly as a rubber band that may snap at any moment.

Lore left the black dress where it was on the rocker's arm in favor of putting on the green flannel first. The fabric sliding on her arms felt like a warm hug from someone who may have known her before. Before this little adventure in the world of Thimbleton.

She rolled her eyes as she slid off the itchy white stockings. *Such a silly, nonsensical name.* As she folded the knitted stockings and placed them beside the black dress, the larger garment fell. Inside of the folded dress, a pop of green peeked out at her.

Lore tilted her head as she knelt down and unwrapped the black dress revealing a pair of cotton green stockings. She peeked over her shoulder at Minifred. *I didn't have these on when the night I came. At least, I don't think I did.* Lore plopped down on the floor and put them on. They matched the dark green squares on her flannel to a tee, it brought a smile to her face. *This was a nice surprise. I'll have to thank her somehow.* As she was about to loudly announce how much she liked the new cotton stockings, she saw Mathilde approach her sister. They were whispering something back and forth, and Lore could make out some words. *Paw prints. Father. Can't trust. Outside of town.*

She slowly got up and ran a finger along the mantle. It came away coated in dust. *Does this have to do with the fox prints we found?*

The glass mushrooms, the guardians of the hearth, were sleeping. Her finger gently caressed the blue-spotted cap of one as it lay there. *I wonder if they dream. Wonder what they dream of?*

A little statue awoke with a stretch.

Lore continued to pet the creature's cap. "You aren't so bad."

The glass figurine fussed away from Lore, using its limbs to push her finger away.

"Oh, this is a no-pet zone," Lore whispered. "Sorry."

The mushroom shook its head.

"Human," Mathilde's voice called.

Lore looked over her shoulder to see the mouse already halfway out the door. She quickly turned to tell the little glass mushroom bye, but it was gone. She brushed it off and rushed to the door that Mathilde had left wide open behind her.

Minifred grabbed her forearm as she passed. "Keep her safe."

Her heart stopped at the request. She could barely keep up with the adventurer, let alone keep her safe. But the older mouse's eyes were pleading.

Lore swallowed hard. "I'll do my best."

Minifred freed her iron grip, and Lore quickly laced up her stone-gray canvas shoes. Then she barreled out the door.

Mathilde was tapping a foot impatiently, looking down at an old chained pocket watch. "We're going to be late." Without further explanation, the mouse disappeared down the cobblestone street like an autumn breeze.

"Late? Late for what?" Lore called as she chased after her down the shadowy road that led away from town.

TWENTY-TWO

Lore panted like a dog in the humid heat of summer trying to catch her breath. With each stride, the town of Charmsend was shrinking behind them, the sounds of the celebration of life ceremony shrank with it. The only noise in her ears was the croaking of some frogs in the distance, and her legs screaming to slow down.

She was following Mathilde to… where? She didn't dare try to fathom. *Perhaps to the ends of Thimbleton.*

The farther from town they went, the less lighting there was and Lore's eyes felt strained from focusing on Mathilde's quick figure in the dark. Her vision would blur every time her foot hit the ground as she chased after the mouse, and a small phantom would take Mathilde's place, and then she was racing after a shadowy figure with pensive golden eyes instead of her friend. With every switch, her heartbeat quickened and the nape of her neck became chilled with a cold sweat. And as soon as she thought she could reach out and grab the figure, Mathilde's bold, red jacket would blindside her.

The melding of memories and reality lasted until the sound of their feet beating the cobblestone path faded and was replaced by the breeze whistling through a thicket.

The mouse finally came to a stop.

"You know, I never even knew this house was out here." Mathilde put her hands on her hips as she scanned the area below. "And so close to the barrier."

Lore doubled over, hands braced on her knees as her lungs ached.

The moment she had finally caught her breath, it was gone again with one look upward.

The dark blue-black sky held millions and millions of glittering stars that overlooked the valley. On the hilltop where they were standing, she felt like she could reach out and steal a star for herself. It reminded her of a scrapbook. Like the sky was a base sheet, and the two moons were cut from a pristine pearl paper with a beautiful glossy sheen was placed over them, giving an iridescent shine. And some powerful creator had placed the celestial bodies with care on the page.

Her eyes scanned below them. In the silvery moonlight, she scanned over an open field surrounded by trees. In the center of it sat a rundown house.

Mathilde's steady voice followed the sound of paper crunching. "That's it. That's where the intruder is."

Lore's eyebrows knitted together. "Don't you mean *murderer?*"

Mathilde shook her head and shoved the letter in her pocket. "No. Just an intruder."

"Uh-huh, an *intruder*. Who just so happened to show up when your dad was got. Okay."

Mathilde's eyebrows raised. "What's got you all riled up, Human?" she teased as she started heading down the hill.

"You don't think this could be some elaborate trap?"

"Nope."

Lore felt her cheeks heat with annoyance as she followed. "Why not?"

"Because if I thought that way—" Mathilde faltered, shook her head. "then I'd be like any other mouse in Thimbleton. Safe at home, trapped by routine, and living an *illusion* of a happy life."

She pursed her lips and the tips of wheat hit her palms as the two walked to the house. "What if it *is* a trap, though?"

Mathilde's tail flicked in agitation. "I guess that's why I have you 'round. To plan for that sort of thing."

Lore rolled her eyes. As they neared the cabin, she felt her gut resemble a can of soda that had been shaken. She clenched her clammy palms shut, snapping some of the wheat grains from their stems. She swallowed hard as the air seemed to become thicker. Lore glanced down at Mathilde, who had already scampered up onto the porch. She chewed the inside of her cheek as she felt the house's heavy atmosphere press down onto her shoulders.

"You comin'?" Mathilde called as she pushed open the decaying door.

"Unfortunately," Lore answered as she stepped onto the shabby step, testing to see if the moth-eaten wood could hold her weight. With a sigh of relief, she was able to proceed up onto the porch. She lingered in the old door frame as the mouse investigated the inside of the worn home. She watched as her guide—and now responsibility, thanks to Minifred's order—interrupted the stillness of some dust-laden items, poking and prodding them, picking them up, and looking them over.

The walls were adorned with old paintings, but they were so dusty or mildewy, Lore couldn't clearly see the subjects. There was a large oval mirror that had a spiderweb of cracks throughout it, and the reflection was so clouded she doubted she would be able to see herself in it. Even with a light on. It hung over a fireplace that appeared to not have been properly used in years, but inside the soot-covered brick hearth, there was a small stack of charred sticks that smelled like they had just been put out.

"Mathilde," Lore hissed.

Her companion turned, her large round ears high and alert. "What?"

"I don't think this is a good idea," Lore said as she crossed her arms, shifting her weight back and forth. "We shouldn't be here."

Mathilde rolled her eyes. "It's fine, Human." As the mouse walked into the center of the room among the sheet-covered furniture, the floorboards let out a ghastly groan. Her eyes shot wide open a moment before she disappeared through the floorboards.

Lore's stomach flipped and flopped on itself. "Mathilde?!" she shouted, her voice being carried on the crisp night air that was blowing through the cracks of the boarded windows.

She didn't even scream.

Lore's brows pulled tightly together as she set one foot further into the house. *So far so good.*

Another step in and the wood splintered under her weight. Shit. Shit. Shit. "Mathilde?!" she called again. Her voice was strained as she remembered her promise to Minifred.

Still no answer.

Another step from Lore made the rundown house let out a miserable moan. The butterflies in her stomach swirled together like a little tornado as she took another few careful steps to peer over the Mathilde-sized hole. Lore squinted, searching for her friend. *Where is she?*

As Lore was thinking about all the ways Minifred would bite her head off for failing to keep her sister safe, Mathilde ran into view.

"Human! You *have* to come down here!"

Lore's knuckles whitened as she gripped the broken wood. "I was just yelling for you!" she growled. "Why didn't you answer?"

The mouse's ears drooped as Lore scolded her, but it wasn't long before a sly grin painted itself on her face. She folded her hands behind her back and rocked on her heels. "Why don't'cha come down here and see for yourself?"

Lore rolled her eyes, but before a semi-witty response could fall from her mouth, the choice was taken from her when the boards collapsed under her weight and she hit the cold dirt with a loud thud. It felt like a baseball bat had knocked the wind from her chest. She huffed and rolled over on her back. Her head pounded in agony, and the shower of splinters around her pricked at her skin and stung like a million little paper cuts against her legs and cheeks.

I'm really done with falling. She began picking wood chips from the long-sleeved flannel. *Falling through floors, out windows, and through realities.* She tossed the pieces carelessly in all directions around her. *It's tiresome, and the only thing I want to fall into is a deep sleep.*

Mathilde leaned over, her emerald, sass-filled eyes sparkled with delight. "Glad you could join me," she teased before offering a hand up.

As Lore stood to her feet, she quickly realized she would have to hunch over to walk under the house. The pale moonlight trickled through smudged windows and her eyes fell on a grime-covered table that had piles of books, a handful of beakers, and bundles of herbs covering it.

Above the table, a large square painting hung. The subject's large, gold, almond-shaped eyes bored into her.

Lore felt like an icicle had pierced her heart. There it was. The shadow that brought her here. A bitter cold spread to her fingertips, making them tingle.

Down the well to Charmsend.

"Isn't this interesting?" Mathilde asked as she picked up some beakers, rubbing her fingertips around the residue that clung to the glass brim.

Lore couldn't say anything. Her gaze stayed fixated on the portrait.

"Human?" Her companion tilted her head and sat the containers down with a clink on the table.

Lore shook her head and wrapped her arms around herself, trying to hide that her hands were still trembling.

"Are you okay?" Mathilde pressed.

"Yeah, fine." She looked back at the portrait. Her heart dropped. The rest of the painting showed a happier white wolf, a younger alligator, and a smiling Sir Crinkle standing with the bat posed in front of the orange well. Lore held a shaking finger out. "Who's the bat?"

Mathilde rubbed her hands together. "Exactly! I've no idea." As the mouse continued on with any and every idea of who the bat was—from an assassin to a local nocturnal farmer—the rest of the world melted away like wax from Lore.

It was just her and the golden-eyed bat, him taunting her with a smile and wave of his hand. A flash of memories, like a set of polaroid photos, ran through her mind.

Her head began to throb anew, and the ice piercing her chest felt turned into cold claws that grasped her heart. She grabbed her temples as the pain intensified.

A sleepy little town, a wooden raven flapping in the rain and wind. An old woman with a warm smile. A field of daffodils with a small crowd gathered at the field's edge. The earth under the crowd stretched, carrying them further and further away from her as she stumbled to approach them.

Then the vision—or was it a memory?—became a blur as she felt someone shaking her shoulders.

"Human!"

Lore's head felt like it was spinning right off her neck, as she tried to focus on the small figure in front of her.

"Human! Snap out of it!"

The clouds that hung in her eyes slowly cleared, revealing a deeply desperate Mathilde staring back at her.

"I—I'm so sorry," she stammered as she attempted to stand.

Mathilde firmly held Lore down by the arms. "I think it'd be better if you sat down for a while." Her voice was gentle, like Minifred's when calming the other sisters.

Lore didn't fight. She didn't have the energy inside her to do anything but follow the mouse's advice. So, she sat there, replaying the captured images again and again in her mind.

Mathilde sat across from her and silently fidgeted with the end of her tail. She looked toward the desk, covered in the assortment of belongings that she was so thrilled about discovering, then back at Lore. The moonlight danced through the dirty windows, and the smell of musk hung in the air. Eventually, the mouse broke the few moments of silence they shared. "Are you okay?"

Lore felt the chill in her chest spread like frost on a window. She shrugged. "I think I will be."

Mathilde leaned back onto her hands, the fur above her eye raised like a human eyebrow. "If you don't want to talk about it, that's fine."

Lore hugged her knees up to her chest, fighting back the tears that welled in her eyes. "I must be losing my mind."

The mouse leaned forward, curiosity piqued. "Or regaining it," she countered, a ring of optimism in her voice.

Lore rested her head on her knees and took a ragged breath. "I feel insane. Down a well to a magical world." She scoffed through her sniffles. "How utterly pathetic and senseless."

"You're right. You're mad." Mathilde stood up and paced a circle around

DOWN THE WELL

Lore. "I'd even say moonstruck… Completely batty." She stopped pacing and her eyes fixed on the portrait hanging on the wall. The mouse's ears pricked up. "But you know what, Human? You're also fantastically and miraculously you." A slight pause filled the room before Mathilde finished her thought. "And I think you are pretty great."

Lore looked at her with bloodshot eyes, then smiled softly and wiped the stray tears from her cheeks. "You aren't so bad yourself."

The mouse grinned. "Oh, I know I'm fucking amazing." She put her hands on her hips and shrugged her shoulders nonchalantly. "It's like I'm the main character or something."

Footsteps above their heads squashed any possibility of continuing the uplifting conversation.

That's right. We're here on business.

The two nodded to each other and followed under the thumping. Lore held her breath as they closed the distance between the desk of dusted collectibles and the hole they both created in the center of the room. They stood there frozen like deer caught in headlights, waiting for someone else to make the next move. The anticipation spread like bugs under her skin.

The steps halted at the hole in the floor. *Were they going to jump down here?* To make matters worse, Mathilde went to stand right under the figure and peered through the cracks, her eyes widening.

Her eyes darted back and forth, searching for a way out. But not even Mathilde could squeeze through the dingy windows. Lore swallowed hard, fear going back down her throat felt like sharp rocks scratching her esophagus. *I guess we just walked head-first into the mouth of a predator.*

Her heart froze over when a sudden thud hit the ground. But no one fell through. Then, much to her surprise, a rope ladder fell down the hole.

"Well, come on," a voice called down casually. "Can't bargain with ya bein' down in a hole. Never make a deal without lookin' someone in the eye."

Mathilde narrowed her gaze and walked back toward their end of the opening. She mumbled something Lore couldn't hear, then climbed up the rope ladder with a huff.

Lore looked over her shoulder and saw the slick, oil-painted gold eyes watching her from the shadows. She quickly bolted to the ladder. Her hands couldn't take her up fast enough, and if she wasn't so panicked about getting away, maybe she would have worried about slipping. She sighed a relieved breath when the thin slivers of the splintered floor poked her fingertips. She pulled herself up and sat, pulling her legs close to her body, careful to not let them dangle into the pit. The adrenaline softened like the warm, dying glow of a candle's wick.

"Oh, lovely. The human hasn't been chased from the town into the Twisted Wood like Frankenstein's monster," the voice teased.

Why did that sound familiar? Something from her *world? Wherever that was.*

Mathilde climbed atop the cloth-covered couch to get eye level with the newcomer, who was standing in front of the window that looked out onto the fields of wheat. "How did you not fall through the flimsy floor?"

The boarded windows concealed his face from the pallid moonbeams, but that didn't stop his sparkling half-moon smile from being seen. "I knew that spot of the room was weak, hence the rug on it."

Lore could practically see the annoyance radiating from Mathilde before the mouse responded—well, exploded.

"A rug?! You thought a piece of fabric was going to deter folks from walking on it?!" she shrieked, finally losing control after all the events surrounding Gannon's death.

The smiling figure flicked something into the hearth. A few sparks crackled and suddenly a blazing fire rejoiced for life inside the smog-filled brick confinement. The yellow and orange flames lit up almost every corner of the living room.

Lore's eyes bounced between Mathilde and the stranger. "Who are you?" she asked as she regained her feet. She didn't want to be sitting if things went south.

The figure stepped into the amber light, making his rusted orange fur glow against his brilliant blue, high-collared jacket. The crisp breeze that snuck between the boarded windows playfully picked up the two pointed coattails. His crescent smile cracked across his face and his white-tipped tail flicked back and forth with what Lore guessed was a twisted sort of excitement.

"I'm Killmoore."

TWENTY-THREE

The fox—Killmoore—ran his tongue over his pointed, yellowing canines with a too-relaxed smile. Then he reached a hand into his jacket. Lore's eyes narrowed as she saw the glint of sharpened metal. Her mind froze but her body shot up to get to Mathilde, who was still inches from the cryptic stranger. Her arms easily picked the mouse up and swung her over her shoulder like a bag of potatoes.

The fox raised a brow as he pulled out a slip of paper. "I'm a bounty hunter." His voice was flat as he flipped the sheet toward them. Lore stared at the image. Little splotches of ink were scattered across the page, and it looked like the picture was drawn in a rush. The illustration showed a gaudy greenish gem that Lore has seen quite a few times around Charmsend. It rested atop a familiar staff. *Crinkle's staff.*

At the bottom, there was a short description of the object, but she didn't have the luxury of reading those details because a set of tiny, balled fists started pounding on her back.

Mathilde wriggled and squirmed until Lore let her slide down to the floor. When she was standing on her own again, the mouse yanked hard on Lore's flannel so they were eye to eye. "I don't care if someone has a sword to my throat," she spat and shoved a finger into Lore's face. "*Never* do whatever that was again." Her words were sharp but clear.

Lore furrowed her eyebrows. "He has a weapon," she muttered by way of explanation.

Mathilde's eyes flashed with anger. "What did I just say?!"

Lore rolled her eyes. "Whatever. Have it your way."

Her friend let go and faced the bounty hunter, who was still holding the paper out to them.

Mathilde scampered over and rubbed her chin. "What does this have to do with us?"

The fox shoved the sheet back inside his coat pocket. "I'm glad to see you got my letter, and even more ecstatic you came to this little hideout," he said in a honeyed voice as he walked around the couch by the hole in the floor where he picked up his ladder. He shoved it into a brown leather bag that he swung over his shoulder, then plopped down in the chair by the hearth, stretching out his limbs with a yawn. When his snout snapped shut, he propped his head on his hand and looked at Mathilde and Lore with sleepy eyes. "I've located the item, and I will need some local help to retrieve it."

Mathilde crossed her arms. "And what's in it for us?"

Lore nodded in agreement and carefully watched the fox. He popped a golden tael coin in between his index finger and thumb. "Because," he mused as he flipped the coin across the tops of his half-gloved fingers, "I saw how that gator died."

The color from Mathilde's face washed away, like water down a drain.

His toothy smile twisted on his face again. "And I didn't bring in any Grayshade when I crossed that fancy barrier the opossum is so proud of."

Lore stared at the fox sitting in the chair. "We help you, and you tell us everything?" she asked firmly.

The amber flecks in the bounty hunter's brown eyes sparkled with a mischievous playfulness. "That's right." His gaze darted to Mathilde, who seemed rather silent at the possibility of knowing what exactly happened to her father.

"Mathilde?" Lore prompted.

The mouse gave Killmoore a sideways glance. "Why would a profes-sional bounty hunter need the assistance of two folks unskilled in that line of work?"

The fox bellowed out a laugh and tossed the coin in the air before snatching it in his palm. "I need someone familiar with the target."

Matilde gulped.

She knows who we have to steal from. If I know, she has to.

"You give us a bit of information about how you crossed the barrier first. Then we will go with you and steal from Sir Crinkle." The mouse's voice was tight.

The stagnant silence filled the air. It weighed heavily on Lore's shoulders as she and Mathilde waited for Killmoore's answer.

The bounty hunter rolled his shoulders and tilted his head as he stared into the lively flames. "Call it luck. The intricate webs the Wielder wove, or just plain coincidence, but there was already a hole in the barrier."

Mathilde took a step back. "But how?" She wore a look of desperation as she glanced at Lore. "Who would open up the town to a Grayshade?"

The fox shrugged and leaned forward to toss another log on the fire. "Beats me, but there were some dried herbs left at the scene. Whoever it was, they were not as clever as they think," he scoffed and eyed the two carefully up and down. "I followed the trail, and it led me to the town square where the murder happened."

Mathilde nodded. "Right. Then I know who we need to see," the mouse assured herself aloud.

Lore's gaze locked with Killmoore's playful one. "Who's your client?"

"First rule of bounty hunting is don't give away any client information to riffraff," he said matter-of-factly.

She rolled her eyes.

"So, who are you going to see, little mouse?" he pressed.

Mathilde's gaze speared him with sharp, emerald eyes. "That's confidential information. The kind that you don't share with any outsider who unexpectedly finds themselves *in*."

He tossed his head back and laughed. "Fair."

With that, Mathilde spun on her heels and went to the flimsy door.

Lore lingered on the threshold for a moment, but her friend was already out on the porch, eager to return to the village. Killmoore waved at her, then hummed as he returned his sight back to the unsteady, glowing flames. "See you here tomorrow at dusk." The words rolled off the bounty hunter's tongue like marbles on flat pavement. Smooth. Quick to the end, and leaving a scattered mess for Lore to walk across.

"Human!" Mathilde's voice was laced with annoyance. "Come on! What's taking so long?"

She carefully closed the moth-eaten door, afraid it would crumble to dust when the latch hitched shut.

Mathilde's face looked unamused while she tapped her foot quickly. It was becoming a habit.

Lore gestured behind her. "He said to meet him back here tomorrow."

Mathilde didn't respond and jumped off the porch.

She followed behind and admired the night sky. The two moons hanging in the sky with the twinkling stars made her feel as if she were being engulfed in a warm wool blanket.

"Something's not right with that fox," Mathilde spat out like the words were a sour candy.

Lore shrugged. "And what makes you say that?"

She was ready for some ridiculously, unreasonably paranoid conclusion, but it never came.

"Who names their kid *Killmoore*?" she blurted out. "And, he took a job he can't even do alone?"

Lore chuckled under her breath.

"Well, I'm glad one of us can find the humor in this, Human." The mouse's voice was threaded with sarcasm as she crossed her arms.

They walked down the dark forest trail, and Lore's eyes drifted through the trunks of trees. Despite the fog that was rolling in, she saw the lights were off in Charmsend.

Mathilde suddenly stopped in her tracks. Her eyes widened, and her ears curled upright in alarm. Her arm stretched out in front of Lore to halt her from walking as well.

Right as Lore was going to ask 'what's wrong now?' she heard a faint voice being carried with the brittle biting night air. The two followed the melodic sounds of the nocturnal siren and they found themselves at the edge of the forest line. The song could be heard a bit clearer now.

> "In the valleys of emerald, there lives a
> white hare,
> As swift as the swallow that flies
> through the air."

The lyrics moved in her mind like brush strokes painting an image of what this Emerald Valley once looked like, with swallows gliding on the breeze.

Mathilde and Lore wandered to the edge of the graveyard. The iron fencing chilled Lore's fingers as she touched it.

> "You may tramp the world over, but
> none will compare.
> To the pride of the valley, the bonnie
> white hare."

Mathilde climbed through the rungs while she carefully climbed over the top, too big to do the same as the mouse. Their feet were silent as they moved over the sacred earth of the eternally resting. The two crouched behind a grave marker that was a stone carved in the shape of a tree stump.

Mathilde's eyes widened and Lore covered her mouth as a gasp escaped.

Through the gray fog was a recognizable white wolf. Lyudmilla was kneeling on the fresh dirt of Gannon's grave. She continued to sing, tears flowing down her furred cheeks.

> "One clear autumn morning, as you
> will suppose.
> Oh, the red golden sun, o'er the way-
> ward mountains rose."

Lore's heart ached as Gannon's friend hugged herself in the alligator's absence. She went to take a step to approach her, but Mathilde quickly grabbed her flannel and pulled down, shaking her head.

They both watched on as Lyudmilla continued her ballad.

> "Larken Dreadway came down to the
> valley, and he did declare,
> 'This is the day I'll put an end to that
> bonnie white hare.'"

DOWN THE WELL

The wolf's sobs became uncontrollable as she threw herself onto the ground on Gannon's grave. "Things were simpler back then, weren't they?" she asked. As if her friend's spirit would answer. "Before Crinkle…" She trailed off, then continued to draw out this one-sided conversation. "When we'd chased bad guys and saved the day." Her sobs turned to a wail-like howl. "Those days were simpler."

Her clawed hand clutched some of the soft earth. As she squeezed it, the dirt fell out, back onto Gannon's grave. "He's not even a shell of who we once knew." A brief silence filled the graveyard while she steadied her breath. "He's a rotted version of himself." Then she continued to weep.

"Come on," Mathilde whispered, her face void of emotion. "It's time to go." The mouse's voice sounded numb, shaken by the display.

And so, they slipped away, back over the fence, and back to the stone path that would take them to the now empty streets of Charmsend.

TWENTY-FOUR

Lore pulled the pillow over her head to muffle out the yells and demands that traveled through the yellow, mayoral manor. *The walls are so damn thin.*

Thoughts of Lyudmilla crying by Gannon's grave swirled around her head. She tossed and turned in the bed, desperate to get comfortable and drift off to a semi-restful sleep. But the call of a rooster's morning yodel made it impossible and left her grumbling with frustration. She slid out of the bed and made her way for the door. Then she heard a yelp and an alarming *crash*. She rolled her eyes and tried to brush her flyaway hair into some sort of place as she scrambled down the stairs.

As soon as her feet hit the landing, she saw one of the twins comforting a sobbing Mildred. She walked over to the mice as she heard Minifred's voice thundering throughout the mayoral mansion.

"*Mathilde!* I don't care how late you are out playing detective, but that doesn't give you the right to *trash Dad's room!*" A burning, righteous anger clung to her words like a sticky film.

Lore leaned over Mayberry and Mildred in the doorway and scanned the room. Pictures were ripped from the walls, the frames busted and sparkling broken glass littered the parts of the floor that were still visible underneath a huge mess. Drawers from the dresser lay strewn throughout the room, all mostly empty, the contents blanketing the ground.

Mathilde's tail flicked rapidly back and forth as her front half was busy under the bed. Lore carefully walked over to the bedside.

Down The Well

Minifred put her hands on her hips. Behind the angry mouse, Lore saw a few holes punched out in the plaster.

"I didn't do this." Even though her voice was muffled from under the dead alligator's bed, Mathilde sounded strained. "But it's obvious whoever did it was looking for something."

The oldest sister rolled her eyes. "I get it!" she spat. "This is your way of grieving. That's fine. But stop dragging the rest of us down this road with you!" Her silver eyes were shooting more than bolts of lightning. Lore wouldn't have been surprised if they produced actual electricity.

Then a rapid knocking at the front door made the tension in the house stiffen even more.

"If you want, I can—" Lore began.

But Minifred motioned for her to save whatever spiel she had as she marched to answer it herself.

Lore locked eyes with Mayberry, who still lingered in the doorway to the room. "I'm sorry," she mouthed.

The gray mouse only shook her head with disappointment.

Lore crouched down and peeked under the bed. Mathilde was there, but the brim of Gannon's top hat hid her face.

"Are we alone?" she whispered from the corner of her mouth.

Lore looked to the other sisters huddling in the doorway.

Mathilde nodded and pushed a green book over the Lore. No title was on the cover. The only symbol was the same four silver circles overlapping each other, like the charm on Petra's necklace.

Oh. Petra. The library. Lore's stomach sank further, and she felt like hiding under the bed with Mathilde.

"It was under the floorboard but it was inside a fancy box that was locked up good," the mouse explained. A sly smile spread on her face. "But luckily I mastered lock-picking back when I was seven."

Lore's sight stayed on the book as Minifred's words to Mathilde echoed in her head. *This is your way of grieving.* She glanced back up at her constant companion in Thimbleton, who returned to fidgeting with the peculiar box. It resembled a three-dimensional diamond and had odd carvings embedded in the glossy metal.

"This is a perfect replica of what Petra had at the library," Mathilde muttered. "He wrote it in for hours and hours."

Lore shrugged. "So, this is the original?" *It had to be, right?*

Before Mathilde could say anything, the floorboards pulsated. They locked eyes.

"Minifred," the mouse mouthed. Pushing the book towards Lore.

Lore quickly concealed Gannon's little green book inside her flannel. Mathilde shot out from under the bed and Lore followed suit. The only difference was she wasn't nose to nose with a fuming Minifred, who had returned from the front door.

"Someone would like to speak with you."

Mathilde shrugged. "Okay." She went to shove past her oldest sister, but Minifred's hand shot out, stopping her.

And then the silver-eyed mouse pointed her sharp expression towards Lore. "Both of you."

Lore's feet felt frozen on the cluttered floor. Mathilde huffed and grabbed her hand and pulled her along.

"Sorry," Lore mumbled to Minifred and the others as her friend bulldozed past her two sisters who still hadn't left their spot where Lore found them during the loud argument.

Mathilde released Lore and flung the door open without a second thought. There on the porch swing, swaying forward and back in the cool autumn air, was none other than Sir Crinkle.

"Good morning, dears," he purred as he sipped from a to-go-styled cup of coffee.

Mathilde crossed her arms. "I hope you come with good news," she declared, as if the disaster that happened inside didn't exist.

The opossum shook his head and let out a sigh as he sat his cup down on the porch. "'Fraid not."

Mathilde's eyes narrowed. "Well, if you've got no good news regarding the killer, did you at least find a way for the human to return to..." Mathilde looked Lore up and down. "Wherever humans come from?"

DOWN THE WELL

Crinkle shook his head again and stood up, towering over both Mathilde and Lore. He leaned forward, putting his weight on his staff. The gemstone twinkled in the early morning light. "There seems to have been another," he paused and whispered the rest of his sentence to assure no passerby would hear the bad news, "incident."

Mathilde raised a curious brow, playing dumb despite knowing fully what he was referring to. "What do you mean?"

"I guess you could say Petra has finally freed herself from her cage." His tone was grim as he looked off into the distance at the animal folk heading toward the market square.

Lore noticed something in his eyes. It wasn't grief or distress. It was a searing disappointment. She ignored Mathilde's gaze on her and pretended to also look off into the distance so she could be spared being a part of the conversation.

"Well, we have things to do. Places to be," Mathilde announced as she skipped down the steps.

Crinkle's thin fingers drummed against the stone atop his staff. "You know, Minifred told me about Gannon's room."

The adventurer's tail straightened. "What happens under our roof is none of your business." Her voice was flat and her fists clenched.

The opossum gestured for Lore to go down the steps as he spoke to the mouse. "It is when someone is breaking into my dead friend's house when his daughters are asleep and vulnerable in their beds."

Lore pursed her lips. But *Minifred was dead set on her sister being responsible for the destruction. Did Crinkle know something?*

Mathilde's clenched fists loosened. She shook her head, probably dispelling a similar thought. "We really need to be going now. We got a hedgehog to see. And I'd like to go before she gets her afternoon rush."

With that, Lore and Mathilde headed south. To the edge of Charmsend.

Crinkle chuckled and unfortunately followed them. "Well, isn't that a coincidence? I'm also heading that way."

Lore held her breath as the tall opossum wedged himself between her and her friend.

"Hmmm. Aren't we lucky, Human?" Mathilde said, sarcasm heavily lining her voice.

He ignored the surly mouse and looked down at Lore with a twisted smile. "Lucky, indeed."

The words sent a shiver down her spine, and a chill lingered around her fingertips as they walked.

"So…" Crinkle continued, his staff beating against the ground in a rhythmic pattern, "what business is taking you to the Iron Rose?"

Lore waited for the mouse to answer, but it seemed the mouse had taken up a silent protest.

"Mathilde is finishing the tour of the town," Lore lied. Her eyes barely caught the faint glimmer of a grin that pulled at the small animal's cheek.

Sir Crinkle tilted his head, curiosity sparkling in his beady, dark eyes like freshly polished obsidian. "And what do you make of our humble little community?"

Lore sucked on her cheek for a moment as her eyes scanned the wild foliage. It was becoming denser, and the morning sun now only peaked through the bare treetops that wove together, leaving the path rather dim. "I think it's…" she paused, running her tongue against the back of her teeth, searching for a word, "charming." Just like its name.

"Why are *you* going to the Iron Rose?" Mathilde's voice was so loud and clear that it seemed to echo down the empty moss-covered path.

Her little silent treatment lasted longer than I thought.

"Well, we have to get this human back to where it came from somehow, right?" The opossum laughed and nudged Lore's shoulder as if they shared an inside joke. "Sable should have the ingredients I need."

Mathilde rubbed her chin. "So, what do you make of Petra and whoever broke into our house?" Her voice dragged low against the cobblestone overgrown with greenery.

The opossum stopped. "Since when did you care so much about what I think, Mathilde?" The flatness in his tone did not hide the greedy gleam behind his expression.

Down The Well

Mathilde narrowed her sight on him. "Everyone is a suspect," she uttered.

Crinkle circled the mouse, tapping his staff against the ground every so often. "Ah, you sound so grown up, Mathilde." He said the words with sticky honey dripping from his voice. "Gannon would be proud."

Lore took a step back. She was now off the path and she felt the leaves tickle the backs of her knees.

The sunlight breaking through the gnarled branches made the yellow stains on the tip of Crinkle's fur shine golden as he stopped to face Mathilde, kneeling down so he could peer into her soul.

"You think you're so clever, don't you?" His words held a threat and rang like steel swords clashing.

Lore took another step back into the tree line that kissed the path they were all three huddled on. A man and woman shouting was a faint echo in her ears. Then the hair on the back of her neck stood straight when the sensation of a warm breath caressed it.

In a swift motion, Crinkle shot upright and in a single fluid movement flipped his staff so the glowing gemstone was shoved in Lore's face. The stone had a brilliant blue light that sparked until a solid bubble enclosed the three of them. Its creation produced a jolt of energy that sent Lore flying forward. She fell onto Mathilde with an *oof.*

As she pulled herself up, she looked over her shoulder. On the other side of the brittle and magical blue dome was a living mountain of matted, slate-gray fur. Unnaturally elongated arms wrapped around the bubble, trying to break in. The barrier cracked as long, sharp claws penetrated the shield above them. Lore's eyes trailed the thin arms back to the creature and her chest became tight. *Those gleaming gold eyes continue to haunt me.* Within seconds, their only protection shattered and fell to the ground around them like icy shards that dissipated immediately like melting snow.

Mathilde shoved Lore out of harm's way as the clawed hands came crashing down on them, sending her rolling along the narrow path, stones scraping her legs.

Lore immediately looked toward the dust cloud and saw the monster was searching for something when a clunk of stone hitting stone made the creature turn. Its long, thick tail dragged across the path. Then a stone, the size of Lore's fist, flew through the air and bounced off the tangled fur of the beast. Mathilde's voice rattled through the air. "You *stupid* creature!"

Although the dust cloud was still swirling with life, Lore could hear the screams of rage-filled tears streaming down the mouse's soft cheeks.

"You belong in the forest!"

Mathilde continued to hurl stones, and they continued to roll off the beast's back. Thudding against the path.

"You horrendous murderer!" The venom in her voice didn't phase the creature either.

Another stone was thrown, and Mathilde's next shrill declaration shook Lore's heart like the monster's footsteps against the ground.

"*I hate all of you!*"

Then, just as a Herculean-sized paw was moments from snuffing out Mathilde like a light, a sturdy hairless tail curled itself around the creature's clawed paw like morning glories trailing up a post.

Crinkle.

With one step backward on the opossum's part, the creature was pulled towards the opossum. *Away from Mathilde.*

Lore found her footing again and as she stood behind him now that the creature's gaze had shifted to her. The creature bellowed a deafening wail that made Lore's bones shudder. Like the one that she and Mathilde had heard Lyudmilla make outside the graveyard the day of Gannon's funeral.

The glittering eyes suddenly had small silvery-purple streaks peeking through the main gold color. Another ear-splitting cry from the beast cut through the air. With a hasty jolt, the monster charged forward, completely stomping over Crinkle.

Lore snapped her eyes shut, expecting the worst. She could not run. Her legs stood stiff like a pair of jeans left out in a blizzard to dry. She heard the *whoosh* of metal fly by her. Her eyes opened to see a brilliant blue light glowing from behind the beast. Growing brighter with each second.

A groan and a whimper from the mighty creature sounded, then it toppled her and the sheer weight of the creature felt like a giant boulder being placed on her ribcage. She expected to hear her bones snap in half, but she heard the tear of fabric and her chest felt warm with adrenaline.

Lore forced her eyes open and saw blood trickling down the creature's face as the monster took its last breath.

As it died, the bright and haunting golden eyes faded to a rich shade of violet. Her hands were shaking as the beast's face, frozen in a yowl, stared emptily down at her. Her body felt like it was bracing against the weight of the heavens. Then the clouds, the morning sky, and the surrounding trees began to blur and spin. Engulfing her like a tornado of personified fear.

Mathilde's light footsteps came towards her. The mouse pulled the hand ax from the monster's head and tossed it to the side, then wrapped her thin, fuzzy digits around Lore's hand. "Don't worry, Human. I got'cha."

The sound of the mouse's voice grounded Lore from the whiplash-inducing spiral that she found herself in.

Her body jerked as Mathilde pulled on her arm. With each tug, Lore felt a sharp pressure digging deeper and deeper against her.

"Mathilde," she gasped out. Her lungs stung with each word. "Stop. Something is stabbing me." Her whispers were more pleading and pathetic than she wanted them to sound.

The mouse dropped Lore's arm and scampered somewhere out of sight. She heard her companion call into the clouds of dust around them. "Crinkle!"

It was becoming harder to breathe and, with each rise and fall of her chest, Lore felt the pressure penetrating more into the flannel. Her eyelids became heavy and as they fluttered shut, she heard the footsteps of Mathilde return to her.

"Help me get this thing off of the human," Mathilde demanded as buried her hands against the creature's matted gray fur.

The opossum scoffed and crossed his arms. "Why do a brute's work when magic can do it for you?"

As she imagined Mathilde giving a huff, a soft blue glow illuminated her eyelids, and as she opened her eyes again, she found her next breath easily. It still felt like she was inhaling static, but at least she was successfully inhaling now. She started to turn on her side, but a sharp pain stopped her.

A sudden brushing of Mathilde's hands against her made Lore plop flat on her back again.

The adventurer eyed the blood-soaked stab wound with concern. "Is that the human's blood or the Grayshade's?"

Crinkle leaned over, his nose turned up, and waved a hand. "Mathilde, be a dear and prop the human up so I can get a look."

The mouse rolled her eyes and Lore felt her friend's gentle touch on her back. As Mathilde pushed, pressing her back against hers to prop her up, Lore could now see Crinkle's eyes, looking like freshly painted buttons.

The opossum brushed his hairless fingers against the gash. When Lore didn't flinch, his snout twitched, and he pressed into the wound. Blood coated his thin fingers.

Lore sat as solid as a garden statue.

"Interesting," Crinkle mused.

She felt the mouse start to shake under her weight and did her best to help support herself.

"It appears," Crinkle mused, "that the creature's blood dripped from one of its fatal wounds."

Lore eyed the opossum and watched every twitch of the corner of his mouth and every time his red-stained fingers fluttered as his thoughts twisted and turned.

His hand slipped behind the buttons of her green flannel, and Lore's jaw tightened. "What exactly are you doing?" she all but snapped.

A smile as sharp as a present moon spread across his face. "Seeing what we have to thank for stopping that Grayshade's claw from dipping into your heart." His voice was hushed, almost at a whisper as he fingered the spine of Gannon's green book. "Ah!" Sir Crinkle announced.

But before he could pull it out, Lore's hand shot out and gripped his wrist. It felt more brittle than she was expecting. Her stone-colored eyes sharpened, and Crinkle's smile shattered.

He quickly snapped his hand back and rose to his feet, eying her up and down with calculating, beady eyes. He waved his staff and blue light fell atop Lore. The bruising aches on her body washed away with the magic. As if he dipped her in a running creek. She stood to her feet, the small book heavy against her chest as she watched him pace over to the lifeless Grayshade.

Mathilde scampered around Lore, looking over where every scrape and tear had been.

The mouse narrowed her gaze at Crinkle's back and with a scoff said, "Well, this little encounter still doesn't change that the human and I still have business at Iron Rose." Her voice wasn't as sharp as before and now had a hollow quality.

"Well, you two can't go alone. Especially after that attack." Crinkle protested.

"So, we're bringing the body with us?" Mathilde asked with a humorless laugh.

The opossum snapped his fingers. "Good idea."

It only took a few words to fall from the opossum's lips for another blue hue to shine around the corpse and raise it in the air. It floated behind them the rest of the walk to the greenhouse.

"You don't think carrying that thing around like that will stir panic?" Lore questioned, taking a few steps backward. Her heel caught the hilt of the ax that had saved her. Before Sir Crinkle could turn to face them, she kicked it to the weeds and brush off the path.

"What a valid concern," Crinkle mused, still withholding an answer.

Mathilde looked up the path that wove its way to Charmsend, cutting through the hillside and under the almost naked treetops. "This was awfully close." Her attention was directed back to Crinkle, who was straightening out the wrinkles in his plum suit and murmuring spells to dissipate the bloodstain on the suit's green trim.

"It was, but after visiting the Iron Rose, I will speak with Lyudmilla." He tucked folded the emerald handkerchief back into a neat triangle and stored it in his pocket. "Perhaps we need to do another patrol."

Mathilde's tail flicked back and forth like a pissed-off lemur. "That's it?" She threw her hands up in exasperation. "Just another protocol, no extra spells?" Crinkle's mouth opened, but Mathilde continued to talk. "Are we just s'posed to sit here like hens waiting for a fox to enter their coop?" Her words were pointed, but Crinkle seemed unfazed as he rubbed the blueish stone atop his staff with his silk sleeve.

"If you're done, Mathilde." His voice was firm and stopped the mouse's tirade. "I understand your passionate feelings about the situation." His gleaming obsidian eyes flicked up from the stone and made him look like a hawk about to swallow its prey whole. "But I assure you we are doing everything we can to protect our *henhouse.*"

A breeze billowed inside the treetop-covered pathway, and it sent a shiver through Lore.

Crinkle chewed the inside of his yellow-stained cheek. "Well, it isn't much farther now." He turned, and the floating corpse of the Grayshade turned with him.

After silently exchanging an uneasy glance, Lore and Mathilde followed behind.

TWENTY-FIVE

L ore stared at the ornate greenhouse comfortably nestled under the swaying amber treetops. Light fell through the leaves and twinkled down like starlight to the forest floor. As they approached the building, she noted a pointed and rusty iron fence protected the perimeter.

A crisp breeze blew down the winding path they just emerged from, the memory of the beast leaping from the forest border echoing in her mind as she stared blankly at the lifeless creature hovering above the forest path.

Sir Crinkle opened the gate door. It was barely hanging on its hinges and had embossed roses twisted upon it. "After you. Beauty before age."

Lore furrowed her brow. "I don't think that's how the saying goes."

Mathilde rolled her eyes and grabbed Lore's forearm, pulling her along.

The path inside the iron fence was covered with brush and overgrown brambles. There were a few thorn-tipped vines that kissed Lore's skin. Not enough to stab her, but enough that she was aware they were there. The sound of the gate snapping shut, made her stomach flip. Its thunderous sound was unexpected for such a fragile thing. As they closed the distance between them and the doorway, Lore noted the small water fountain in front of the greenhouse that was overtaken by the pointy plant. Her lips pursed. *It's a shame. I bet it'd be beautiful if the weeds were better managed.*

She followed Mathilde through the door and saw the inside was much smaller than she initially thought it'd be. Years of dust and algae buildup tinted the windows. She couldn't even see outside. Half of the building looked like it was being devoured by an amalgamation of the same, thick blue-tipped greenery outside. Except these were about the size of Lore's forearm.

They just happened to also have the most beautiful blooming orange flowers. The petals looked like the tips of the warmest flame, the centers like a burning red ember.

"*Sable?*" Crinkle called as he walked away from the entrance, leaving the dead body of the Grayshade to float alone. As he walked, the thud of his cane reverberated off the walls in the seemingly abandoned space.

Mathilde tapped her foot impatiently and rubbed the scruff on her chin. "That's an awful lot of fire flower," she muttered as she shoved her hands in the pockets of her red jacket.

Lore ran her hand along the wood of the raised beds. *Fire flower?* The words ran through her mind, but the voice that said it belonged to a man. Lore tried to navigate through her memories, but it felt like she was looking at a mirror that kept fogging over. No matter how many times she wiped the glass clear, more mist would appear in its place. She gave up and her eyes shifted back to the garden beds. Most of them were empty or had only dried plants remaining in them. *A bit odd.*

Crinkle spun on his heels. "I don't have time for this," he spat.

Lore studied his flattened ears. He shoved past both her and Mathilde on his way back to the floating corpse in the doorway. *What caused this sour shift in mood?* As he turned, the sound of the opossum's tail whooshed through the air.

Mathilde pulled on the back of Lore's flannel just in time. If she hadn't, Lore would have had her legs taken out from under her.

Sir Crinkle's triangular face scrunched. "When you *do* find her, tell her I have some important business that needs the nurturing care of someone with a green thumb." With that proclamation, the monster floated back outside, following Crinkle before the pissed-off animal slammed the door shut behind him with so much force it shook the very foundation of the Iron Rose.

Lore looked at her friend. "I don't think there's anyone here with a green thumb."

Down The Well

Mathilde shook her head, her eyes fixed on the hallway that was engulfed by the fire flower vines. "Sometimes her thumb is *too* green," the mouse said under her breath as she proceeded towards the plant-infested hallway.

"Are you sure that's a good idea?" Lore asked as she followed,

"No."

"Those thorns look pretty sharp." She was pleading now.

Mathilde looked over her shoulder. "Then don't get stuck by them," she said flatly.

Lore furrowed her brow. *DoN't GeT StUcK bY ThEm.* As if it were that easy. She huffed and watched the three-foot-tall mouse nimbly walk around each sharp obstacle.

"Well, come on, Human," the mouse encouraged as she delved deeper into the shadows of the crowded hall.

"What if I *do* get stuck by one?" she asked as she carefully edged herself around the pointy, blue-tipped thorns.

"It'll burn like the fire of a thousand suns," her companion's voice casually called back. As if the answer was obvious.

Lore's heart immediately began to race. She could barely see and she did her best to listen for the mouse's footsteps to guide her. When she came 'round a corner, it felt like she had stepped on a cord.

"Human! Get your foot off my tail!" Mathilde squeaked.

"Oh, sorry!" Lore could feel sweat trickle down from the nape of her neck. *One wrong move and we are both in for a painful time.*

Then the creaking of wood splintered against their ears, and a sliver of dim orange light poured into the hallway. A figure was hiding behind the door, but they peaked through the crack. Lore couldn't make out any facial features, but the soft light illuminated raised a set of spikes on the individual's back.

"Is *he* gone?" a spooked voice called.

"Sable? Is that you?" Mathilde called out. "You sound different."

"Is he gone?" Sable asked again, her voice flustered.

"Yes." Mathilde made her voice small and soft. "Crinkle is gone." Her tail wrapped around Lore's ankle. "Just me and the human."

Sable opened the door all the way, revealing a kind face. She waved her hand and the dense vines retracted back to her, rattling the halls as they did so. "Come quickly, then."

They bolted down the emptied hall to the dim glow of the orange light.

The hedgehog held her arms out, embracing the mouse in a tight hug.

Mathilde pushed away from the embrace. Her eyes were pointed sharply, but her voice was one of confusion. "Where have you been?"

Their host ran her hands over her wrinkled green apron that had many swirling silver designs embroidered in it. Then she closed her hand into a fist, and the thorny vines again flooded the hallway before the door slammed shut.

Lore jolted from the unexpected speed of it all.

Sable's eyes were staring down at her own twiddling thumbs. "Hiding."

Mathilde gulped and reached for a chair that sat in front of a bulky desk. She played with the collar of her shirt as her gaze fixated on the shy hedgehog. "Why are you avoiding Crinkle?"

The greenhouse owner's tear-filled eyes locked on Lore. "It's not just Crinkle." Her dark quills bumped the drying herbs above her. Her masked face softened when she looked at Mathilde. "I've had many unwanted visitors lately."

The mouse rested her cheek on her hand and gestured vaguely with the other. "Who?"

Sable shook her head. "Doesn't matter. What is it you want?"

Mathilde sighed and waved a hand for Lore to sit next to her.

She lingered in the doorframe, unsure. *I don't wanna scare the poor thing further.* "I'm good, thanks." She smiled and scratched behind her braid.

Mathilde rolled her eyes and turned to face Sable again. "Is there anything Gannon spoke to you about regarding specific herbs and the uh—" her voice became a low gentle whisper, "barrier."

"No, but someone did."

"Can you tell us who?"

The panic returned to the hedgehog's eyes. "It was someone," she repeated without any further details.

Mathilde's furry forehead wrinkled. "Can you describe this *someone?*" Her voice was patient and placid.

"They were cloaked in shadow and came on the stormy night Gannon—" Sable began to choke on her tears. "The night Gannon—" Her voice cracked, and she reached out for the desk to steady herself. "The night he died."

Mathilde's eyes softened as she watched the hedgehog collapse in a chair.

Lore's eyes were busy looking around the room, the conversation happening at the far edges of her attention.

"What herbs did they want?" Mathilde pushed.

Lore focused on the orange blossoms emanating little bioluminescent orbs from its center.

"I can't tell you but—"

The sound of a tome being thudded against the desk brought Lore's attention back to them. The book was at least a foot thick.

"If you happened to look here while I did something else…" Sable trailed off, her suggestion clear. She went over to water the fire flower that was pouring out from a single terracotta pot.

Mathilde wasted no time and hopped up on the desk. Her face dropped, and she closed the leather cover shut just as quickly as she'd opened it. She leaped off the desk and scampered beside Lore.

"We'll be going now." Her voice was hollow again.

The hedgehog didn't turn, just waved her hand and the sound of the vines retreating rattled through the walls. The door opened and while Lore was eager to leave, Mathilde lingered a bit, looking at the clearly magically gifted animal. Another Wielder.

"What's it Crinkle wants you to do?" the mouse asked in a low voice.

The expert gardener didn't turn to face them and continued to water her plants as she uttered, "The most unnatural of acts."

The words haunted the two as they walked out. Without the dangerous foliage filling the space, it was clear the floor in the greenhouse had suffered some claw marks.

"Now I understand why she has all that fire flower," Mathilde murmured as they passed through the busted gate.

The sun was low in the sky. Lore furrowed her brow. *Surely that much time couldn't have passed?* She looked down at Mathilde, who was being rather silent. "Where do we go next?"

The mouse sighed. "We need to return to the scene where the Gray-shade attacked us."

Lore felt like her heart was frosting over, but she gulped down her anxiety. "Okay."

The two raced out of the glass structure and back up the weaving path. Lore's lungs stung against the crisp night air, and her eyes strained to focus on Mathilde in the dusk light—or lack thereof. Then they halted.

"I think this is the place," Mathilde said, rubbing her furry chin.

Lore slowly turned in a circle. "I don't know how you can tell. It all looks the same in the dark."

"Human? You mean to tell me you can't see the monster's blood staining the ground?"

Lore squinted as she looked at the path. Her eyes caught the sight of a faint outline. "Barely," she uttered.

"Where is the ax?" Mathilde hummed to herself, searching the area for the wayward weapon.

Then the sound of voices carried down the tunneled path and as Lore froze in place Mathilde quickly leaped into the tall thicket, motioning for her to do the same. Just as the grass sprang back, concealing them, they saw the flickering firelight against the stone path. Shadows grew along it as the voices grew nearer and nearer.

"What do you mean? There was another one?" Lyudmilla's voice cut through the cold air.

Between the blades of the tall grass, Lore saw a trio of the pink-eyed wolf, Sir Crinkle—whose scrunched face signaled his sour mood, and a familiar lamppost between the two.

"Someone who I thought I banished is back," the opossum replied. "Gannon's death can't be a mere coincidence."

There was a thick stillness in the air that weighed on Lore's shoulders. She could hear her heartbeat rushing in her ears.

"You think someone is trying to pick us off?" The wolf's voice was riddled with apprehension. "Dreadway wouldn't have any more followers to do that. They all died with him."

"No, this is someone closer to home." The once polished and keen onyx eyes of Crinkle were dull like used lumps of home. "We need to cover all our bases, so you'll have to tell your little girlfriend that you can't see her for the next few nights."

The sound of metal slamming against stone rang in Lore's eardrums.

"Grimace all you want, but unless you want that pretty calico skinned by a Grayshade, you will patrol while I work on putting extra charms on the town." Sir Crinkle's order was laced with every ounce of authority he owned. Then he dramatically turned to walk back up the path.

The lamppost clumsily chased after the opossum.

As the shadows engulfed Lyudmilla in their embrace, Lore leaned back on her hands. A twig snapped beneath her palms. The wolf's pink eyes snapped to the thicket, and Lore felt her heart race as she thought Lyudmilla was looking right through her.

The breeze was gently blowing the tops of the grass when a snow-colored snout poked through the dying greenery of the thicket.

Lore felt as if ice was solidifying in her veins as sharpened pink eyes glowed in the darkness, boring into her. She swallowed hard. It felt like broken glass scraped her throat.

Then an otherworldly howl echoed through the valley.

Lyudmilla's pink nose pulled away. She rushed down the path, brandishing her battle ax.

Mathilde yanked on Lore's arm. "Quickly now," The mouse then switched tactics and began pushing against her side. "It's under your big butt!" she spat.

Between Crinkle's concealed fear coming to light and someone wanting to kill off the citizens of Charmsend, Lore didn't know what else to do but laugh at Mathilde's comment.

"Human, get it together. There's too much at stake for you to lose it."

She stood up. The thicket tickled against her stomach and forearms as Mathilde grabbed the hand ax.

The mouse flipped it over again, trying to notice any details. Then a creeping smile spread onto her furred cheeks. "What'd'ya make of this?" she whispered, placing the hilt into Lore's palm.

The wood was cool and sleek against Lore's skin, like a stone smoothed by years of weathering rushing water. As her fingers curled around it she felt the indentation of a letter A. She pursed her lips. "So, does this letter represent the someone that has Crinkle so flustered?"

Mathilde's green eyes flickered in the dark. "There's only one stranger in town to ask."

TWENTY-SIX

Killmoore didn't even jump when Mathilde burst through the door of the rundown cabin. He kept his back to them and looked at the wall he had covered in papers. Red strings from all corners of the display came back to one point in the center of the web.

"We need to talk," the mouse announced.

The fox's ears twitched. The back of his blue coat brushed against the dusted floors, his back still to them as he scribbled something down on one of the papers. "Have you come back to put another hole in the floor, or are you going to help me?"

Mathilde's large ears drooped. She turned to her and held an expectant hand out.

Lore gingerly placed the weapon in her companion's hand. She held her breath and watched the mouse march inside. Then her eyes drifted back to the fox, who was clearly fixated on whatever scheme he was planning to steal Crinkle's gem.

Without warning, Mathilde drew her arm back and launched the weapon forward.

As it spun in the air, so did Lore's nerves. *Why was everything act now, ask later with the little rodent?*

The blade crunched into the shack's moth-eaten wood walls and landed a whisker away from Killmoore's face.

He casually pulled the ax from its target, as if such close calls were a regular occurrence. Maybe they were. Once it was extracted, a few pieces of his paper fluttered to the ground like a butterfly whose wings had been ripped off. He turned, tossing the ax up in the air and catching it again. "If you wanted to help plan all you had to do was say so. No need to throw a tantrum." A toothy grin spread across his face as he looked down at Mathilde, as if he were amused by almost being cut by the flying blade.

She shoved a finger in his face. "Did you let in that Grayshade?!"

He tilted his head and returned the ax to its holster that was strapped across his back. "Can't say that I've left here at all today, but thanks for finding that." His attention returned to the wall.

Mathilde huffed. "Did you bring it in with you?" she asked again, her voice strained.

Killmoore shrugged as he crossed his arms. "I guess it's not impossible one could have squeezed through that hole. But, as I said before, I didn't enter with one."

A brash scream of frustration escaped Mathilde's lungs. Then she scampered past Lore and out onto the porch.

Lore looked back to the fox, who had his chin resting in his hand.

"Yeah, you'll want to go get her."

She sighed and stepped outside.

The adventurer had her knees pulled up close to her chest and her face buried in her hands.

Lore couldn't explain it but, she felt she had been in the same position a handful of times. She sat beside her. "Hey," she whispered.

Mathilde sniffled, her face still hiding behind her hands.

"I know you've dealt with a lot here lately, and I'm sure it's not been easy." Lore rested her elbows on her thighs and looked out into the meadow that was flooded with moonlight. She began to pick at the skin around her nails. "You know, I don't know what a raccoon at a fair looks like. And I still don't know how humans went extinct in Thimbleton." She looked at Mathilde.

The mouse's face was no longer hidden behind her hands and now showed a pair of furry, tear-stained cheeks.

"But what I do know," Lore continued, "is that there is nothing that will keep you down."

The mouse smiled softly and wiped her nose with her jacket sleeve.

"At least not for long," Lore comforted. "Because you are too fiery and vibrant to be snuffed out."

Mathilde fidgeted with her tail. "You know," she said with a raspy whisper, tears pooling in her eyes, "It feels like I'm try'n'a swim."

Lore nodded and gave her a sympathetic pat on the back. "Yeah. After a while you just get tired."

The mouse shook her head and tried to steady her breathing, "No, not like swimming for a long time." She paused, trying to center her cracking voice. "Like I'm try'n'a swim in the ocean during a storm."

Lore looked at the shadowy tree line in the distance. She understood. Images of her hands fighting against the shadow in the well flashed in her mind. At least she had felt a similar experience of fighting waters working against her. "Maybe in my life before I felt what you're feeling. Maybe I'm here to get you through."

Mathilde squinted her bloodshot eyes. "Human, don't speak such clear nonsense."

Says the talking mouse.

"Listen, I don't know why I am here, but I do know that you're like my only friend." A small smile pricked at the corners of Mathilde's mouth as she listened to Lore continue. "And if you need one, I'll be your lifeboat."

Silence.

Lore's nostrils flared as she took a deep breath in. "You know I didn't know when would be the right time to tell you this."

The mouse's round ears perked with curiosity.

Lore's gaze drifted back to her fingertips, now picked raw. "But I've been hearing some things and I think it's a hint of my life before." She shook her head, not believing her own hopeful words. "Nothing concrete, of course, but—"

"Human," Mathilde interrupted, speaking from the side of her mouth. "That's great news." The red-clad mouse tried to sound as peppy as she normally was. But she didn't quite manage it.

"Not everything I hear is pleasant, though."

Her friend sniffled, stood up, and looked out into the field, drowning in the pale light. "Thank you, Human. Once this is all over," she looked at Lore, a gleam of seriousness behind her eyes, "I promise I will do whatever I have to, to get you back home." She offered an open hand.

Lore took the mouse's palm in hers and stood up. "Let's go question this fox."

Mathilde nodded, her fire reignited. "Got to focus on the mission in front of us."

Whatever helps us stay afloat in this ocean of grief.

"Ah, you've returned!" Killmoore chimed as he positioned two chairs in front of the wall. "So, the gemstone." He tapped a pointed blade of a knife on the papers behind him. "Are we ready for the rundown?"

Mathilde wiped her cheeks as she sat down in the chair, her hands folded neatly in her lap. "Actually," she said matter-of-factly, "before we help you do your job, I have one question."

A spark of amusement danced across the bounty hunter's face. "And what question is that?"

"Why does your weapon have an A carved into it?" Mathilde held the fox's gaze. "Your name is Killmoore."

The bounty hunter shrugged. "Family heirloom."

Mathilde narrowed her gaze. "I don't buy that."

"I found it." His voice was flat.

Her eyes drilled into him and her nose twitched. "I don't know why you insist on lying to me."

"Fine," he spat, his tail swooshing back and forth under his royal blue jacket. His eyes looked back at the wall of papers and red thread. "I stole them. Happy now?"

Mathilde crossed her arms. "I still don't believe you."

The fox let out an audible groan and pinched the ginger fur between his eyes. "Sounds like a you problem." He turned back to face them and tapped the tip of a sharpened knife on the wall again. "But what will help you get the answers to whatever burning questions you have, is by helping me." He paused. His eyes darted between Lore and Mathilde. "So, help me help you."

Lore looked down at her friend, who waved a hand casually.

"Just get on with whatever hodgepodge of a plan you have," the mouse said.

TWENTY-SEVEN

The sticks and bramble poked Lore as the trio hid in the shrubs of Charmsend's market square. It was even more uncomfortable than the shrub she'd hid in when she'd seen Gannon's dead body.

"This isn't promising," the bounty hunter murmured as they all peeked through the leaves at the stationed guards.

"It's probably 'cuz the Grayshade that attacked us on our way to Sable's," Mathilde added under her breath.

Lore chewed her bottom lip. The lamplight sparkled off of the freshly polished swords of the witching hour's watch. Her stomach felt like it was trying to digest pins and needles. "So, what now?"

The fox's amber eyes gleamed as he looked them over. His tongue clicked behind his teeth. "We aren't in a position to do a direct attack, let alone one without them alerting others."

Mathilde narrowed her gaze in protest. "I think you underestimate us. In case you didn't notice, we *survived* the attack."

"Listen, do you wanna chance it because you've got something to prove?" Lore could hear how stupid the fox thought that choice was. "Come on, how bad would it look if you were caught with me? A human and an un-vouched-for outsider?"

He had a point. A lot of the animals already hated her. She didn't want Mathilde to get in trouble for associating with more strangers.

A loud whistle pierced the night air and disrupted the sleeping carrier crows perched on the iron street lamps. Then the sound of clunking boots made them fall silent in the shrub where they were hiding. The armored body halted in front of the thicket. The metal clanged as the animal's legs snapped together. Lore looked at her warped reflection in the polished steel as the striped tail of a raccoon swayed from side to side. Lore ran a hand over her chest pocket where the hole in her flannel was.

Would metal be enough to stop the talons of a Grayshade? Her hands instinctively ran over her heart and her fingertips kissed the frayed thread of the hole in her flannel. *I mean, I guess if a simple book can, metal should suffice.*

Tension clung to the air like the stink on shit. Until it broke when another whistle cracked through the atmosphere like lightning during a summer thunderstorm. The armor-clad raccoon moved to another point in the town square.

"There's an opening to sneak through," Killmoore said quietly.

Mathilde nodded, and Lore felt whatever nerves she had left get taken to a back alley and shot.

Her voice wavered. "Are you sure that's the *only* option?"

The fox's face was expressionless. "Oh, no," he said in mock horror. "It appears I have forgotten I possess The Warden's key." He dug around in his satchel. "It appears I *can* open a portal to the opossum's house, after all."

Mathilde tried to hold back a giggle with her hands.

Lore just rolled her eyes. "A simple no would have sufficed. You don't have to be such an ass—"

The whistle sounded again. The trio held their breath waiting for another guard to halt in front of them, but it didn't come.

Mathilde eyed the market square and the dimly lit street lamps. "Appears to only have three watchmen in this area," she noted.

The bounty hunter nodded and rhythmically drummed a gloved hand on his chin.

"Why are you even wearing those if they just cover your palms?" the little mouse teased.

"Because," the fox said matter-of-factly, "someone among us has to have style." He pulled on the bottom of the black glove that wrapped around his wrist.

Another whistle blew. Another guard shift. This time, a squirrel's curled fluffy tail greeted them. It almost looked like it had a blue sheen under the moons and stars' light. In the flickering lamplight, the lush fur practically called Lore to touch it.

She lifted her hand to do just that, but Mathilde quickly smacked her hand away and shook a finger quickly back and forth in her face, accompanied by an angry scowl.

Lore tilted her head. "I wasn't actually gonna do it," she mouthed.

After another few moments of silence, the whistle blew a fifth time, becoming like clockwork. The squirrel moved to a concession stand a few feet away.

Killmoore's eyes shifted. "Alright. The next rotation, we move."

Mathilde nodded.

"We'll have to be quick," he added.

Lore raised a brow. "Oh, I thought we were aiming to be slow and steady."

He smirked. "Don't worry, lass. Everyone's first quip or two isn't the funniest."

Lore narrowed her eyes at the teasing fox. Before she could say another word, the signal they were waiting for echoed through the air.

The fox bolted from the shrub like a shadow across the path, followed by Mathilde close behind. The two animals quickly and quietly leaped over the hedge box outline that enclosed a tree.

Lore stumbled out after them. Luckily, the light emanating from the iron lamps didn't give her away. She leaped over the hedge surrounding an abundant apple tree and landed on the bounty hunter with a thud.

He shoved her off with an annoyed side-eye.

A few apples fell from the tree, but the guards didn't seem to notice. *Thank goodness.*

"When it goes again, we are gonna be trying to get to that empty stall. Okay?" The fox's expression was heavy with the consequences of what would happen if they get caught.

Like Lore or Mathilde wanted that any more than he did.

The rotation whistle sang over the somber square. As the guards moved, the trio slinked to the empty wood stall. The ratty, green fabric covering some merchant's booth flapped haphazardly in the crisp night air. Under it, there were shelves lined with sweet-smelling teas and salves.

Mathilde picked up a tin of salve and looked at the painted logo. A gray rose. "Sable," she whispered as she quickly pocketed a handful of the merchandise.

Lore looked to Killmoore, who was peering around the edge of the stand for their next vanishing point.

"Where are we going next?" she asked.

"Shh. I'm thinking," he said as he scanned the area. The whistle echoed once more over the area, but the fox didn't move.

The makeshift counter above them released a raspy sigh as a large brown bear leaned its weight against the stand.

His eyes grew as wide as the second moon that hung oh so low in the Thimbleton sky and he quickly huddled next to her and Mathilde by the merchandise. His face said it all. They needed to be silent.

Lore's heart thudded against her ribcage hard enough that she thought the bear would surely hear it. As the trio pressed themselves against the flimsy pine, waiting for the damned whistle to blow, Lore's foot slipped. The sound of her shoe squeaking against the cobblestone square made ice shoot down her spine. *Was this it?*

The bear adjusted his weight while Killmoore's hand lingered over a hand ax, ready to strike when a whistle called the guard away, saving him from an untimely death. The heavy footsteps shook the ground and shrank as the bear receded until the ground was still once more.

A relieved breath whooshed out of all of them.

The fox slithered over to the end of the booth to peek around it. Then he quickly popped his head behind the pine wood planks again to face Mathilde and Lore. "That's where we'll go."

Lore peered around the side and saw the hydrangea bush she had hidden in the morning Gannon's body was discovered. She gulped, but followed the plan. When the high-pitched sound rattled through the air, the trio bolted. One behind the other, so close that their shadows combined when cast against the stone, looked like a misshapen caterpillar.

When they all crouched within the bush, the fox was already crawling to the back. Even this close to him, he was still hard to see.

Killmoore cupped his hands around his muzzle to muffle his words. "We should be able to exit here and go down this alley. But we'll have to be careful."

"Who knows where Crinkle has guards stationed?" Mathilde added with a head nod.

Lore's neck began to ache from being hunched over into tight spaces. She peered through the leaves and past the flowers. And the stillness of the moment sent a haunting chill up her arms.

The three guards appeared painfully bored. The raccoon hung over a concession stand, tail waving in the air as he scooped up whatever goodies were behind the counter, and the squirrel was admiring their reflection in their polished broadsword. Heavy snores erupted from a nearby spot.

Lore's heart skipped a beat when she laid eyes on the brown bear sleeping propped against an iron lamppost. She shrank back into the overflowing hydrangea bush.

The only one who seemed to notice was the living lamp post.

Her jaw dropped when it tipped his hat to her. Did it recognize her? Was it the same one that helped her and Mathilde find the footprints in the bush or was it another one?

"Mathilde," Lore whispered.

"Not now, Human." The mouse waved her worried friend off as she and the fox looked over a makeshift map.

The streetlight wriggled, trying to free its thin metal body away from the dreaming bear. Lore shook her head in disbelief. It waved with a creaking iron appendage at her. With the thud of the bear against the cobblestone path, the sentient iron fixture began to make its way over to the bush, a clink and clank echoed with every rushed step.

"Hey what's Grian doin'?" a nasal voice asked aloud.

"Dunno."

A grunt of frustration followed by quick footsteps scampering against the path made Lore fall backward. Luckily, her hands caught her weight.

The silver blue squirrel stood in front of the bush, arms wide open. "Grian, what are you doing? Get back in position."

The lamp flapped its squeaky appendices.

Mathilde's hand gripped Lore's shoulder. "Come on," the mouse urgently whispered.

The broad sword swayed in its hilt as the squirrel tried to herd Grian back to the guards' corner. "We've a job to do. If you goof off like this, who knows who'll slip through?"

The lamppost stomped one of their four metal feet in protest and crossed their arms.

"Let's go, human," the fox said, moving to the back of the bush.

She followed behind Killmoore, though she didn't have much of a choice with him dragging her by the forearm. Once they cleared the bush, he released her.

As the trio wove in between trash bins down the narrow alleyways of Charmsend, she could still hear the faint echo of a whistle sounding and clinking metal. She halted behind Mathilde to avoid running over the mouse.

Killmoore wasn't as quick and almost mowed down Lore.

The mouse turned and held a finger up to her mouth. She pointed, and Lore's eyes followed to see the flashing pink neon sign for Dina's pub.

She was still open?

It was clear from the packed seats behind the fogged glass paired with the sound of the band and Tansy's voice pouring out of cracked windows into the empty streets that not even a Grayshade on the outskirts of town would keep the folk of Charmsend from enjoying themselves. As they gawked at the pub, another figure emerged from the dark alley.

White fur glistened in the pale light of the moon. Pink eyes lazily scanned the area before Lyudmilla huffed and collapsed on the steps of Dina's.

The door opened and the calico cat handed the wolf a pint of something and some mutton. They appeared to be talking about something, but Lore couldn't make out what it was.

The concern on Dina's face was hard to miss when every time before she seemed so cool and collected.

"This is bad," Mathilde murmured. She whipped around and tried shoving them back down the alley.

"No. Let's see what happens," Killmoore insisted.

"So you can meet the sharpened edge of her battle ax?" Mathilde quipped, pushing the two further and further back down the alley. "For a fox, you aren't very clever."

His face scrunched at her last comment.

"I know another way," the mouse insisted. "A safer way."

The bounty hunter finally gave in, and the band of heroes slunk down a few more back alleys.

They all looked the same to Lore. "Are you sure this is the way?" she pressed. At this point, she was convinced Mathilde was taking them in circles.

"Yes." The mouse didn't even turn to face her, but the tone of her voice was as flat as the stone path they were walking on.

Lore felt the inside of her flannel, her fingertips brushing Gannon's little book as the trio stepped out into the lit path. She recognized their location and remembered the library once stood to their right. A shudder went down Lore's back as she tried to forget the snake launching herself at the door in one last attempt. Their shadows elongated against the building beside the rubble.

Mathilde pointed to a lane that headed to the north side of the town's perimeter. "Just a bit further," she said before marching in the indicated direction.

The walk was eerily quiet. A thick mist swallowed the stone lane whole, along with the stealthy trio. Even though she couldn't see it, Lore felt Mathilde's tail wave wildly in front of her. She reached out a hand and felt it curl around her fingers. Then Killmoore grabbed Lore's shoulder, his grip a bit stronger than what she imagined. Soon, green lights glittered in the distance against the white puffy fog.

"We're here," Mathilde murmured. The gray mouse led them to a handful of large rocks that were almost too conveniently placed by the rickety house.

Lore sighed as she crossed her arms. "You know, for someone who dresses as fancy as he does, this isn't the type of place I imagined Crinkle living in."

Mathilde shrugged. "Maybe it's a preference?"

The bounty hunter scoffed. "Preference? Darlin', I bet it's to go along with whatever front he has up."

They both squinted in Killmoore's direction.

"He probably has items in there worth more than any house's value could imagine touching," the fox added.

"So, do you just hate rich folk?" Mathilde asked innocently enough.

"No," Killmoore snarled. "I hate *thievin'* folk."

Mathilde held her hands up. "Okay, that's fair. No need to bare your teeth at me." Then the mouse looked over the top of the boulder. "Do we want to wait till this fog clears a bit?"

"What do you mean *wait*?" Killmoore protested. "It's the perfect cover."

Lore couldn't place a finger on it, but an anxious pull on her stomach didn't like the situation the three of them found themselves in. A dark cloud of trouble loomed, but her companions didn't seem to notice as they continued bickering about where to enter the building and when was the proper time to do it.

Then she heard something heavy dragging against the ground. She looked to the lane the group had just walked down and there was Lyudmilla, pink eyes weary. A bit busted up. Blood matted her milky fur. Though her free hand was covering her arm, blood still spilled out. The blood loss did not stop her from gripping the ax tightly as she walked to Crinkle's door.

Mathilde's jaw gaped open at the sight.

Luckily, the wolf was too preoccupied with not falling down that she didn't pay attention to the mouse's gasp.

"What do you think happened?" Lore asked in a whisper, kneeling next to Mathilde.

"There's no mistaking it." The mouse's voice trembled. "That's the work of a Grayshade."

"More have come through?" Killmoore asked aloud. "It'd be probable that one had, but two or three?" His eyes gleamed as he thought through the likelihood of it happening. "More than a bit odd."

"They travel in packs though, so it makes sense," Mathilde quickly countered. "We're lucky more than that didn't get in."

Killmoore rolled his eyes. "Never mind."

Lore chewed her lip as she watched Lyudmilla collapse on Crinkle's doorstep.

"Crinkle!" the injured wolf yelped. "Crinkle!" she howled when she didn't get an answer.

She could only try to imagine the pain she was in.

The door flung open. "Do you have to make such a ruckus?" the opossum snapped.

Lyudmilla ignored his callousness. "I need to be healed." Her eyes drifted to her bleeding arm.

The opossum grumbled and turned on his heels. "If you must, but don't get blood on the good rug."

The trio watched as the albino wolf barely pulled herself up onto her weapon and stumbled inside. Mathilde winced as the door loudly slammed shut.

"So, is there a back door we could slip through?" the bounty hunter pressed. "As sad as it is, if the 'possum is healin' ol' wolfy, it can prove useful for our sake."

Mathilde rubbed her chin. "There are a few basement windows. I'm sure I could squeeze through one."

Lore pursed her lips. "I'm not sure I like that idea."

The gray mouse dusted her red jacket off. "And why not?"

Lore twiddled her thumbs. "I don't know." A frustrated sigh escaped her lips. "I just don't think we should split up."

Mathilde narrowed her eyes. "You don't think I can do it?"

"That's not what I said."

"Yes, it is," the mouse argued.

She crossed her arms, "Listen, I know this place is your home and you know every nook, cranny, and alley. But you're just gonna leave me with—" she looked to Killmoore warily, "a stranger?—No offense," she added to the bounty hunter.

Mathilde sucked on a tooth, trying to find the right argument, but nothing came.

"How about we find the windows first and see if we all can't fit, and go from there?" Killmoore offered.

"If I get caught, I can pull an excuse from thin air," Mathilde insisted. "If we *all* get caught, how will I explain that?"

"Also a good point." The fox nodded. "One we can analyze later."

Lore nodded in agreement.

Mathilde huffed and crossed her arms.

"Okay, so where are these basement windows?" the bounty hunter asked again as he slid his ax's from their holster.

Mathilde's ears flattened. "Follow me."

They pitter-pattered around the warped house, sneaking under windows and around dead rose bushes.

"He really doesn't have a green thumb," Lore noted.

"No, Gannon used to tease him about being rotten," Mathilde giggled.

As they rounded the back of the house, a large shadow appeared.

Lore froze.

"It's okay. Just Crinkle in the kitchen," Mathilde assured.

The sound of the glass panes being slid open sounded like two scratchy rusted pieces of metal being rubbed together. Mathilde motioned for them to follow her. The bitter taste of copper clung to the air escaping through the window.

"I wouldn't have to waste my time with this if you weren't so careless in combat." The opossum's words were laced with venom.

"They're getting faster." Lyudmilla's voice was ragged.

"You disappoint me," they heard Crinkle say.

"Damn," Killmoore muttered. "What a hard-ass. Is he always so mean, or is he just mad that he's losing some of his beauty sleep?"

The group continued to slink under the cover of the fog.

Then Mathilde stopped in front of a single window that was hugged between two blocks of sandstone. "Here it is." She leaned down to wiggle it open. No luck. "I guess we can find another way."

The fox ripped a piece of his dark shirt and wrapped it around his hand. "This'll do."

"If you break it, he'll hear it," Mathilde spat.

Killmoore nodded. "And you'll intercept him, darlin'."

"Stop calling me that," she said through gritted teeth.

"That still splits us up," Lore added.

"Human, you'll just have to deal with my company," the fox said, clearly a bit annoyed. "You and I will slither in and get the gem while mousey here talks a big game to Sir Sourpuss."

"But what about Lyudmilla?" Mathilde added.

"What about her?" Killmoore shrugged. "She's injured."

Mathilde shook her head. "Crinkle is a master healer."

The fox leaned down by the window. "Then I guess we better be quick, huh?"

Mathilde frowned, and before Lore could offer any other solution, the echo of broken glass rang through the foggy air.

As expected, the looming shadow in the kitchen quickly disappeared.

Killmoore laid the scrap of fabric on the broken glass and easily slid inside. He held a hand out for Lore to follow.

As she lowered herself through the window, she saw her friend run to the corner of the house where Crinkle would surely be going.

"Mathilde?" His voice called out a little too close for Lore's comfort as the bounty hunter pulled her down.

The opossum's shiny black dress shoes walked by the window.

Killmoore sighed. "That was close. Come on, human." He scanned the basement for the stairs.

As Lore followed behind the fox, she heard Mathilde's voice loud and clear. "'Bout time! What do I have to do to get your attention?"

"What are you talking about?" Crinkle's voice was strained. "I'm dealing with something at the moment."

"I knocked on the door, and there was no answer." She could imagine the smirk on Mathilde's face as she kept the charade. "It's about who broke into Gannon's room."

"Oh, that so?"

Lore stayed close to the window, listening to every lie Mathilde let spill from her small mouth.

"Human, come on," the fox called as he pulled down the trapped door.

Lore hesitated but bolted to the rickety stairs that she and Killmoore carefully climbed up.

The bounty hunter gently lifted the floor piece where the entrance to the basement was. They paused and scanned the area's black and white tiled floor and dingy gray walls from underneath a table. A sink full of dishes sat on the far end of the room. *If I had magic, you'd best believe the dishes would be doing themselves.* Then, as a double-sided ax slammed on the ground in front of them, they knew their window was even smaller. Lore could see her own fear reflected back at her in the polished steel blade.

"Crinkle?" Lyudmilla groaned as she pulled herself from the table above them. Her feet gingerly touched the tiled floors. "Crinkle, where are you?" she called again as she stumbled through the kitchen, her weapon doing the bulk of the work of keeping her steady.

"Quick, human, where do you think the gem is?" Killmoore asked, his eyes wide as he quietly climbed from the hole.

"His staff," she huffed as she took the fox's arm, lifting her weight out of the basement.

Killmoore whipped his head back and forth. "You go there." He pointed to the hall Lyudmilla did not go down. "And I'll trail behind."

Lore didn't have time to think about how she was feeling at that moment. Her legs quickly carried her across the kitchen floor and to a carpeted hall.

The bounty hunter pressed a hand against her back. "We're good," he whispered. "Lead the way, human."

Lore squinted in the darkened room. A study? Her hands quickly began feeling the walls. She couldn't find a light switch.

"Little gem, of the ocean blue, show us the way back to you," Killmoore hummed.

In the corner of the room, a weak blue glow flickered to life. It looked like the soft sun rays shining through warm summer waters, the way it rippled against the wall.

"There," he said.

Lore silently stepped her way closer and closer to the staff. When her fingers wrapped around the blueish-green stone, it felt like she was dipping her hand into cool, refreshing waters. It almost took her breath away.

Then the sound of metal clashing behind her gave her heart a sudden jolt.

She looked over her shoulder and saw Killmoore had blocked a downward blow from Lyudmilla.

Her pink eyes seemed redder than usual. "I thought I smelled a dirty fox."

Lore turned on her heels to face the staff again. She gripped the stone as tightly as she could and pulled. But it didn't budge.

"Any time now, human!" Killmoore called, sweat breaking across his brow as he tried to fend off the wolf's sheer strength.

"I'm trying," she said through her teeth as she continued to yank at the glowing gemstone.

"Try faster!"

The fox quickly sidestepped, and the weight of the blow crushed the carpeted floor where he just stood. "Come on!" he called as he rolled over the hunched friend-turned-enemy, trying to pull her weapon from the floor.

Fear ate away at Lore's stomach and chewed harder when she closed the distance between her and the injured animal. *Run away from the danger—not towards it.* As she went to slip past her, a bloodied paw grabbed hold of her arm.

"Not so fast there, human," Lyudmilla snarled.

Lore looked out the kitchen window and saw Crinkle's back facing it. A wide-eyed Mathilde leaned around the opossum's figure when Killmoore's shadow gave away that he picked up a wooden chair from the table.

The next few moments blew by like a whirlwind. Lore ducked, and the chair hit the white wolf head-on. Just as they *thought* they were threat-free, a loud crash resounded through the house.

The opossum spun on his heels and his eyes seemed to be filled with a brewing storm. He said nothing, but with a snap of his fingers, the staff shot out from the study and thumped Lore on the back of the head.

DOWN THE WELL

She fell to the ground, the image of Crinkle waving his staff fading away from her as Darkness welcomed her back into its embrace. The last sensation she felt was someone lifting her up.

TWENTY-EIGHT

The early morning sun trickled through the broken glass of the basement window, casting a fractured rainbow light against the sandstone walls.

Lore's head felt like it was spinning. She weakly pulled against chains that connected her to the wall.

"No use, human," Mathilde groaned.

She squinted and saw some bruising beginning on the little mouse's face.

"I'm sorry," Lore uttered. "This is all my fault." Her eyes stung as she fought back the welling tears. "I did this to you."

Mathilde cocked her head and tried to adjust the heavy-duty iron cuffs that weighed down her hands. "No. Crinkle did." She didn't sound like herself. Anger was behind each word.

Lore looked around the small dim basement. "Where's Killmoore?"

Mathilde pursed her lips, and as if on cue, a blood-chilling wail echoed through the old bones of the house. "That answer your question?" the mouse spat as she continued pulling at her cuffs.

Lore furrowed her brows. "Well, what do we do now? We've got to have a plan, right?" She couldn't hide the naivety of her pleas.

Mathilde stopped and the chains hitting the floor triggered a flash of light in Lore's mind. The mouse's gaze narrowed at Lore. "We try to survive."

The trap door above them opened and a dingy yellow light flooded the basement. Crinkle then tossed the bounty hunter's body through the hole.

"Should I go and chain him?" Lyudmilla asked.

Down The Well

The opossum stared down with a twisted smile. "No, he won't be moving for some time now." He let out a deep laugh.

Mathilde's face twisted in a scowl. "I don't know what you're scheming, but this clearly isn't something Gannon would approve of!"

The opossum craned his head down through the trapped door. "Precisely why he's dead, girl."

It was at that moment Lore felt whatever hope she was clinging to leave her body.

The fighting fire Mathilde had been storing seemed to fizzle out with the downpour of their captor's storm.

Crinkle laughed like a cackling old witch and slammed the door shut.

Even in the dark space, Lore saw Mathilde seethe with anger.

"Killmoore!" Mathilde yelled, jerking at the chains confining her. "Killmoore, get up!" she demanded as she stomped her foot. The mouse let out a rage-filled scream that made Lore's blood freeze in her veins.

Hours had passed, marked by the moving sun. The light dwindled and was soon covered by planks of pine wood. At times, they would hear footsteps above them. Other times, it was dead silent.

Afraid to speak too loudly, Lore whispered, "Killmoore."

The fox was still unresponsive.

"No use, human. He's probably already dead," Mathilde huffed with her arms crossed.

Then his blood-soaked tail twitched, and he lazily tried to lift his head.

"Killmoore!" Lore pulled against the chains holding her, trying to get a better look.

"I'd defy Death just to spite you, mousey," he teased through bloody coughs.

"I told you to stop calling me that."

"You told me not to call you *darlin'*...Mousey."

The mouse in question chucked a stray rock at him.

"Mathilde! He's really hurt. Don't do that," Lore scolded.

Her belligerent companion turned her nose up. "He's so battered, he probably didn't feel it."

The fox rolled over on his back and looked at the joists that supported the warped and twisted home. "Your shrill little cries were really what hurt the most."

"Okay, both of you, can you just stop?" Lore spat, rattling the chains over whatever cruel thing they were going to hurl at each other next.

"Then what do you purpose we do?" Mathilde chided.

"I don't know, but we can't just go at each other's throats. That won't solve anything."

The mouse's ears folded back in anger.

"The spirit is admirable, human, but I feel they will dispose of us soon," Killmoore rasped.

Mathilde shook her head. "No. You two, maybe." She began to pace in the limited space she had. "But he wouldn't do that to me."

Lore raised a brow. "Mathilde. He basically alluded to having your dad killed. You're also in danger here."

"Who's to say he isn't the one who did it personally?" Killmoore added. "He's sick enough to. That much is clear."

Lore tried to steady her breathing. Her mind was going a mile per second as the silvery moons' light seeped through cracks and crevices of the boards across the window.

Then the hatch above the trip sprung open. A fully-healed Lyudmilla stepped down into the pathetic pit of a basement.

"You!" Mathilde shrieked. "How could you!"

The wolf's head hung in shame, her pink eyes looking over the battered body of Killmoore. "You aren't the only one who's got folks they wanna protect," she muttered, hoisting the fox over her shoulder. She then took two heavy steps toward Mathilde and freed the chained cuffs from the wall. She took the metal links and wrapped them around her fist. "Just don't open your big mouth or anything during this next part, and everything should be okay." She jerked the mouse up the narrow brittle staircase of the trapped door.

They disappeared upstairs, and then she was in the dark again. Alone. Not that Lore was complaining, but it did tickle her curiosity. *Why is she leaving me?* She sat there in the musty underneath of the house watching

DOWN THE WELL

dust particles float gently in the light seeping through the planks covering the window. Dead air left an itch in the back of her throat and her head still throbbed.

The door opened above her again, and a familiar shadow loomed.

The musk stench on the opossum's fur made Lore scrunch her nose as he descended into the basement. She shot up, her arms still bound.

He took a few steps towards her, towering over her.

"*Tsk tsk,*" Crinkle mused. "Look at the little lost human. Who are you?" He asked as he unlocked the chains from the wall.

"Even if I did remember, what makes you think I'd tell you?" Sweat formed on her brow as the words fired from her mouth.

Her captor chuckled and yanked her towards him by her chained wrists. She fell over her own feet, and his pointed nose came close enough to her ear that his whiskers tickled against her skin. "I don't know who brought your kind back here, but whatever it is," he jerked and forcefully spun her round and up the stairs, "can't be good for me or my legacy."

Lore gulped as Crinkle forced her out his front door. His staff in one hand and a free hand to shove her. He pushed her toward a large cage connected to a carriage, but she couldn't register anything other Killmoore and Mathilde who were already inside the iron bars.

Crinkle locked the chain links of Lore's cuffs to the back. "Won't hurt you to walk to the rim of the town," he said under his breath. Then he walked around and sat next to Lyudmilla.

She heard the snap of reins. Instead of immediately taking off, the carriage lulled forward, then suddenly, with a jerk against Lore's wrists, they were moving — fast. They rode through town, which was a great deal emptier than usual. She heard a metallic clinking against the stones with every step, but no matter how hard she tried to peer around the cage, she couldn't see if it was pulled by horses, cattle, or a donkey.

201

The otherwise eerie silence dampened the town's charm. Not even a sound escaped from Dina's pub. She looked at the empty streets. When they passed through the square, she saw the guards stationed there the night before were gone as well.

The cart continued to jostle the cuffs around Lore's wrists. The iron began to sting against her raw, pinkened skin. She ground her teeth together, refusing to make any sound of pain, and she thought Killmoore gave her a wink. Or it could just be his eye swelling shut.

The only being around was the dancing flame of a familiar light post. It tipped its hat and Lore gestured with her head for Grian to follow. *There's no way this will work, but it was worth a try.*

Whether it was out of spite or the Weavers of fate threading it into existence, the iron post trailed behind them.

The babbling of Crinkle and Lyudmilla seemed to confirm they were comfortable enough in their victory that they didn't notice their little follower.

Soon, the carriage wheels rolled past the large yellow manor. The porch light was on. *Surely Mathilde's sisters were worried about her.*

Lore watched as Grian halted in front of the house and hobbled into the grass to hide. *Well, that didn't last long.*

As the cart continued to the outskirts of town, Lore could no longer see the flickering firelight behind her. She grimaced and redirected her sights to try to see where they were going. The square footage of everything under the barrier couldn't be *that* much. Soon, another familiar sight was growing small behind them. The graveyard.

Lore's eyes narrowed on the wolf who sat passenger to their moving prison. Was it only the other night that Lore and Mathilde saw Lyudmilla crying on Gannon's tomb? And now she was helping Crinkle do who knows what to the alligator's mouse daughter.

The animal's words echoed in her mind. "You aren't the only one who's got folks they wanna protect."

She tried to ignore the warmth she felt around her wrists by coming up with questions. *Who was she protecting? Why did Crinkle want to hurt them? Why did he kill or have a hitman kill Gannon? What was the opossum's creepy fascination with humans? What was his end goal?* No matter the questions she toyed with, she didn't have a clear answer. Lore's mind felt like it was trying to undo a puzzle that didn't have one set picture when the pieces were placed together. *Frustrating, really.*

What was even more annoying was the damn jerkiness of the cart. She didn't know how much more abuse her wrists could take. Then they stopped at the bottom of a hill. Her heart was racing.

"Don't worry." Crinkle's voice was steeped in honey as he delightfully took the chains binding her in his hand. "Come on. Just a bit further."

Time slowed as Lore passed the cage. She looked at the grinning fox and the mouse, whose anger burned like a restless fire. *What waited at the top of the hill for the three of them?*

Crinkle pressed into Lore's back with his staff. The jagged edges of the gem felt like ice now instead of the lapping of a cool spring. "Go on now, human," he continued.

Lore looked over her shoulder as she walked up the path. Lyudmilla was getting Killmoore and Mathilde.

Maybe this bad dream will end soon, then, she thought as she looked down at her feet. With each step, it's like she was walking between realities. One minute, she was crunching red and orange leaves beneath her sneaker. The next, she was splashing in spring puddles.

Occasionally, her eye would catch the figure of an old woman smiling at her in the reflection of the water. It sent shivers down her back. She looked up, and it wasn't much longer until she'd find out what beast lay in wait for her. A tear escaped down her cheek. *I could die before I remember who I am, or where I'm even from.*

A gentle voice, not her own, countered her thought with a positive one. *Or perhaps you'll simply wake up.*

Lore shook her head, trying to silence the fleeting thoughts. The anxiety chewing at her stomach felt too real to be a dream. The sting around her wrists felt too painful to be a figment of imagination. She looked back down the hill at Mathilde fighting the opossum's enforcer with every step, and Killmoore slouched over the wolf's shoulder. *Her friends were too real for this to not be real.* Lore gulped in what she thought was her last breath as the next step brought her to the top of the hill. Her heart froze as she saw the backs of townsfolk all huddled together in front of a podium.

"Ahem," Crinkle cleared his throat. The crowd turned to face him.

Lore wished she could say there was a shock that washed over their faces, but that didn't happen until they saw Mathilde being drugged along by Lyudmilla.

The loathsome opossum inched his way to the stand. "Fellow folk of Charmsend," he began as he gave Lore's chains a jerk for show. "It has come to my attention that we were bewitched by this human." His smile cracked like fractured glass across his face as the murmurs of the gathered crowd began.

Lore braced herself for the untrue words that were being hurled at her.

"Lowly, human."

"Should've done away with her on the spot."

"Murderer."

"Never trust a human."

It was the last one that really pushed Mathilde over the edge.

"Never trust a human?!" her words burned through the crowd. "I trust this human more than any of you!" Her eyes shot daggers pointed with disgust.

"Ah, yes," Crinkle added. "And it seems with the mouse and the fox, we have our three alligator butchers." His smug smile was more than enough to make Lore want to chuck a brick at his face. *I get pinning the murder on me and Killmoore. But Mathilde? His daughter? How would anyone believe that?*

The crowd began an uproar of angry boos and insults.

"Now, now," Crinkle raised his arms to calm the crowd, "it is true. The mouse tried to cover the tracks for the fox and human." He admitted, "But she did such a poor job," Crinkle's beady eyes held Mathilde's gaze. "She isn't as clever as she thinks she is."

Then he continued. "The fox is an outsider that the human smuggled in, thanks to their distasteful magic."

"I have no magic!" Lore spat.

DOWN THE WELL

The outburst from the human riled up the crowd again, and Lore quickly recalled the other tidbit of information Lyudmilla had said to Mathilde. "Keep your big mouth shut and everything should go okay." She bit her lip, and Crinkle laughed, taking pleasure in the spectacle.

As the chatter died down, the opossum began his spiel again. "So because of their offenses, I think it only fitting that they be banned to the Twisted Wood."

There was an eruption of cheer from the crowd Crinkle was slowly working into a mob.

Mathilde's eyes widened and Killmoore was only just finding the strength to stand.

"Unhand my sister!" a familiar and stern voice bellowed. Minifred marched through the animals and stared at Crinkle.

"Minifred, what are you doing here?" Mathilde's eyes were on the verge of letting a waterfall of tears spill over.

"Because it's obvious you need to be pulled out of whatever mischief you found yourself in." The coal-colored mouse flicked her tail and directed her gaze to Crinkle.

"I'm fine," Mathilde uttered. She tried her best to lie, but the clear bruises on her body weren't helping her silver tongue.

The villain leaned against the podium, not wavering under Minifred's glare. "So you admit your sister was stirring mischief."

Then a soft smile spread as Lore saw a gentle warm light flicker above the angry mob.

Grian. The crowd parted and revealed the other three sisters huddled up around its post.

The eldest's silver eyes pierced the opossum like a needle pricking a balloon. "Don't think I don't *know* what you're doing."

"I'm serving justice to your father's killer isn't that what you all wanted?" He prodded as he pounded his staff against the ground.

Minifred's head snapped back toward her captured sister as fog enveloped the trio of prisoners, Lyudmilla, and Crinkle. It dissipated and quickly reappeared by the tree line.

Crinkle dangled Mathilde at eye level with him. "If you want your sisters unharmed, you'll go through without an issue." His threat slipped through a lily-livered smile.

She narrowed her gaze. "Deal, you slimeball."

With a snap of his fingers, the cuffs fell from their hands. "Your options are to take a gamble with the Grayshade beyond the border, or stay and let us deal with you." It was clear what he wanted them to do.

Without any further fight, Lore and her animal companions stepped through the invisible shield.

The last thing they heard was Minifred crying out, "Mathilde!"

When they looked back, all the trio saw was an empty field.

TWENTY-NINE

Mathilde collapsed onto her knees and wailed, "Minifred! My sisters—I'll never see them again!"

Lore knelt beside her and traced circles on the mouse's red jacket. "We'll find a way back through."

"It's impossible," Mathilde choked through tears. "I tried to keep them out of this and do what Gannon willed by protecting you." She crawled away and pulled her knees up to her chest. "I've failed him."

"Impassible," Killmoore said, pointing to the unseen barrier. "He wants you to think it's impassible, but fear not, darlin'. Because nothing is *impossible*."

Lore nodded in agreement and offered a hand to Mathilde.

The gray mouse took it. "So how do we get back through, then?" she asked as she rose to her feet.

A haunting howl shook the mangled treetops and sent goosebumps down Lore's arms.

"I don't think that's our biggest problem right now," Killmoore said softly, staring into the darkness of the Twisted Wood.

Mathilde nodded. "We need to go."

The trio filed down a small embankment to their left and followed the first clear path they saw.

"So, since we have the time now," Mathilde began walking behind Killmoore. "Tell us, how'd you find the town?"

Lore grinned when she saw the fox's ears twitch.

"Well, it wasn't that hard." He stumbled over his words. "After all, I am the greatest bounty hunter Thimbleton has to offer."

"That doesn't tell us anything," Mathilde huffed.

Killmoore popped his collar. "It tells you that I'm a good tracker."

Lore put her hands behind her back and looked at the interlocking bare branches above them. "So, you wandered this whole forest until Lady Luck had you stumble upon that hole in the barrier?"

The fox stopped dead in his tracks and whirled around, his fur sticking straight up. "We are in a bad spot and all you two can do is make jokes?!" He turned back around, holding his tail between his hands as he soothed himself. "I'm sorry. My body just aches, and I don't wanna walk for hours. But if we stop, we risk being monster food."

Lore spotted another embankment and when she went to peer over it, she saw a rather cozy-looking entanglement of tree roots. "We can rest here for a moment."

Mathilde helped Killmoore over and the three of them piled into the cool hole in the ground.

"A rather snug burrow," Mathilde chimed, a spark finally returned to her voice.

The fox said nothing, just picked the stray twigs from his tail.

"So, human," Mathilde started. "What are you gonna do when you return to your world?"

Lore folded her knees to her chest so Killmoore could bring his legs into the burrow. "I'm not sure." She thought about the old woman she saw in the puddles of spring rain. "I think maybe see my grandma." *Because who else would that old woman have been?*

Mathilde tilted her head. "So, you *are* remembering things?"

Lore shrugged as she ran a finger through the cool dirt. "From time to time, but nothing groundbreaking."

The gray mouse adjusted her jacket, and her grin warmed the atmosphere. "What about you, foxy?"

Killmoore rolled his eyes and peered out the mangled tree roots. "Really? *This* is what we're gonna do to pass the time?"

Down The Well

Lore looked at the fox, whose body and pride were now riddled with injury. "You know, Killmoore…" She then leaned back into the wall of dirt, not minding the bit of fallout in her hair. "I think you're pretty crafty."

The bounty hunter's ears perked up, though his eyes were still fixed on their shadowy surroundings. "Shh."

Radio silence, only the occasional howl carried on the breeze.

"Oh, come on," Mathilde said as she leaned forward for a playful tap on the fox's shoulder. "Don't be like that. She's just try'na make nice."

"I said hush," he snapped as he squinted into the fog. "Something's coming." He pushed himself as far back as he could into their current hiding spot.

They could see a figure in the distance that towered above the dead gray path below.

Mathilde crawled into Lore's lap wearing a *don't you ever talk about this if we make it out alive* written across her face.

As the beast came closer, Lore noticed its eyes were different from those of the Grayshade that had broken through. Its eyes were a beautiful shade that resembled a jar of honey when the sun hit it just right.

The creature sniffed the air and seemed to follow its nose. *This* Grayshade shook its long gray foliage from its back that looked like a bunch of clumped hair, causing the ground to shake just enough to make Lore and Killmoore's butts slide in the dirt. The creature stood on its hind legs, still sniffing at the air, then fumbled down another path, completely passing the trio. It didn't seem to notice or care.

After a few moments of waiting, the three let out a relieved sigh.

"Good hiding place, human," Killmoore chimed.

"What do you think it was looking for?" Mathilde asked.

Lore put a hand to her chin. "Maybe something to eat?"

"We would have been a great meal," the mouse objected, ironically offended at *not* being eaten. "I mean, look at us. Killmoore may be a bit grisly, but the human and me we would make a fine five-star course."

The fox laughed. "You two aren't so bad, I guess," he said as he looked back at his tail.

The trio dozed in and out of sleep. As Lore did, she felt like she was falling through the air once again. She landed in a field of daffodils and a large, snow-colored stag stood across the field. His antlers looked like they carried the forest with them.

Lore started walking towards the animal, but as she did, the ground beneath her stretched. It was getting farther and farther away, no matter how fast her feet carried her. Soon, her lungs begged her to stop, and the powdered blue sky began to swirl with dark clouds. She froze in the yellow field.

A voice boomed like thunder from the clouds.

"Human!"

Lore felt the ground shake. As the field of daffodils cracked open, she slipped and tumbled down, down, down.

"Human!" the voice called again, sharp as lightning cracked across the sky.

Lore's eyes shot open and Mathilde had been shaking her and whispering in her ear.

"Good, you're finally awake," Killmoore called softly from outside the hiding spot. "We need to move. We've been sitting here too long."

"And you know what they say about sitting ducks," Mathilde added as she climbed out of the cozy abandoned hole in the ground.

"Are we sure that's a good idea?" Lore asked, a bit desperate to return to her dream and the white stag.

Mathilde and Killmoore both delivered a similar expression, clearly stating *yes*.

"Fine," Lore huffed. As she crawled out, Gannon's little green book fell from her flannel.

"Mathilde!" she squealed as she picked it up off the ground. "I think we might find a way back through with this." She turned and presented the book.

Killmoore smiled, and Mathilde beamed with hope.

"You've been quite the lucky charm, human," the mouse mused. "Maybe that's why Gannon seemed set on me sticking close to ya."

DOWN THE WELL

Lore tilted her head as she flipped open the green journal. "Why would he say that?"

Mathilde shrugged. "Not too sure myself, but I'd say all the answers we need are in this book."

Killmoore led them away from the mangled tree roots. "I wanna know why Crinkle and swing-happy wolfy didn't take it off ya."

Lore pursed her lips. "I guess Lady Luck was on my side?"

The fox shook his head and his eyes drooped. "Doubt it. That fickle broad is so particular about choosing who she wants to help."

Mathilde looked at the empty holsters on the fox's back. "They took your weapons."

He didn't turn to chat. "Which is why I would like to not take a chance about facing off with those beasties."

Lore flipped through the pages. It was Gannon's account of finding Charmsend. How the four of them were welcomed by a lush green forest to the valley. Her nose shot up from the book. "Four of them?" she said aloud.

Mathilde stopped. "Curiouser and curiouser." She gestured for Lore to hand the book over.

"But I'm reading it right now."

"Human, that is my—"

Lore leaned down at eye level with the mouse. "Your *what*, Mathilde?"

Mathilde huffed and crossed her arms. "*Nothing*, Human. I can read it later."

"Don't count your blessings that there will be a *later*, lasses." The bounty hunter lunged at them and they crashed behind a large boulder.

"Another one?" Mathilde mouthed.

Killmoore nodded.

Lore quickly closed the book and slid it back inside her flannel again for safekeeping.

The earth didn't shake beneath the might of this Grayshade. In fact, Lore could barely tell one was there. She peered around the side of the large rock just to be sure that Killmoore wasn't being too paranoid. She met the eyes of a shadow that was casually strolling through the fog-ridden area. Lore never turned back so quickly before. Her hand hovered over the book that rested above her heart, but she could still hear the pounding in her chest.

They stayed there just like sitting ducks as Mathilde had said while the mouse scanned the area for any sort of weapon—whether it be a fallen branch or a stray stone. Killmoore searched for an escape route. It was quiet for the longest five minutes of her life.

Lore slid the book from the safety of her flannel, dying to soak up anything else before they were potentially slashed and left for dead. Her eyes ran over a bunch of words that talked about Gannon's day until a name that she hadn't heard of popped out to her.

"Who's Merlin?" she whispered to Mathilde.

The mouse furrowed her brow. "Now really isn't the time, human."

A smiling face suddenly swung down in front of them. "'Tis I! Merlin the Magnificent!"

The three scattered with a shrill scream coming from Killmoore.

"Oh, now don't be like that. You all are late!" The dark purple bat cheered, hanging upside down from a walking stick. His face moved toward theirs, then backed away with each swing from the oversized rod. "Come now, don't you all know what time it is?" He flapped down to the ground.

Mathilde looked at Lore, then back to the bat. "No?" But the animal's unexpected appearance didn't stop the small adventurer from stepping closer to the seemingly mad loner. "What time is it?"

Merlin smiled and pulled a pointed hat from thin air that went between his tall triangle ears. "Well, it's time for tea, of course!"

THIRTY

The house the cloaked bat had led them to seemed like something out of a fairytale. It was a small, cozy cottage at the heart of the dead forest, but still wasn't as lively or inviting as what Lore had been hoping for. The only sign of life was the bioluminescent mushrooms that covered the ground and tree trunks of the area.

"You live here?" she asked, craning her neck to take in her new surroundings. It wasn't like they mayor's mansion in Charmsend.

Merlin waved a hand. "Yes. I can't remember how long, though."

She looked to Mathilde, who shrugged.

"So, what kind of tea is the right kind for you?" the bat inquired as he opened the door to his home.

"Uh…" Lore's stomach churned in on itself with nerves as she looked over the skeletal remains that were poking out from the quaint cottage's foundation. "We'll have whatever is easiest," she finally answered.

Merlin eyed her up and down and pursed his lips. "It all cooks the same, you know."

As Mathilde went to collapse in a chair at the dining room table, their host waved a finger at her.

"Tsk tsk." The bat pushed the chair back in. "This way." He led the tired trio through a back entrance and down a step to a patio that had an absurdly long table. "Here," their strange host said as he pulled a chair that rested atop a human skull out, "is the tea table." He patted the wooden chair. "Take a seat!"

"Yeah...no. Not until you tell me where you got those skulls, batty," Killmoore said, pointing to the long-dead pile of bones.

"Oh?" the bat asked, clearly distracted. He turned and saw what the bounty hunter was talking about and exclaimed, "*Oh!*" Merlin took off his hat and held it gingerly in his green-gloved hands. "Those were already here," he said with a friendly smile. As if stating that wasn't still super creepy.

His gold eyes sent a suspicious shiver straight to Lore's fingertips, but she didn't let it show. Maybe she was wrong, and it was just the skulls that were freaking her out.

"They're from, you know," the bat continued, gesturing about with a hand as he searched for a better explanation, "from when the humans were practically forced to flee into the woods—where the Grayshade devoured them on site. Cross my heart!" The little bat made the gesture as he said the last words.

Mathilde huffed with annoyance—at what, one could only guess—but took a seat without further delay.

Lore hesitated another moment, but followed suit.

Killmoore was the last to sit, and he made it a point to sit the farthest away from the wacky bat.

Merlin waved a hand. A teapot, matching cups, and saucers floated down onto the table. He winked, and a spark flew from his fingertip. The light grew into a larger flame that feathered out like a fan under the floating teapot.

He was a Wielder.

He leaped onto the table. "Fancy yourself one lump of sugar or two?"

"One," Mathilde hummed.

"Two," Lore answered.

Their host looked down the table to the melancholic fox, who seemed wholly uninterested in what was happening, but that didn't stop him. The bat got a scampering start on the tabletop, then he leaped into the air, gliding above the table and perched across the wide top of the tall seat before peeking down at Killmoore.

"One or two?"

"How about none?" the bounty hunter sneered.

"No sugar?" Merlin seemed quite concerned as the tips of his ears withered flat.

"No. No *tea*!" Killmoore spat as he crossed his arms.

"Oh. Oh." The winged animal mused as he leaped onto the table. "I see. You're a coffee kind of guy. Well, I have that, too. Let me just get it—" he moved to magically gesture again when the fox interrupted.

"What?!" Killmoore slammed his hands on the table and narrowed his gaze on the bat. "Didn't you hear what I just said?"

"Yes, quite clear." Merlin chuckled. "No tea, which means you must prefer coffee."

The fox groaned as their host magically gestured a cup towards him. Then he lashed an arm out and sent it flying, shattering against a tree. "Enough with the stalling! Get to it already! What do you *really* want from us? It can't just be our company for some silly tea party. There's no way you could have know we'd be here."

"Oh. *Oh*…" Merlin whined. "That was my favorite cup, too."

"Killmoore!" Mathilde gasped. "He's just trying to be hospitable."

The grumpy fox held a hand up as he demanded, "But why?"

Something clicked between the bat's ears. Maybe it was his brain catching up to the conversation, or maybe it was something else entirely. Who could tell with someone so—*batty*? "Oh. *Oh*," the Wielder began to moan, as he walked back down the table. "Because I have something for Lore," he said on a quiet exhale, almost thoughtfully to himself and not to his guests.

Mathilde almost fell from her chair. "Who?"

Merlin pointed to the human. "You know, Lore. Lore. The human girl?" He cupped his hands together. "Is this not the human named Lore who came to Charmsend?"

The three of them sat there, jaws on the table.

"I am the human that randomly found herself in Charmsend," Lore admitted. "Not that I've figured out how."

Mathilde's head whipped to look at Lore, "You mean to tell me your name isn't *Human*?!"

"What do you have for her?" Killmoore cut in, his voice the only one still sounding of reason. And sounding like he was ready to bolt the moment they got the answer.

"Glad you asked!" Merlin chimed. When the tea kettle screamed, he snapped his fingers, making the flame whittle back down to a single spark, and returned to its origin inside him. Then he turned to Lore and pulled a silver bracelet from his sleeves. "Does this belong to you?" His eyes glittered with excitement. One could practically hear the squeals of excitement he was fighting to hold back.

She reached out to grab the piece of jewelry. "I think so."

Merlin snatched it back and leaned close. "You think so? Or you know so?"

Lore chewed the inside of her lip. "I know."

He handed it over, and muttered under his breath, "Good. You don't know the deal I had to make to get it."

She took the bracelet in her hands. The cold, silver chain links felt refreshing in her calloused hands. A single charm flipped itself to face her. Looking at the gold, embossed daffodils felt like home, and the deer shed wrapped in the two flowers made her recurring dream quite clear. Her mind had been trying to lead her to this piece of jewelry.

Her eyes connected with the bat's keen, golden gaze—collided, really...*with Merlin.*

Creepy tea party aside, their host didn't seem that bad. Maybe a bit too hyper and friendly, and perhaps *batty* just like his species, but nothing too awful. At least, nothing as bad as Killmoore seemed to think of Merlin. But she still had a weird feeling about the bat, too, so maybe it wasn't crazy that the fox didn't like him.

Lore lay in the only bed upstairs and tried to fold herself into a position that was comfortable enough on the bat's four-foot-long bed. Perhaps it was the time in isolation among the Grayshades in the Twisted

Wood that drove him to lose a few marbles.

She heard Mathilde and the Wielder talking beneath the floorboards. From the sounds that rose like heat to the ceiling, they were swapping stories about Gannon.

"A gator of great strength, and even greater heart," Merlin declared. "Oh. Oh, we went on the most thrilling adventures together. The four of us were quite the team, you know."

"Oh, yeah?" Mathilde's tone begged for more details from the buffet of Gannon stories Merlin was recounting.

"We called ourselves the Order of The Golden Dawn." The words were said on a wistful sigh. The bat was likely remembering his glory days with his friends.

Lore could picture the clear smile on Mathilde's face as she shared some of the most cherished memories she had of the gator.

"Whenever we were sick," she heard the mouse reply, "Gannon would tuck us into bed and give us a goodnight kiss on our heads with a cup of mint tea within arm's reach. But all five of us would end up piled in his bed before the night would end." Mathilde let out a belly-filled laugh to punctuate the happy memory.

Based on the family photo she'd seen, the scene wasn't too hard or too far-fetched for Lore to imagine.

"He's always been a giant with a soft heart," Merlin chimed. "How's Lyudmilla?" The excitement in his voice was as clear as the blue-green gem Lore hadn't been able to pry from Crinkle's staff.

She flipped over in the bed at the thought of it. She was trying to sleep, after all. That's when the room below fell silent.

"She's doing just fine for herself," Killmoore jested.

There was no response from the bat. But Lore could hear Mathilde stomping her foot in annoyance at the fox's yet-to-be explained grudge.

"Oh, you're just mad she bested you," Mathilde said as if Killmoore hadn't endure hell in Crinkle's house the night before.

"Bested me with a Wielder on her side who is also a healer." The fox's voice was coated in crumbs of a conniption.

"I don't understand why would she have attacked you three, though?" Merlin's voice wavered with confusion. "That's not at all like the Lyudmilla I knew."

"Well, however long you've been out here, that rotten opossum seemed to have sunk his claws into her good," Killmoore spat.

Then the sound of footsteps coming up to the bedroom made Lore snap her eyes shut. *I didn't hear any of it. I didn't hear a thing.*

The door opened, and the bounty hunter tried to silently move across the floor to a rocking chair in the corner. "Hum —" he stopped himself. "I mean, *Lore.* I think it's been a long day."

Lore rolled over. "How'd you know I wasn't asleep?" she whispered.

"I don't know how anyone could have slept through that," he said with an eye roll.

She stayed silent, and sank further into her blanket burrito.

The echoes of Mathilde and Merlin's banter flowed back outside of the quaint cabin.

The fox shot up and went to the round window on the other side of the bed. "I don't like that bat," he said flatly, peering out the window. "He's preying on Mathilde's grief."

Lore propped herself up on her arm. "I think he seems pretty decent, and she's just relieved she is around someone who was so close to her father that isn't trying to kill her or her friends."

The fox shook his head in displeasure. "It's more than that. There's something else. I just know it." Then his pair of intense amber eyes held her gaze. "You need to promise me you won't be dazzled by his little magic tricks."

Lore furrowed her brow. "I don't see what the big deal is, but okay."

Killmoore paced back to the rocker and collapsed in the seat. "If he was so chummy with this Gannon, what's he doing out here, huh? Why wasn't he in Charmsend to protect the mayor? Or taking care of Mathilde and her sisters?"

"I'm sure he'll tell us tomorrow."

The bounty hunter crossed his arms. "Promise me, Lore."

"I already said okay?" Her confusion was hard to hide. What else did he want from her?

"Exactly." The fox wrapped a knitted blanket that was hanging on the chair's back around him. "You said *okay*. That's not a promise."

"*Okay*," Lore sighed as she cocooned herself even deeper into the purple comforter. "I promise, Killmoore."

THIRTY-ONE

The aroma of roasted apples roused Lore from a surprisingly deep sleep. She looked to the corner of the room to see the fox absent from the rocking chair. Her eyes searched the walls for the movement of the flowered wallpaper. Of course, there was nothing.

Lore flipped on her side, and the bed frame rasped revealing its old brittle age. She pulled the comforter over her head. She always had a hard time falling asleep. The warmth enveloped her, but her stomach pushed against that temptation with a twisting ache. She tried to close her eyes and drift back off to sleep. *Alone, once again. Just me and my thoughts.*

Lore swung her legs over the side of the small bed. Her feet felt the splintering of the hewn wood beneath her. She took a deep breath in and stretched her arms up and the tips of her fingers traced the ceiling. *This really was a tiny cabin in the woods.* She stood, only needing to tilt her head the slightest to move around.

As she walked to the staircase, she felt a shooting pain in her neck. Then a burst of vivid color traveled to the forefront of her consciousness, bringing with it the dreams of last night.

It was like watching herself through a fisheye lens camera. Chasing after a gold-eyed shadow. The sound of a man's voice stopped this version of her. She didn't see his face, only the back of his black, unkempt hair. Her heart leaped, and as she and the man talked, their conversation was drowned out by the rushing sound of water.

She looked past herself and the person—friend, she somehow knew—

whose name and face she couldn't recall, and saw the shadow wiggle a finger for her to come closer. She did. Ripples broke around her like the fabric of reality was nothing more than wrinkling water reflecting the surrounding landscape of towering treetops and a field of hued yellows.

As she got closer to the blue well, a deep vibration began to hum in her ears. Words whirled on the wind rushing past her. *Meet the shadow at the wishing well, for he has secrets to tell.* Lore continued to close the distance between her and this shadow perched atop the blue bricks of her grandmother's well. Another gust of wind whipped her braid wildly and the same voice slithered past her ears again. *Secrets of time undone and spells that were spun.* Lore felt a hidden presence pulled her hands out, urging her to brush her fingers against the chipping blue paint. The air burst from behind her one last time. *Meet that shadow, not the shell, after the final farewell.*

Then shadow's thin mouth curled into a smile as he leaped into the dark waters below. Suddenly, the perspective shifted again, and she was watching herself through broken glass. She watched as she leaned over the well, and without warning, the shadow lunged from the inky water below and dragged her down the well.

Back in the present, her hand trembled against the doorknob. *I wish there was a simpler way to remember my life before. But, no. Instead, I get to play piece-the-puzzle-together with trippy dreams and cryptic phrases.* The silver circle of the bracelet caught the morning light trickling in through the window.

"Lore!" she heard Mathilde's voice call loudly, just on the other side of the door.

She shook her head, gathering her thoughts. It was nice, not being called *Human. And even if I have nothing else in this world, at least now I have my name.* She took a deep breath. *I have my shit together.* Lore opened the door and went down the flight of stairs. The smell of caramelized apples hung in the air, thick as smog in the city sky.

"How'd you sleep?" Merlin asked as he came through the back entrance. He laid his cloak on the more reasonably-sized table where Killmoore sat reading some random soot-covered book that the bat must have kept stored in a dust bunny nest.

"Good," her voice chimed as she looked at the delicious browned apple slices in the pan Mathilde was carefully watching.

"Most splendid!" Merlin walked around Lore and, with a wave of his hand, opened the cupboard by the front door. Plates and cups floated out to greet him. It was then as the Wielder rose his hands to direct the dishes that Lore noticed Merlin's ornate necklace. A piece of golden ribbon hung around his neck. A gemstone about the size of a nickel dangled from it. The outer rim was breath-stealing hues of purple swirled with a dark, rich blue. Thin veins of pink coiled inward towards the burning orange center. Looking closer, she swore the colors pulsated with life. As if the flimsy piece of jewelry trapped a tiny galaxy.

"Breakfast, Lore?" Merlin asked, seeing her staring off into space.

Her eyelids fluttered at the sound of her name. "Yes!" She shuffled in and pulled out a seat beside Killmoore, who raised a brow but kept his nose buried in the book. "I'm starved," she added as the tableware gently descended to the tabletop.

Merlin smiled and gave a nod as Mathilde brought in the cast iron with gloved hands.

Lore didn't wait to dive in. Notes of cinnamon and nutmeg danced across her tongue with every bite. "This is delicious," she said, pointing her fork at her friend. "Compliments to the chef."

The mouse's whiskers twitched, as she scratched behind her ear. "Thanks," she added between sticky bites. "They're not as good as Mildred's, though. If I'm remembering right, this was something she'd make on Gannon's birthday every year." Her friendly smile couldn't hide the yearning to be reunited with her sisters. Her eyes practically screamed the desire.

Merlin drummed his fingers against the table. "Guess there's only one way to find out."

Killmoore's ears jerked at the bat's statement as he ate absentmindedly, his eyes still racing across old inked words across onion-thin pages.

"We'll have to go back to the town and see which sister does it best," Merlin said playfully.

Right as Mathilde swallowed her bite to say something, Killmoore snapped his book shut.

"Ah, yes. Because it's not like there's a power-crazed opossum that kicked us out—and is keeping the town and its folk trapped."

Merlin patted his mouth with a napkin. "You're too easy to rile up, Mr. Fox."

"My name isn't *Mr. Fox*," Killmoore growled and stood, towering over the Wielder with his hands spread out on the table.

"Ah, right," Merlin said as he climbed onto the table to stay eye-level with the bounty hunter. "Mr. Fox must be your father. How silly of me." He moved around Killmoore's display of intimidation with casual grace. "So, ladies. We have a big day ahead of us." The bat sounded like a dad talking to his children on the morning of their big ball game.

The fox's amber eyes gleamed in a reflection in the back door's glass. They looked like they had just come off a forge.

"I think Killmoore has a point," Lore said as she stabbed a few more slices of apple onto her fork. "Crinkle is going to be a problem. We can't ignore him."

"And how are we going to even break through that barrier?" Mathilde asked, her lips smacking loudly as she chewed. "Killmoore just got lucky finding a tear. Surely we won't be lucky enough to find something like that again."

The bounty hunter grumbled. His chair's legs scratched against the floor as he pulled it out with a sudden yank.

Merlin paid no attention to the fox's clear surge of annoyance, and his gloved hands clasped together. "Fear not! This is something I have been preparing for." The bat's gold eyes glossed over and his voice died down to a whisper. "For a long, long, long time, actually." His fingers drummed against his chin. "Years and years spent planning."

The trio sat there in silence, waiting for their host to pick up where he left off, which he did rather quickly.

"Righto!" Merlin chimed. With a click of his middle finger against his thumb, the wall in front of Lore and behind Mathilde's seat, glowed red.

Heat radiated from the wall in a rounded red rectangle. Then the Wielder turned to face it and snapped his fingers again. The glow of dying embers swirled into the center, leaving behind charred remains that revealed a map of the forest, including their location, as well as Charmsend's location.

"The barrier, while impressive, was something that stemmed from one of my spells." He leaned down a hand over his mouth as he stage-whispered to Lore, loudly enough that the others could still easily hear him. "He never was great at coming up with original charms, bewilderments, or otherwise beginner's hocus-pocus." Merlin chuckled to himself, then looked at the charred map on the wall. He walked until his foot was on the edge of the wood.

Mathilde gasped as Merlin took another step. She was expecting him to fall, but there the bat was. Walking on air.

"So, it's simple, really." He spread his clasped hands, revealing a thin rod of wood. "We'll enter through a crack that'll be here." He smacked the tip of the rod against the wall, circling a spot that looked to come out into a clearing on the southern side of town.

Mathilde turned in her chair. "You'll just *break* the barrier? Something that's been there for about fifty years?" She shook her head in disbelief. "Why didn't you do it before and come in and take care of all this?"

Merlin's eyes seemed to twinkle as they fixated on Lore. "Because we didn't have someone like her."

The mouse turned to follow his line of sight, a burning question on the tip of her tongue but the tapping of the rod against the wall called their attention back to Merlin.

He seemed eagerly rocked on his feet, ready to continue. "Mathilde, I'll need you positioned somewhere away from the danger."

The adventurer's face dropped at the prospect of missing out. "No, I need to be where all the action is happening. For Gannon."

"*That* is why you won't be putting yourself directly in harm's way," Merlin said with the stern care of a parent.

Lore could hear the frustration in the huff the mouse made when she turned away to continue eating.

Down the Well

"Lore," Merlin circled a burnt image of a poorly drawn well on the map. "You have the most important job."

"That charm bracelet of yours—it ties you to our world." The enthusiasm radiated in Merlin's voice like a warm ray of sunshine.

"How?" Lore asked as she flipped the circle charm between her fingers beneath the table as Killmoore watched carefully.

"It's special." Merlin pointed to her. "It's tied to the magic of the well and it should act as a key."

"A key?" The fox's voice was flat as he crossed his arms.

"Yes, a key," Merlin explained. "One that can lock the magic, meaning Crinkle's magic source will be cut off."

"You're still putting these two in a direct line of danger—without any sort of combat training." Killmoore's voice was tight, daring Merlin to balance on the weight of his words.

"I know I can't train them in a single night. Not even with magic," the bat admitted as he removed his pointed hat. "But magic will give us an edge."

"Why do you care so much about cutting off the magic from Crinkle?" Killmoore's eyes narrowed.

Merlin nodded his head, absorbing the question as he pressed his back against the wall. His hands gripped the brim of his hat tightly as his eyes fluttered back to the table. "Tell you what... you tell me why you seem so concerned with my town and her problems first, and then I'll tell you why it's so important to me."

Killmoore shrugged. "Deal." The fox pulled his chair closer to the table and rested his elbows against the wood. "I'm a hired blade by the romp clans of the south to retrieve a sacred artifact of theirs. The stone in the opossum's staff."

Lore watched as the bat slid against the wall. Now seated on the ground, he chuckled softly. "Oh, how funny the Weavers can be."

Killmoore gritted his teeth but stayed silent.

"Oh calm down," Merlin teased. "I remember the day the madness first curled its fingers into Crinkle's soulfire. I told him not to do it." His

225

eyes paled as he recounted the tale. "You see, the four of us we weren't necessarily a group of heroes. But we also weren't villains, either. Gannon always said life wasn't black and white like that. So, the method of how we took jobs wasn't, either. We lived in this gray area the rest of the world wasn't ready to accept—you can imagine there were regions where we weren't welcome. It didn't matter how many times we saved Thimbleton." He paused and began rubbing the amulet around his neck.

"Well, now you know why I am here. I'm being *paid* to return that gem," Killmoore edged in.

The bat nodded but continued his story as if the fox didn't comment. "So, after that little escapade, we were banished from ever crossing the southern borders again. We grew tired of being travelers and hungry adventurers. We were welcomed by an old friend to seek sanctuary in the Emerald Pass." Merlin looked out the window. "She picked up the rot from the well that's entwined with Crinkle's magic. One day, I wish to see her lush and green again." His eyes drifted back to the table. "Just like I dream of freeing all the folk that left their home to settle in this valley with us. The folk of Thimbleton believed in us and wanted to settle with us. And now their descendants are trapped. I could not just leave with that knowledge haunting me."

"So, how was it you ended up on this side of the barrier?" Lore's voice seemed to echo in the silent house.

Merlin sighed. "As the last humans that were already hidden in the valley welcomed us to join them in their Eden, Crinkle started obsessing over the magic that flowed from their wellspring. It was the most refined source we'd come across in all of Thimbleton. And he was too weak to fight temptation. Not even I would dare take an ounce of magic from it. But Crinkle..." the bat trailed off. "He went a step further and fused his rotted casting magic with the wellspring's power. So, naturally, his rot spread," Merlin sneered.

"I thought Crinkle was a N.O.T, though? How is his casting rotted?" Lore sat her fork on her empty plate with a clink. "Aren't N.O.T's the most powerful casters?"

Down The Well

Merlin scoffed. "The last N.O.T I laid eyes on was deep in the dark forests of the Umber Valley. And that was ten-ish years before we founded the village."

"So he lied?"

"If that surprises you, Lore, then let's skip to the part where he waged a campaign to get rid of the humans who so happily welcomed us," the bat replied. "How he forced them into the dying forest that once protected them and reveled in the screams of their slaughter by the guardians that were corrupted by his rot-infused well. He cast me out because I spoke against it. Then laid the barrier and rewrote history, thanks to the help of a simple memory charm." Merlin's chest was rising and falling quickly as he tried to find his center, using the wooden rod to help him stand. As he did so, green, yellow, and golden orbs the size of water droplets glimmered above them in the room.

The smell of spring storms and pine tickled Lore's nose. She could practically feel the spring rain against her freckled cheeks.

"That is why I will heal you three, and we will rectify the past."

The magic burned the bruising away from her skin. The sensation was quick. *That wasn't too bad. Only hurt a little.*

When he was done healing the others, from his hat, Merlin pulled out a silver bow with bronze veins that swirled into the most ornate designs, along with a matching quiver full of purple-tipped arrows. "Mathilde, this bow hardly misses its mark."

"*Hardly?*" the mouse said with a shrill squeak.

Merlin shrugged. "Well, magic can't do it all."

Killmoore actually laughed.

Merlin pulled two familiar hand axes from the hat as well.

"How?" the fox asked as he reached for them.

"I can reach in from time to time, but it takes a lot. And I can't bring that much back at once. How do you think I got letters to Gannon? Who do you think planted the idea for the CHS in the mayor's mind?" Merlin explained. "Got to somehow preserve the correct accounts of history." Then he pulled two bronze cuffs from the pointed hat. "These are power

227

braces and should even your strength out with Lyudmilla."

"Thank you," Killmoore said in a whisper as he snapped the braces on his forearms. Obsidian swirls spread across the shining surface as he did so.

"And this is for you, Lore." Merlin pulled a ring from his hat. "This is the Band of Life, made from a branch of the Mothertree, and will protect you from Death's embrace."

As Merlin placed the wooden ring in her palm, the weight surprised her. It felt ancient and from a different plane entirely.

She slid the jewelry on her finger, and a radiant green aura hugged her form.

"You all are welcome to relax today, but tomorrow in the early hours, we go and kill that bloody opossum." The bat's voice was firm. A rallying cry.

Killmoore nodded in agreement.

Eager to get paid, I'm sure. Lore's eyes drifted to Mathilde, who was still looking at the archery equipment in her lap. The mouse's forehead wrinkled as she gently touched the tip of the purple arrowhead.

Tomorrow was going to bring change. Change Lore didn't know if she was ready for.

THIRTY-TWO

With Merlin a part of the group, Lore could appreciate that everything about the Twisted Wood had a strange sense of beauty. A rolling gray mist swept the forest floor and coiled around her legs as she followed the bat, almost as if it were begging her not to leave. Air hissed past her ear and left a cool kiss against her neck. Morning dew shimmered in the soft light of a fading night sky. Mangled treetops were sort of sculpture-like, with each tree a little differently shaped and misshapen in its own way. Even the occasional calloused wail of hunger that echoed down the abandoned paths embellished them with a sense of adventure that was long forgotten.

A Grayshade walked ahead of them on the path as if they weren't even there. Merlin called it a cloaking spell, but it was bizarre seeing the faces of these beasts up close without being in danger. Their slow and heavy pace was reminiscent of a child whose favorite toy was taken away. They carried the weight of a forgotten kind of sadness.

Lore started to wonder if their cries were just for a time before when they weren't stalking the woods outside of the town. But then, the same question would always pass through her head as the four trudged on in the stillness of the dawn in the Twisted Wood. *What were they before? Before the rot had settled into their bones and hearts?* Their golden eyes pulsated with power, and Lore remembered how it felt being on the bad side of that power and want. A shudder down her spine. But even with that in mind, she couldn't help but pity the creatures roaming with no purpose.

The tree line thinned, and soon they saw an open field of wheat blowing in the gentle wind as the second, smaller moon began its descent behind the horizon.

"Alright, you three stand behind me. This will only take a moment," Merlin said with a confident wave of the hand.

No one protested, perhaps because of the adrenaline and anxiety fighting in the pits of their stomach for dominance or because there was nothing to protest about. The Wielder was the only one who could use magic, after all.

The tips of his pointed ears drooped. His eyes closed as he let out an exhale of controlled breath. An orange spark spurred around his fingers then flames began to weave between his digits like a fish swimming over and under a coral. He then pressed his hand gently on the unseen barrier and inhaled deeply, causing the flames engulfing his hand to flicker. With another exhale, they grew with new life. He continued this until the heat spread and cracked the barrier like a rock that had just been thrown at a window. It fractured and split then came down like a glass ceiling, crashing as it landed in the meadow.

Lore looked down at Mathilde, who was gripping the silver string of her 'hardly misses' bow. It looked like it weighed on the mouse. Her expression was an intricate puzzle of mixed signals. Anger burned behind her eyes, but her brows were turned upward. Her tail flicked with unbridled nerves, and her knees trembled. The reality was settling in that her arrows may pierce the skin of those who had a hand in her rearing.

Killmoore rested a hand on Mathilde's shoulder and gave her a playful smile. "We got your back." His voice was gentle with reassurance. It was the first time Lore's heard it without a sarcastic ring or double meaning.

It was nice.

And with that, they stepped over the threshold.

"They'll surely know we are here, and there's no mistaking it that Crinkle will know I am not only alive and well," Merlin said with some pep as he led the trio through the wheat fields, "but that he will need to cling to whatever power needed to save his delusion of a *perfect* town."

DOWN THE WELL

"Speaking of," the bounty hunter spoke up, "the townsfolk—what will he do with them?"

Merlin adjusted his cufflinks. "If we are lucky, just lock them up somewhere." he halted. "If we are not so lucky, we may be walking into a bloodbath."

Mathilde gulped and gripped the string of the bow harder. As if strangling the bow would somehow do the same to Crinkle before he could lay a finger on her sisters.

"Minifred won't let that happen," Lore added, trying to sound optimistic. "Come on, could you imagine Crinkle trying to lock her up?" She playfully nudged Mathilde.

The gray mouse said nothing, only a nervous smile spread on her face.

"You're right, Lore," the fox added as he looked at his reflection in the copper armbands. "She'd scold him and give him an earful leaving him wishing for Death."

Mathilde giggled at the image.

Then Lore saw a familiar silhouette on the horizon.

It was the rundown house where they first met the bounty hunter. As they closed the distance between them and the worn home, Merlin began to slow his pace. Falling behind Lore and Mathilde, and eventually behind Killmoore.

"What is it?" Mathilde's voice was barely audible.

Merlin's lip trembled, and his hands balled into a fist. "The humans that used to live there gave me guardianship of their home after we were able to secure their safe passage."

Lore looked back to the house, rotting away in the open field.

"A dear friend and I were able to channel enough power to create a split in the fabric. Send them to a safer world while the other humans were being chased into the Twisted Wood." His voice cracked, and his head hung low. His pointed hat sagged as well. "We couldn't save them all, though."

Lore walked over to the bat and knelt in front of him. She took his small fist and gently cradled it with her hand, then rested the other hand

231

on top of it. "You did what you could. And I am sure that the human family you were able to save was so eternally grateful."

His bloodshot eyes looked past Lore's freckled face to the dilapidated house. "I did not do their many kindnesses to me any justice."

The sound of the wheat rattling in the morning breeze was the only sound that filled the stillness of the moment.

Killmoore shoved his hands in his pockets and looked at the orange and pink clouds of a new sunrise.

"Then let that justice be served today." His voice was firm.

Merlin exhaled a shaky breath. "I s'pose the past is behind us for a reason." His gaze bounced to Mathilde. "There is nothing that will change the course of what's been done." To Killmoore, he said, "The only thing we can do is make better choices to become better ourselves." Finally, his softened expression landed on Lore. "You hold the same compassion behind those storm cloud eyes as they did, you know?"

Lore's chest felt tight, "Thank you."

"Thank *you*." Merlin looked to the other two of the trio. "Thank you all for being brave enough to start to heal the ugly history that built this town."

Killmoore rocked on his heels, a grin curled up into his cheek. "I don't know if I'd call more murder healing."

Merlin burst into laughter, a tear escaping, and he quickly marched ahead. "Well, let's waste no more time. I still have one stop to make before I am welcomed home."

The only sound in the graveyard was Mathilde's muffled wails into Lore's chest. They stood in front of Gannon's headstone. No supernatural presence lingered.

Merlin rested a hand on the stone. "I am so sorry, my friend, that the quest I set you on became your undoing." His voice was low. "And now I ask your daughter to go into this battle on your behalf, along with the human we so desperately searched for."

Lore's arms ached under the weight of the mouse's grief she finally couldn't bottle any longer. It poured out through snot and tears.

Down The Well

"You were a great leader, and I always wanted to be like you when I grew up." The bat paused through sniffles. "It may have taken you a while, but you always ended up doing what was right in the end. You were the moral compass of our little band of adventurers. I see you in Mathilde. Her headstrong nature was one of your most admirable qualities." He took a few steps back and sighed as he placed his hat between his ears. "As much as I look forward to our reunion, Gannon, I hope that day isn't today."

The group stood there as the alligator's daughter's tears eventually ran dry, and all that she could choke out were painful sobs.

Lore leaned into her. "Hey, let's go home."

Mathilde steadied her breathing and hugged the headstone before she placed a trusting hand in Lore's.

THIRTY-THREE

The curtains of the yellow manor wiped over the sharp edges of broken glass—the remnants of the windows tore at the sheer threads. And the heavy oak door was off its hinges, but this was what all the houses looked like, or close to it. When the party walked up onto the porch, the steps didn't groan the same as they once did.

Mathilde's hands trembled as she went inside.

Lore followed closely behind. She wasn't sure which was worse—the inside or the outside. The kitchen table was knocked over, the mushrooms were missing from the mantle, and the flowers on the walls were still and lifeless. No fire burned in the hearth, and no pitter-patter of mouse footsteps came down the staircase to greet them. The house was completely sacked and empty.

Mathilde balled her hands and Lore had a hunch that the knuckles beneath her velvet soft fur were stark white. Her jaw pulled as tight as her bow as she notched an arrow, pulling the string back. Ready to fire. "Let's bag an opossum," she muttered, holding the weapon with such ferocity that if Lore was spat up from the well today, she never would have guessed this was the mouse's first day holding a bow.

Their footsteps echoed in the empty town of Charmsend. There was not single a trace of the villagers anywhere. Just abandoned houses and glass glittering on the ground. Not even the street lamps were spared from whatever rampage had sailed through the town.

DOWN THE WELL

The air felt like it was shrinking and thinning the closer to the market square they walked. The once colorful area was now muted shades that left the taste of ash floating amongst the settling dust clouds. It made Lore's lungs sting. *Closer to the well.* Lore began twisting the Band of Life on her finger, the silver chains of her bracelet clanged as she did. The jingle carried on a breeze that blew past them, announcing their arrival.

Her eyes fell onto the orange well, whose bricks were cracking. A flickering green light emanated through the open veins. She shifted her focus to the three bodies that circled the wishing well. First was Lyudmilla, whose blank expression revealed she was somewhere far away from the eye of the storm. Then she locked onto the withering figure of Sable, trapped in a blue orb that seemed to be devouring her very essence. The magical sphere was attached to none other than Crinkle, who radiated an aura that froze the atmosphere around him, like the first layer of Winter's frost.

"Where are my sisters, you monster?!" Mathilde demanded with the silver string pulled tight, ready to launch her very first shot.

Crinkle let out a laugh so low it sounded like it dragged across gravel. He waved his staff. The blueish-green rock glowed. A rush of water followed it from the well like liquid metal to a magnet. As he spun the tip of his staff the, water spun into a flat circle that took the shape of an oval mirror. Behind the swirling liquid, the figures of the townsfolk became clearer behind the iron bars that imprisoned them. "I'm keeping them safe, sweetheart. I was always keeping you all safe." Crinkle's voice walked a fine line between genuine softness and rampant madness. At any moment, he could contort one way or the other.

"Lyudmilla!" Merlin called. "Lyudmilla, I know you remember me. I know deep down you are better than this."

The wolf's stoic face twisted in a painful expression. "I don't know what I'm supposed to know," she uttered. Tears left the corners of her pink eyes as she heaved her ax above her head. "I know I want freedom and Dina's safety. And you're *in my way!*" She swung her double-sided ax downward, missing Merlin by a whisker.

VERONICA KING

The last sound Lore registered was her own gasp at the sight of a Grayshade Crinkle magically unveiled. She didn't hear its hungry cry, only felt the ground shake under the beast as it charged them.

The next few movements happened fast, Lore could barely catch her breath as she felt her body be pulled to the side just in time for a blue beam to crackle through the air and burn the spot she was just in. Everything felt like moving through water—slow with an invisible weight crushing her from above and pockets of air far too away from her lungs. Just like her journey down the well that landed her here in the first place.

She saw Killmoore locked into a standoff with Lyudmilla just like they had been back at the mad Wielder's home. The only difference was that now, with the magical braces of power, the fox didn't lose any ground.

Merlin leaped on Lore's back and launched into the air to hurl a series of fireballs at Crinkle, whose skin was splitting to reveal the same magical and radiant blue light that held Sable captive.

The opossum flung the weakened hedgehog in front of him to absorb the fiery blows.

Lore swallowed down the fear rising in her throat and bolted toward the well. It was then she felt a sudden pain in her stomach as the Grayshade's tail flung her away from the orange bricks. She rolled to her side and coughed so hard, her throat burned from the dryness.

The earth trembled once again as the beast charged her—only to be stopped by a rain of purple-tipped arrows. Most of which hit the beast head-on. One even stuck out from its pulsating electric blue eyes. An angry howl bellowed from its chest as it stopped in its tracks, too pained to continue its attack.

Lore scanned the area but couldn't find Mathilde anywhere.

Merlin waved fiery fists that formed into a flaming rope. He whipped it around Crinkle's staff, making it smoke as the blaze licked the wood.

Lore saw an opening and began to close the gap between her and the well. Her fingertips itched from the memory of running them over the crack—the keyhole. Another step closer.

Another bolt of magic was loosened from Crinkle's staff.

Lore flinched, but this time, tentacles of green smoke emanated from the Band of Life and absorbed the blast. She took another quick step.

Killmoore was sent sliding across the stone, but quickly shot back up and ran back to the jaws of peril. Lyudmilla was unyielding as she swung her weapon at him. Anything near her was liable to break under her strength. But the fox moved quickly and struck faster. In and out, a dance of hit and dodge.

Another roar erupted from the Grayshade as it stormed toward Merlin's unprotected back.

"*Behind you!*" Lore shouted.

Without missing a beat, Merlin blew a single puff of air from his mouth to the ground and it shot him up into the sky. The beast ran right under him and crashed into a smoking Crinkle.

The bat's gold eyes shot over his shoulder. "Quickly, now! The—" But his words were cut short by the sound of ice shards hissing in the air. His attention shifted, and a dance of ice and fire ensued.

She watched as arrows fell from the sky between Lyudmilla and Killmoore, keeping the latter safe as he put a bit of distance between himself and the white wolf.

Lore was so close to the well now, and she was finally able to draw a filling breath. She lunged, and her hands felt the smooth orange paint. They shook frantically as she tried to unfasten the bracelet.

The face of an old woman sat with her at the helm of her thoughts. "You can do it," she cooed. "There's nothing you can't do, Lore." Her honeyed voice felt so close, yet she wasn't there at all.

The sizzle of magic behind Lore made her freeze. Her ring absorbed another attack.

Another rain of arrows fell from the sky, successfully stalling the Grayshade stomping towards her.

Another blast of ice shot over Lore. It made contact with a building an alley or two over. Pink sparks erupted as it froze over. The weight of the ice crumpled the structure in on itself.

Her heart dropped and her fist tightened. *Mathilde.*

Despite her worry, she saw nothing else aside from the keyhole. The cries of battle, clashing of metal, and magic smoke melted away as she felt a rush of cold water pool over her. The silver charm gleamed in the glimmering green light, as Lore pushed it in like a quarter in a quarter machine. She tried to turn it to lock whatever door was powerful enough to seal the magic away, but nothing happened. The liquid around her became colder and colder, lulling her into a dangerous sleep.

Behind her heavy eyelids, she saw a ghostly stag standing on a crescent-shaped lake. It made no sudden movement and posed no sign of threat. It only stood there staring with eyes deep and as blue as a rage-filled ocean.

She walked toward it. Each time she plunged into the water, an unseen weight dragged her under. She fought to the surface to gasp for breath. She didn't dare look down at whatever was getting in her way. Until she didn't have a choice.

When she did, she saw her own face. The glowing silver light of the stag emanated as it walked on the water above her. She kicked against herself and tried to swim to the surface, only to be dragged down once more. She kept trying until she couldn't dish any more punches. Then she allowed herself to be pulled down to the bottom of the lake, where she heard the sounds of her own cries. The darkness of the deep waters curled around her as she searched for herself. To find a little girl hiding, crying.

Uncomforted. Unloved. And alone.

Lore felt tears warm her own cheeks as she pulled the shadow of her younger self into a hug.

Her eyes snapped open, and the reflection showed they were now glowing the same deep rich blue as the elusive stag. From her dark brown hair, large, ethereal antlers sprouted, and she felt waves crashing within her. Power she held. Power she could wield. Then the vision—the lake and stag—disappeared, and she was back in the battle.

With a scream erupting from her stinging lungs, she turned the bracelet's charm in the keyhole. The well shuddered and began to crumble, making Crinkle wail in defeat.

As weakness spread through her body, she shifted her gaze toward the corrupt opossum. He was crumbling away as if he was made of sand. It didn't take long for the Wielder to become dust in the biting autumn wind.

With him gone, Sable was freed, and the stolen life force was returned to her. Merlin stood in the ashes of his former friend and picked up the blueish-green stone that still pulsated faintly.

Lore's eyes fluttered over the body of the lifeless Grayshade, its corpse riddled with arrows. She went to stand, only to fall to her knees again. Her gaze lazily landed on Killmoore, who had Lyudmilla pinned against the ground with his axes crossed over her thick neck.

The last thing she saw before completely giving in to the exhaustion was Mathilde running towards her from the alley.

THIRTY-FOUR

Pink blossoms that searched for drops of sunlight welcomed Lore. She saw that the curtains half-hung off the walls and out the busted windows of the mayor's mansion.

"Good to see you awake," Killmoore's voice was smooth as he sipped on a mug of tea in a nearby seat.

She sat up in the bed, noticing the bandages that were wrapped around her arms as she did so. They itched and her head buzzed with a faint recollection of what happened along with a pressure that could be the start of a nasty headache.

"Mathilde!" she called as the image of the frozen roof of Dina's collapsing played in her head.

"She's fine," the fox said as he walked to the foot of the bed.

The door opened and the red-clad mouse leaped onto the bed to hug Lore. Then promptly grabbed her by the shirt collar and shoved a finger in her face. "Don't you ever pull a stunt like that again!"

Lore laughed. "I won't. I promise." When free from the mouse's strong grip, Lore's fingertips played with the ends of her loose hair that had been tickling her cheeks. "It's been so long since I've worn it like this," she admitted quietly. Then she ran a hand through her brown waves and as she went to split it into three sections… then she noticed it. Her jaw slackened and she felt the heat rise to her cheeks. *No, no it can't be, it was just a dream. A vision.* The mortified feeling that welled in her gut must have read obviously on her face.

Down The Well

"It's okay, Lore," Mathilde said in almost a whisper.

But the soft velvet kissing her fingertips at the roots of her hair made it a reality. Continuing her hand up the surface it then became smooth and broke off into multiple Y branches. Lore took a deep ragged breath. The sudden realization made the weight on her head feel all the heavier. *I much rather have a pressure headache.*

"Wha–" She stopped, if she said it then it had to be true. *If a human was a monster then what beast am I now?* A tear ran down her cheek and Mathilde's finger wiped it away. "It's like a crown." The mouse whispered to her friend. "A beautiful crown."

Lore bit her bottom lip. "But I didn't ask for a crown." Her voice cracked as another tear escaped the corners of her eyes. "I didn't ask for any of this." her hands gripped the bed sheets tighter as she bawled her fists.

Killmoore tilted his head and his ears lifted. "Sometimes we get gifts we don't ask for."

Lore's brow pulled tight as her tears turned bitter. "There are stag antlers on my head, Killmoore!" Her voice was strained and tired. "I can't just return to sender, now can I?"

The fox winced at the harshness Lore had not displayed before. Not to the Grayshade that attacked them, the townsfolk who scrutinized her every move, not even to Crinkle.

"I'm sure your family will still love you," Mathilde assured.

Lore's throat tightened more. *Shit. I haven't even thought of that.* She swallowed a now soured sentiment of a happy reunion with whoever was looking for her. "Who could welcome me like this?" Lore's eyes stung at the mere thoughts of rejection. "I'm a monster."

"No, no," Mathilde mused as she ran her small, thin fingers through Lore's glossy hair. "You weren't a monster before and you aren't one now."

Lore's lip quivered as she tried to focus on Mathilde's words. Then the mouse wrapped her arms around the human's neck. "You can't let what others may or may not say about you define who you perceive yourself to be."

241

A warmth radiated from Mathilde and washed away the *what ifs* Lore had swirling around her.

She thought it rather pathetic but all she could muster out was a ragged, "thank you." That was all the mouse had needed though.

Minifred came in with a tray of tea. "Sable said you need to drink this when you woke." She set it on the nightstand where the photo of Gannon with his five mice daughters was still displayed.

"Thank you."

The coal-colored mouse smiled. "Thank *you*, Lore. You're the human who helped save our town from the unseen spell that had ahold of us all." With that, she left. The door silently shut behind her.

Lore waited to see if the other sisters would visit, but when they didn't appear, she looked out the broken window as Mathilde hopped off the bed to pour the water from the kettle into the daffodil mug. *Gannon's cup.* She smiled down at the comforting design.

Killmoore had silently moved over to the window where he watched the folk of Charmsend pick up the shattered pieces of their home in the streets below.

"The well is broken," Mathilde said. "The thing she used as an entrance is now gone."

Lore chewed the inside of her cheeks. "It's impossible then?" her shoulders slumped forward as she began to pick at the skin around her fingernails. "Maybe I'm never going to find my way home." She fidgeted with the wooden ring on her middle finger.

"Don't forget," Mathilde chimed as she handed Lore the teacup. "I made a promise to get you back. No matter what."

Lore's fingers wrapped around the painted gold flower. It truly was a beautiful cup. "But how?" she asked. "Getting home seems like an impossible dream now."

The mouse didn't have an answer, but gently patted her shoulder in an attempt at comfort.

"The well is impassable," Killmoore said as he shoved his hands in the pockets of his blue coat. Then he cleared his throat and his amber eyes drifted back to Lore and Mathilde with a familiar glint of excitement. "But my dear friends," his warm laughter filled the broken room, "nothing is *impossible*."

GANNON'S LAST NIGHT

HARDCOVER EXCLUSIVE SCENE

Gannon took a longer route to Dina's pub, mainly because he felt like there was someone slinking in the shadows behind him. The streets were quiet as the townsfolk were retiring to their homes, surely getting ready for their nightly routine as the sun was finally kissing the tree line of the Twisted Wood goodbye. If one listened close enough to the sounds of footprints on smooth cobblestone whispered just enough, one might hear a handful of Animalfolk making their way to a building whose flickering neon sign acted as the light that drew in moths.

It was no surprise to the alligator when he entered the pub that there was no wait to start the rounds of drinks. The thick clouds of smoke whirled around him as if they were an old friend, welcoming him into a long and unnecessary embrace. They scratched his throat, and he let out a cough.

The clap of a familiar hand landed on his back.

"Good to see ya, old timer."

He fanned away the puffs of smoke. "Glad to see so many showed up tonight, Dina," he admitted through coughs.

The calico cat grinned. "Let me show you to your table, dear founder. There's lots to see tonight."

The alligator nodded and followed the heeled cat to a round table just off the center stage. The lights weren't on yet. They had historical matters to attend to first. He took his seat.

Dina stood looking at all the Charmsend Historical Society members. "We've grown so much since starting," she murmured under her breath.

Gannon looked up at her. "That's always been the plan," he said with a wink.

She smiled warmly and then put on her serious mask. "Alright!" the cat roared, causing the commotion in her pub to dwindle to utter silence. "We'll be starting with artifacts." She sat down beside him.

This town, for its colorful exterior, had its rough edges. He knew the feline had fight in her. But he knew that wasn't who she was at her core. *She just wants her shot at a happily ever after, too.*

A thud against the table reined in his wandering thoughts. His eyes looked down at the object presented on the bar table stained with booze, vomit, or blood. He didn't know, and it really didn't matter. He lifted the item, brushed off the remaining dirt, and brought it closer to his face. "Where was it you found this?"

"On the outer rim of the town, sir," the rabbit replied.

Gannon tapped a claw against the colored metal square. "Did anyone see you there?"

"No, sir."

The alligator's eyes drifted from the stained glass artwork back to the trembling rabbit. He leaned closer to the animal, a smile cracking his mouth. "What do ya' think it is?"

The fluffy animal steadied his arms by hugging himself and rocking back and forth on his heels. "I, uh—I don't know, but it is mighty pretty and would look great with some light." The young creature then gestured to the candle at the center of the table.

Gannon bellowed out a laugh. "Smart thinking." He put the dyed square glass around the flame.

Oohs and *ahhhs* floated in the air.

The gator gave Dina a nod.

She scribbled something down in a notebook and then reached for the item to sit it at her feet.

"No, no," Gannon mused. "Leave it. It adds a nice touch to the place."

Dina rolled her eyes. "Whatever you say." She picked up the notebook and paper again. "Next!"

It went on like that for what felt like hours.

Gannon watched the moon's light travel over the town from the windows and imagined all his daughters at home, sleeping soundly.

When the artifact examination was done, he gave the fox sitting on the stage a thumbs up.

The lights turned on but stayed low as the bandmates gathered on the stage. The mic flipped on, and the vixen began singing a beautiful melody.

"So what's it gonna be for these items?" Dina asked, tapping the artifacts with her boot.

"Take 'em to Petra. She knows what to do with them."

The calico cat nodded as she stood to her feet, and the alligator's stomach grumbled. She cocked a brow. "What's it gonna be for dinner?"

"Oh, it's fine." Gannon waved a hand. "We got food at the house."

Dina grinned. "So you'll have the mutton?"

Gannon met her gaze. *I spose the girls are fine, and one bite shouldn't hurt.* "Alright, alright. But only if it's on the house," he teased.

The cat laughed and headed to the kitchen, stopping at a few other tables on the way to see what the remaining members wanted for a little midnight snack.

Gannon's eyes fluttered around the pub, his clawed hand drumming along to the beat of the music filling the air. The smoke was still thick but not so thick it caked his throat.

A juicy mutton leg plopped down in front of him. He pulled the plate closer. "Well, that was quick."

The cat shrugged. "Just left of what we made this mornin'."

Gannon dug in his suit pocket for his wallet.

"It's on the house, old timer."

He laughed as he pulled out some taels. "Oh, Dina, it was only a joke."

"I think what you're doin' is admirable. Folks should know the true history of the homes they're livin' in."

The alligator's face fell as he dropped the coins onto the table. "I shouldn't be praised. It's the bare minimum at this point."

"Well, regardless, I think it's something." The cat pushed the currency back toward the mayor.

"At least let me tip my amazing waitress. I hear the boss 'round here doesn't pay enough," Gannon said with a masked smile all his own.

She let out a heavy sigh. "Fine." As her clicking heels walked away, she added over her shoulder, "I have you know, she's meaner than a rattlesnake, too."

The gator laughed and sank his teeth into the meat. In between bites, he kept looking out the window. All seemed normal until he saw a hairless animal peeking in. His heart thudded against his chest. Now? As fast as he saw the creature, it disappeared. He shot to his feet and headed out the door, not saying a word to anyone.

As he rounded the corner to the alley, the sinking feeling halted.

"Mathilde," he groaned. "How did I know you were the root of this mischief?" He paused for a moment, giving his youngest daughter a chance to collect herself. "Go on, explain yourself."

Mathilde began twiddling her thumbs. "I was exploring."

"Exploring?" he questioned with a boom. "More like snooping in on CHS affairs, little lady. I thought I told you to stay home."

"Yes, maybe I was, *but* if I weren't snooping around, the human I found stalking about would have caused a panic," she pleaded as she poked and prodded at the human.

Gannon knelt beside the human and tilted its head toward his snout with a taloned hand. "Mathilde, do you know what this means?" he said slowly, recalling the many letters that have been coming to his window for about a year now. A flutter began in his stomach.

"Yeah, Gannon. Humans aren't extinct, like we originally thought." Mathilde was doing a very poor job of containing herself—per usual. "Are we going to tell the Society now?"

"Do you know *who* this is?" he asked in a soft rush, ignoring his daughter's question.

"Uh…" Mathilde scratched her chin and rocked on her heels. "A lady kind of human?"

The alligator shook his head at his daughter.

Before he could say what he wanted, she quickly added, "But I don't wanna assume."

"Where were you going to take it?" he grumbled.

"Well, I haven't gotten that far yet," Mathilde admitted, voice lifting in defensiveness. "I was going to take it back to the house, bandage it up, and then show you when you got back." Her eyes were eager, searching for his praise.

The alligator let out a deep groan. "Bandages won't heal this up. We'll need to be careful." Silence settled for a moment more before he added, "We'll have to send a carrier crow. It shouldn't take that long." Gannon hoisted the human over his shoulder. *This isn't ideal, but I'll have to make do.* "But Mathilde —"

"Yes?"

"No matter what, you can't let anything else happen to this human once she's well again. No matter what anyone tells you." He spoke quickly in a near whisper.

As they rushed towards home, he recalled he was supposed to visit a certain librarian. *Oh, my work is never done.*

He opened the front door, closed it behind them, then dropped the human on the couch by the hearth that the mushroomlings were quickly tending. "Go fetch CC and bring me some paper and my quill," he ordered. "Quickly, now."

Mathilde pitter-pattered across the room. "So, when will we tell the Society?" she asked again.

"We won't be telling them anything," he said sternly. "But I will let the other elders know. This is vital to my work."

"Yes, and I think it's important I be there, too." The mouse's voice was sharp, but more like that of a needle than of a sword. A small annoyance rather than a threat.

"Mathilde, my dear, bring CC here, please. This can't wait."

The mouse held the ink-feathered bird as he scribbled a message.

If you think you're so vital, come and help.

He then rolled it up and put it in the crow's little bag. He walked over to the window, adding, "Alright, now this shouldn't be a long wait, but I am tasking you to look after this human in my absence. They certainly aren't from here and will need guidance."

"But —"

He cut her off. "No *buts.*" He slid the window open and the crisp night air rushed past him.

"You expect me to babysit the human?" the mouse repeated, clearly offended. "I'm not a babysitter! I'm an explorer." She huffed, trying desperately to find a better term. "I'm an adventurer."

His face softened as he walked over to kneel by his daughter, taking in her defeated expression. He placed a hand on her shoulder. Remembering the day he brought them home, a tear formed in the corner of his eye. "Sometimes, my girl, the biggest adventure you can take is getting to know someone else."

Mathilde gave Gannon a nod. He pulled her into a tight hug.

The door opened again, and a musky scent clung to the air.

Good grief. He still hadn't bathed?

Gannon released Mathilde from his protective grasp.

"Oh, Gannon. A human? How?" Crinkle inquired.

"Can you help or not?" he snapped as he rose to meet his bygone friend.

"Of course I can." The opossum's cackle filled the room. "After you take the human to a bed, I'll need you to fetch a few things from Sable's for me," Crinkle purred as he gestured for Gannon to give him a pencil and paper.

As the door clasped shut behind him, his heart raced as he rushed down to the Iron Rose. *Would Sable would even have a moment to spare? She had always been a star-hour kinda gal, and she always filled her orders under the cover of night.*

As Gannon charged down the winding path that was a bit too narrow for him, he felt like there was a shadow behind him nipping at his heels. *Just a bit of paranoia. The quicker we do this, the faster we can get home to the girls and the key.*

He arrived and blew through the iron gate that adorned the perimeter of the greenhouse. He let himself in. The dim glowing of the fire flowers illuminated the hedgehog's face.

She appeared to be testing soil.

"Sable," he rasped, waiting for his breath to catch up with him. I'm not as young as I once was.

The hedgehog's honeyed gaze enveloped the alligator as she rushed over to him. "Gannon, what has you like this?"

He reached up and clasped a hand around her forearm. "The key arrived."

Sable's eyes shot wide open, "Then what are ya doin' here then!?"

"I need," he looked at the scrap of paper Crinkle had given him, "root of Valeriana."

Her face fell. "I took the last of what I had up to the library today as per request of carrier crow."

"For who?!" he tried to control his tone but the rattling glass of the greenhouse told him exactly what a piss-poor job he was doing.

"Petra."

He rolled his eyes as he brushed his hands against his legs. "Well, I needed to visit with her, anyway." His words danced the line of annoyance and seething anger at what appeared to be misfortune looming over him.

As he blazed out the door, he was too caught up in his own head to hear the hedgehog call out to him, "Be safe, please!"

Gannon flung the door to the rundown building with enough strength that it almost flew off its hinges. The statues and stuffed heads began to mutter, but he wasn't paying any attention.

"Petra!" he called with his hands cupping around his snout. "Petra, come here at once!" he demanded.

The rafters rattled as the snake revealed herself. She allowed her body to pile onto the floor, making a mountain of shining obsidian scales.

"I hope you're here about my releassse," she hissed.

"No, I'm here to see if you used the root of Valeriana yet?"

The snake's flat head tilted. "And why would that be any concern of yours, Missster Mayor?"

"The key is here, and it's injured. Crinkle needs that root to heal it."

Petra's orange eyes narrowed on Gannon. "Not until you release me from my contract."

He threw his hands up in the air. "Really!? You want to do this now!? I've got a half-dead human in my guest bedroom and you want to negotiate contracts?!"

The snake grinned, revealing her fangs. "Ssseemsss like the mossst opportune time to, wouldn't you sssay?"

Gannon ran a hand over his face. "You know what you ask is impossible because I'm not the one who bound you here to begin with?!"

"But you have been in communication with him, have you not?!" Venom coated her words.

Gannon inhaled a deep breath as he clasped his hands together. "I am trying to be the middleman for so many right now. If you do this kindness for me, then I will in my next letter bring up your contract."

The snake's orange eyes flickered like a growing fire.

"Seriously!?" His tail jerked. "What more do you want?"

The tip of her tail wove between bookshelves as she pulled a podium from some corner of the first floor between them.

Gannon looked over the gray, leather-bound book and specialized pen beside it. "You really don't trust me?"

The fire in Petra's eyes seemed to be fanned by the alligator's comments. "You expect me to trust ssso easssily after being put in a box after trusssting the lassst one I called friend?" her tongue flicked out over her last few words.

Gannon's jaw tightened as the clock echoed in the silent halls of the library. *I need to return home to my daughters.* "Fine. Whatever will make this end quicker."

The snake's thick mouth spread into a smile. "Sssplendid." She flipped the book pages open with a flick of her tail. "Sssign here."

Gannon looked over the page.

> I, _____, hereby bind my word to my blood. If I
> break my vow, only my blood will fulfill my promise.

The alligator gritted his sharp teeth. "Petra, please."

The tip of the snake's tail only tapped the page. "Do you want the root or not?" she spat.

A rage warmed Gannon's hands as he pricked his finger with one end of the pen. He watched as his blood transformed into ink. His anger continued to rise, but he could only chew on the heated thoughts as he signed his name on the line. "There." he seethed. "The root."

As the snake coiled her tail around the podium, she said, "Of courssse."

After returning the cursed book to its rightful place, she disappeared into the rafters.

Gannon stood there frozen, only half-processing what he just did in order to accomplish the one task that echoed in his head. *Gotta get home.*

Petra returned with a smile as she dropped a brown bag with a rose stamp on it at his feet.

Gannon said nothing as he snatched it from the ground and began a hasty walk for the exit.

The alligator's earth-shaking footsteps came to a halt as his eyes fell onto tuffs of matted gray hair. The creature's long arms gripped the sides of the orange brick well as it bellowed out a howl into the well.

You'll need a tael, if you're making a wish.

Using the stalls as coverage, Gannon tried to walk silently on the edge of the square. Those things have always had a stronger sense of sound compared to sight. *As long as I take this slow, I should be fine.* He watched the creature sulk around the well carefully as he made his way from vendor stall to vendor stall.

So now Crinkle is allowing Grayshade to pass through the barrier?

The throb of his heart pounding against his ribcage reminded him of the real danger he was in. No wandering thoughts could deny that. He steadied his breath as his sight focused on the path home. He was almost there.

Then the winds changed favor, and a gentle breeze carried over the square. Towards the Grayshade circling the well like a buzzard circling a carcass.

Gannon's grip on the bag of Valeriana root tightened and the rustle it made sent a shiver down his scales. His gaze drifted to a Grian that was seated away from a flowering bush. *If only its flame weren't so bright, I'd be able to scamper by riding the shadows all the way home.*

The metal light post took notice of the squatting alligator gawking at it. The fire-lit lamp tilted its glass head, the flame trapped within it flickered with curiosity.

Gannon brought a claw up to his mouth to signal the street lamp to be quiet. Then the alligator peeked over the wooden stall. He saw the Grayshade's back as its tail swept over the stone of the square. *Now's your chance*, he told himself as he inhaled a deep breath. The night breeze carried pollen that tickled his nose. He held his breath to not sneeze. As the moment dragged on, Gannon peeked around the stall once again to check if his opening was still open.

Glowing blue eyes stared back.

The creature let out a yowl.

Without thinking twice, Gannon's tail whooshed through the air and landed a hard blow on the Grayshade's jaw. Hard enough that the disproportionately large Grayshade stumbled back.

Gannon went to flee, his claws clutching the brown bag to his chest. Then his tail suddenly stung. When he turned, he saw the creature's mouth latched on. His blood bubbled and pooled around its mouth. Before he could react, the creature shot upward.

Gannon soared through the air. A trail of blood splattered the ground underneath the airborne alligator, sputtering from where the end of his tail once was.

His body hit the post of another Grian. He looked up at the flame that was shifting from a radiant red to a blustered blue. "Grian," he gasped as he pulled himself to his feet. "I'll need to borrow you for a moment." Gannon's hands gripped the cold iron as he wielded the pole as a weapon, blue fire spurting from its top.

The Grayshade let out another animalistic growl and darted for Gannon, who let out his own battle cry.

Long obsidian claws clashed against the metal.

The alligator shoved the creature off him by putting all his might behind the swing of the Grian.

The Grayshade's claws scratched the ground's stones as it slid away.

Come on, you got this, the alligator told himself as he steadied his breath. His gaze stayed on the Grayshade, already scrambling to its stout legs again. Another yowl echoed in the square. This time, Gannon didn't wait for the monster to strike first. He pointed the blue blaze forward and ran toward it.

The bright flames kissed the creature's face, causing another shrill howl of pain. Then paws the size of a bear skull grappled the glass head of the lamp. Shattered glass tinged against the stone as the Grian's fire was snuffed out.

Gannon's face fell as he dug his feet firmly into the ground. The creature bared its teeth and let out a bellowing roar that made the tail of the alligator's suit jacket flutter behind him.

"You'd benefit from a breath mint."

The creature jerked the cold iron body of the Grian towards it, but Gannon barely moved an inch.

He gave a tug, barely moving the Grayshade. He saw double as his vision blurred. *Blood loss. Damn it.*

The creature capitalized on the moment and, in one fluid movement, swiped the cold iron free from the alligator's grasp.

Cold metal met Gannon's face, and he hit the ground once again. He tried to stand up again, but his back suffered violent lashes from the Grayshade's claws. His eyes fought to stay open.

If I'm not leaving here, then neither are you. Then, with his remaining strength, he lurched forward and snapped his jaw down on the creature's long, thick tail. He then began to spin, causing the tail to wrap around him until it, too, snapped off.

The creature yowled in pain. With a swoop of its arm, it lifted Gannon into the air, revealing the gator's soft belly, and sank its dark claws in.

As its talons sliced down Gannon's stomach, he knew it was over. It burned like the flames of the fires he once set on a wooden building housing that sheltered a cowering horde of humans hiding from the Animalfolk.

As his body thudded against the ground and his blood pooled around him, he watched the Grayshade lumber off into the night. *If only I could look into someone's eyes so they knew to watch after my girls.*

The metal footsteps of the Grian rang out against the stone ground as they rushed to circle around the alligator, trying desperately to close the cuts and reattach the body parts.

The last thing Gannon felt before answering the call to return home was the tip of a frigid knife digging into his mouth.

ACKNOWLEDGMENTS

As vain as it may seem, I'd like to thank my past self for actually finishing *Down the Well*.

This was the first story I ever wrote 'the end' on. I did it as a first-time mom who was writing during nights when my oldest was restless, then continuing to write during the long days between naps, mealtimes, and play. It was something I set out to do as a way to prove to my children and to myself that you don't have to stop chasing your dreams because you became a parent. You can have both, but it will be work. It will be hard, and there will be times you want to give up, but it will be so worth it when you taste the sweet flavor of the victory cake. So, a very *big* thank you to my Moonbeam. I never would have been determined enough to reach the end without you on my hip.

Thank you to Grandpa Robb for printing out my first draft and binding it for me all the way back in 2019.

Thank you to Zara, who not only had the tedious task of fixing this Appalachian's every spelling and grammatical error but also took a risk on signing this trilogy. I appreciated your presence along the way as I cleaned each draft as my editor, but also as my friend. I wouldn't have been able to get through the days that imposter syndrome grabbed me by the throat without you. Thank you for believing in me as much as I believe in you.

Of course, I'd also like to thank the community of friends I have found on the AuthorTube spaces who were able to give me good feedback on my writing. With the feedback from Alpha readers Amanda N. Newman, Hannah, and Stig Dyrdal, I did my best to level up one draft to the next and it's still crazy to me as I am writing this that *Down the Well* went from a very crappy draft to now a good clean story.

Thank you to the talented artists, whose work really makes the magic of Thimbleton come alive, Nia (The Vixen of Fiction on social media) & Grayson (iwritewithpride on the internet) the artwork in this book adds so much character and whimsy that Zara and myself felt the story needed.

A big thank you to Samantha Traunfeld. I don't know how I could have gotten through the crazy process of publication and all the stuff on the backend without our texts and check ins. So glad you are the person I get to call debut buddy, and glad that our friendship was kindled through something we both love so much, Sharing stories. Here's to many more years of friendship and book titles being released!

And last but not least, I'd be lying if I said I could have held onto the threads of my optimism trudging through draft after draft of *Down the Well* without the ongoing support from my partner Logan. Who pushed me to make writing days, continued to make sure I was eating and staying hydrated enough through the process, let me sleep in late on the weekends, and was interested in me reading aloud bits of the manuscript when they don't really enjoy reading to begin with. You took this dream on as if it were your own and for that, I will be forever grateful.

ABOUT THE AUTHOR

Kelli Wright (Veronica's true name) has a deep imagination, and a sail filled with ambition for the sea of opportunity ahead. As a teen, Kelli loved consuming all media about far-off magical worlds. As an adult, she enjoys using her own spellbinding creativity to spin whimsical worlds and charming characters from thin air.

She is a proud Appalachian because you can take the woman out of the mountains, but you can't take the mountains out of the woman. When she isn't crafting a story, she enjoys kitchen witchery, reading to her young daughters, and playing video games with her spouse.